PRAISE FOR

Starry Nights

"As beautiful and sweet as a Cézanne peach."
—**Stephanie Perkins**, author of *Anna and the French Kiss*

"A beautiful, poignant, romantic story about the
mystery and magic of art. Inspiring!"
—**Malinda Lo**, author of *Ash* and *Adaptation*

"An incredibly imaginative, impossibly magical mystery with
an equally magical and impossible love story at its center,
Starry Nights is the art lover's ultimate fantasy."
—**Kendare Blake**, author of *Antigoddess* and
Anna Dressed in Blood

"A cross between *The Da Vinci Code* and *The Night at the Museum*,
this sophisticated fantasy . . . borrows from art history and ancient
mythology as chaos erupts at museums around the world."
—***Publishers Weekly***

"It's Julien's passion for art, for feeling it with his whole heart,
that makes him and the novel different. . . . This delightful
read has enough magic to enchant the most jaded."
—*SLJ*

"Whitney offers Muse dust,
quirks and the ghos
—*Kirkus Revi*

"Readers familiar with European art history will enjoy the many
references to renowned painters and their works."
—*Booklist*

BOOKS BY DAISY WHITNEY

Starry Nights
The Fire Artist

Starry Nights

DAISY WHITNEY

BLOOMSBURY
NEW YORK   LONDON   NEW DELHI   SYDNEY

First published in the United States of America in September 2013
by Bloomsbury Children's Books
Paperback edition published in September 2014
www.bloomsbury.com

Bloomsbury is a registered trademark of Bloomsbury Publishing Plc

For information about permission to reproduce selections from this book, write to
Permissions, Bloomsbury Children's Books, 1385 Broadway, New York, New York 10018
Bloomsbury books may be purchased for business or promotional use. For information on bulk
purchases please contact Macmillan Corporate and Premium Sales Department at
specialmarkets@macmillan.com

Inside cover images courtesy of Bridgeman Art Library:
Inside front cover, clockwise from the top: *Olympia*, 1863 (oil on canvas), Manet, Edouard
(1832–83)/Musée d'Orsay, Paris, France/Giraudon; *Still Life with Open Drawer*, Cezanne, Paul
(1839–1906)/Private Collection/Photo © Christie's Images; *Young Girls at the Piano*, c. 1890 (oil
on canvas), Renoir, Pierre Auguste (1841–1919)/Musée de l'Orangerie, Paris, France/Giraudon;
Starry Night over the Rhone, 1888 (oil on canvas), Gogh, Vincent van (1853–90)/Musée d'Orsay,
Paris, France/Giraudon; *Rouen Cathedral, the West Portal, Dull Weather*, 1894 (oil on canvas),
Monet, Claude (1840–1926)/Musée d'Orsay, Paris, France/Peter Willi.
Inside back cover, clockwise from the top left: *Dancing at the Moulin Rouge: La Goulue*, 1895
(oil on canvas), Toulouse-Lautrec, Henri de (1864–1901)/Musée d'Orsay, Paris, France; *Dr. Paul
Gachet*, 1890 (oil on canvas), Gogh, Vincent van (1853–90)/Musée d'Orsay, Paris, France/
Giraudon; *Ballet Rehearsal on the Stage*, 1874 (oil on canvas), Degas, Edgar (1834–1917)/Musée
d'Orsay, Paris, France/Giraudon; *The Japanese Bridge*, 1918–19 (oil on canvas) (see detail
382336), Monet, Claude (1840–1926)/Musée Marmottan Monet, Paris, France/Giraudon; *Dance
at Bougival*, 1883 (oil on canvas), Renoir, Pierre Auguste (1841–1919)/Museum of Fine Arts,
Boston, Massachusetts, USA/Picture Fund.

ISBN 978-1-61963-436-7 (paperback)
LCCN of hardcover edition: 2013009610

Book design by Donna Mark
Typeset by Westchester Book Composition
Printed and bound in the U.S.A. by Thomson-Shore Inc., Dexter, Michigan
2 4 6 8 10 9 7 5 3 1

All papers used by Bloomsbury Publishing, Inc., are natural, recyclable products
made from wood grown in well-managed forests. The manufacturing processes
conform to the environmental regulations of the country of origin.

This book is dedicated to my amazing friend Theresa.
How lucky am I that our paths crossed so long ago
and that we've stuck together through the years?
Love you so much

PROLOGUE

The Lovers' Bridge

Several Weeks Ago

The padlock glistens with rain. Hooked into a link on the lovers' bridge, it is snuggled against countless other *cadenas d'amour*.

But not for long.

"Bolt cutters, please," I say to my best friend, Simon.

He couldn't be happier to be wingman. He never liked Jenny, and he especially didn't like her when she took off with Christophe last week. I didn't like that either.

"As you requested." He hands me the orange bolt cutters. I press on the handles, slide the metal teeth around the loop of the lock, and slice. Within three seconds, the wet padlock falls into my open hand. I used to wonder if it was the police or fire department that cut old padlocks from the bridge to make way for new promises, but now I know it's neither.

"And with that she's ancient history," I say, hoping she truly will feel that way soon. I tuck the bolt cutters into my backpack and drop the broken padlock in the nearest trash can. Jenny insisted on hanging the *cadenas* a few months ago. As is the custom, she wrote our names in black Sharpie—*Jenny + Julien*—then clamped the lock closed on a link of the bridge. She tossed the keys into the Seine, and I pictured them touching down next to thousands of keys lining the riverbed. Then I told her I was crazy about her and we kissed. Stupid me. Tourists and locals fasten locks with their names to this bridge every day, but I bet few couples stay together for long.

"Now, on to part two of the Purge of Jenny from Pittsburgh," Simon declares as we catch the Metro to Oberkampf.

"Jenny? Who's Jenny from Pittsburgh?" I say, as if I've never heard the name.

"Exactly, Julien. That's exactly the kind of attitude I want you to foster."

On the train, Simon tips his forehead to a pair of pretty girls sitting not far from us. They're dressed for a night out, with low-cut shirts and lots of leg showing. "We should invite them to come along," he says.

"It's as if you can read my mind."

"Or maybe just that my mind is on the same thing all the time."

"What else is there to ponder?" I say, and we knock fists and head over to the blonde and the brunette. Simon says hello and asks where they're going. When they say the same stop as us, he flashes a big smile. "What are the chances?"

It's my turn. "There's a group of us going to this club. We would love it if you'd both come along," I say, and it's the best I can do, given my state of mind, but it's enough, because they say yes, and that's all I really need right now anyway.

We exchange names as the train rattles into the next stop. The doors open, and the four of us walk down the cobbled street in search of a neon-lit door that leads to an underground club. Inside, the music is so loud that I can't hear anyone—not the girls we just met, not any of my other friends from our school, or from nearby schools, and nearby cities too it seems, that Simon has corralled into the dimly lit corner. Everyone dances and moves to the pounding bass from the sound system, including the girls from the train, one on each side of me. I banish Jenny from my mind, and the music helps because it drowns me in a riot of sounds that give no room to think of her.

Soon our group thins, the girls say good-bye, and the night has served its intended effect.

I leave well after the trains have stopped running, and even then I don't go home. My parents are out of town, so I go to the Musée d'Orsay, where I lead tours after school. There's no tour now in the middle of the night, but I'm allowed in whenever I want. This place is like a home to me, and the paintings on the walls are often the best kind of company. I say a quick hello to the security guard and take the stairs to see my favorite Van Gogh. But I don't make it to the second floor because I spot someone in a skirt rushing into a nearby gallery.

There's only one guard here at night, and I haven't a clue who could be roaming the halls. When I turn the corner, I nearly stumble and fall. I grab the doorframe, then blink several times at the scene unfolding before me. A girl is pirouetting across the floor. I spin around, looking for the security guard, looking for corroboration, but he's strolling the galleries, making his rounds, blind to the young dancer twirling in a flurry of white as if she's rehearsing for a ballet in the museum's main thoroughfare.

If I were seeing genies riding on magic carpets while huffing on hookahs, I'd be less shocked. Instead, all my senses are ignited, and my brain is buzzing, and it feels like I'm dreaming, but I know I'm wide awake and seeing art come alive. This girl has danced her way right out of a Degas.

CHAPTER 1

Of Painted Peaches, Cats, and Dancers

Present Day

A peach falls out of a Cézanne.

I grab the fruit before it rolls down the steps and out to the lion sculptures, near where the security guards make their nightly patrols. This peach looks tasty, the kind that would drip juices on your chin and you wouldn't care. I run my thumb over it, fuzzy and tender, begging to be eaten, then bring it to my lips. If I take a bite, I will know whether it's real or a figment of my imagination. But I don't entirely want to know if my mind is playing tricks on me, so I resist.

Instead, I do what Cézanne did—capture its likeness. I rustle in my backpack for my notebook and pencils, then kneel down on the floor, the soles of my heavy boots pressing against the polished hardwood. Quickly, I sketch. When I'm done, I look at the peach, then I look at my drawing, and I see an anatomically correct peach. Nothing more. I have just drawn a page for a how-to-draw-a-peach handbook, not something delicious you want to wrap your lips around. Not the kind of peach that makes the girls swoon, that makes a girl like Jenny leave you for another artist. A *better* artist, like Christophe, the oh-so-talented young sculptor.

I close my notebook and stuff it back into the bottom of my bag, amid the crinkled pages of homework that I've barely glanced at.

I carry the escapee back to its home on the wall and tuck it into its frame, as I have done before. The canvas stretches itself around the piece of fruit, making a sucking sound, like a slurp, then goes quiet. The peach is two-dimensional again.

A black cat rubs up against me.

"Meow," she murmurs.

She swishes back and forth against my jeans, her chest rumbling on my calf as she purrs. No wonder this cat keeps company with Manet's *Olympia*; she is the feline form of that naked woman. Sometimes I think Olympia watches me too; I swear I have seen her eyes flick back and forth, following me as I walk from one end of her gallery to the other. She always stays put though, stretched out seductively on the white silken sheets of her painted bed.

"How did you make it all the way over here?" I say as I scoop up the cat and bring her back to her nearby home. With the fifth floor closed for a summerlong renovation, nearly all our art is camped out here on the main floor. "They say black cats are trouble. That you're a sign of trouble. Is that true?" I ask as I escort her to the edge of the canvas. She is silky, luxurious to the touch. She meows one more time, but the sound is cut in half when she folds herself back into her regular pose—arched back, fierce yellow eyes, completely still.

Almost as if she never leaped out.

I hear soft footfalls from another gallery, the delicate sound of toes tucked into slippers twirling against hardwood floors. My heart speeds up. The dancers—they're gorgeous. I hurry across the hallway. Two dancers in white dresses, including the girl from that first night, have jetéd their way out of a Degas and are now spinning in dizzying circles. They make regular nighttime appearances now, and many others have joined them too. Last week, all the dancers here in the Musée d'Orsay, and a few musicians from an orchestra scene too, peeled away from the paint Degas rendered them in more than one hundred years ago and formed a ragtag, makeshift company to perform *Swan Lake* in the main gallery at midnight. The only thing missing was the male dancers to lift them up. No one painted them. The only men Degas painted were teachers or choreographers, and they never leave the art.

I half want to ask the ballerinas if they'd ever consider adding in a little underground music, maybe even something cool and modern, because I like the traditional as much as I like the avant-garde. I'd have them all do a more streetwise number some night, flash-mob style, down the steps in our main gallery. I could play deejay, cue up my iPod on a set of speakers, and blast some of my favorite tunes from an Internet station that broadcasts out of Brooklyn.

The dark-haired girl dances past me on the way back to her frame but stops short. She turns around, grins wildly, then spins en pointe, again and again, a bravura coda to the impromptu show.

She crashes, crumples to the floor.

I rush over to her and kneel down as she whimpers and cradles her foot. "Are you okay?"

She nods bravely.

"Let me help you," I say. She leans against me, small and lithe, and I loop my arm underneath her. She stands up, wobbly at first, then sturdy again. I've never touched one of the dancers. I've never touched any of the painted people. She feels so real. Warm skin, beating heart. Like me, like life. I don't know what I expected, but then again, I never expected paintings to perform.

A loose tendril of her hair brushes my arm.

"Thank you," she says, tucking the hair into its proper place. I help her into her frame, the canvas wrapping gently around her, sensitive to her wounded state.

The museum is still again.

Or maybe it's always been still.

Maybe it's all in my untamed imagination. It's not as if the dancers twirl during the day for our visitors, or even in the evenings for my mother. But for now, if my life is becoming a Dali landscape, I'm lucky that my mother runs the Musée d'Orsay. Our walls are filled with the prettiest paintings, the kind you long to see alive.

On my way out I catch the spot on the wall where we will hang a new painting soon. *The Girl in the Garden* will look stunning there. It would look magnificent anywhere. It's a Renoir and it's been the most sought-after lost painting for more than one hundred years, a work of art collectors and historians around the world have salivated over. Every several years someone claimed to have seen it, spotted it in an antique shop, caught a glimpse of it at a flea market. But now it's been found. Now, *The Girl in the Garden* is coming here, and she'll be one of the final paintings I show on my tours. I've only seen photo reproductions, but to have her on our walls and become flesh at night . . .

I head out, saying good-bye to the security guards. The gray-haired one, Gustave, gives me a curt nod. He fiddles with a piece of copper wire and teardrop crystals that he bends and twists into a miniature sculpture. He is an artist too.

Aspiring, I should say. Just like me.

"Your piece is coming together," I say.

"Thanks."

"See you tomorrow, Gustave."

As the door closes behind me, I bring my palm to my nose. My hand smells like a peach. I am sure of that.

CHAPTER 2

Silver to Life

I walk home along the inky quiet of the Seine, listening to a California radio station, since they do cool new music in America way better than they do in France. After a few songs, I turn away from the water and wind through the streets to my neighborhood.

I push off my headphones when I hear a rubbery thud on concrete. Next, the back wheel of a bicycle pops up, perpendicular to the rough stones.

It is Simon. King of bike tricks, the unofficial star act of nighttime riders and skate rats in Saint-Germain-des-Prés, and this is his base camp outside a pair of popular cafés.

"Want to know what this move got me tonight?" Simon's back on two wheels now, his feet planted on each side of the fire-engine-red frame of the bike that's far too small for him, especially since he is insanely tall to start with.

Simon and I met at school several years ago and discovered a shared penchant for hijinks. One afternoon when we were both thirteen, Simon found a stash of cheap plastic Eiffel Tower replicas hidden under a blanket near the river, so we grabbed berets and baguettes and did our best to look like forlorn young boys who had to peddle tourist trinkets just to buy bread for the family. Never mind that poor French boys wouldn't have berets or baguettes. We made a killing the next few days outside the Eiffel Tower. Pretty much every American mother buying a tchotchke paid us double because we didn't seem like street scammers, like all the other "salesmen" waggling cheap silver, gold, and copper tower replicas in the faces of tourists.

But our fellow countrymen were none too happy. We'd infringed on the turf of some Algerians, and they ran us off their patch of sidewalk, telling us they'd track down our mommies if we ever tried to horn in on their trade again.

"What did your move score you?" I ask.

Simon executes a quick fishtail on the cobbled street. "The phone number from one of a pair of lovelies here tonight. The one with the long hair may have been custom made for your friend Simon."

"Really?"

"Her name is Lucy, and she is tall, hot, and totally witty. The other I'll save for you."

"Aren't you generous. I suppose she is the wicked stepsister?"

"No. The other one, Emilie, she's just kind of shy. But she's a dancer, so maybe I'll just take both at the same time."

"Have fun with them. I better get on home. My mom will have a fit if I'm any later."

"Wait," Simon says, and for a moment he is nervous. "Um, I have a date with her Friday night. With Lucy. I need you to think of something really interesting for us to do."

"Right, because I'm what? A social organizer? A date planner?" I joke, though there's some truth to it, because fun and games are the only subjects I've ever excelled at.

"Because you're the creative one, idiot," Simon informs me.

"And you're the charming one. Or so you think."

"See! That's why the ladies love us. We can make it a foursome. I'll see if her friend can come along," Simon calls out as he wheels off toward his favorite set of steps, and I turn down the quiet lamp-lit street that leads to the only place I've ever lived.

When I'm inside my home, my mother shuts the door behind me and motions to the kitchen, where we can talk freely. My father must be asleep. He's a professor, and he has an early morning class tomorrow.

"I have something for you," she announces, barely able to conceal the sneaky smile on her face. I pretend to look behind her back as if she's hiding something.

She shakes her head and tsk-tsks me. "You know the rules."

I sigh. I do know the rules. I hate the rules. "I left my paper at school."

"Well, what kind of grade did you get on it?"

"An average one. Like usual. What's this thing you have for me?"

"Don't you worry, young man. It's something you'll want. Are you going to pass your literature class this year?"

"I'm doing my best."

She scoffs. "Your best? That is rarely enough when it comes to academic endeavors, Julien."

I'm never good enough—I wasn't good enough for Jenny, I'm not a good enough artist, and as for school, I'm barely good enough to pass. It tires me, sometimes, my own mere adequacy. "And on that note, I think I'll just head to my room and spend some time with my friends from Brooklyn."

This rankles my mother, as she hates my music with such passion I swear she wishes the Internet were never invented. Bands like Dirty Cat and Protracted Envy are screechy and scratchy, she likes to say. I tell her Mozart is too, even though I don't believe that.

I walk off, but she calls me back. "It's the Renoir."

I stop in my tracks, and my heart dares to beat faster, betraying me. The prospect of the Renoir is more powerful than ticking off my mother. "What do you mean?"

"I mean, if you actually get your homework done, Julien, then you can see the *The Girl in the Garden* before anyone else does."

I turn around. "But it's not coming to the museum for a few weeks, I thought." I've been eagerly tracking the painting's journey since it resurfaced last month, just a few days after I cut the padlock. The collectors are a couple in Montmartre who run a high-fashion line, and their family had sheltered the painting for more than a century. They reached out to my mother and told her that the Musée d'Orsay was the only place they wanted it hung. It's a gift to the museum. Quite the present, indeed.

"It's not. But you can see it tomorrow if . . ."

"If what?" I ask, though I know what's coming. Because the rule is this—if I pass all my classes, then I'm *allowed* to spend my evenings at the museum. Most parents would be thrilled if their kid wanted to hang out at a museum. But I'm the freak, the boy who actually craves the company of paintings, so my insidious genius of a mother uses all-hours access as a carrot for better grades.

"If you're doing well enough in literature. Then you can see it."

"I'll bring home the Molière paper tomorrow."

"Good. I have some final documents to review with them anyway. But just wait till you see the painting, Julien." She places her palm against her chest, as if the memory of the painting is too much. "It's the most beautiful Renoir I've ever seen. You will be in love. I know you. You're just like me. You fall hard."

I am like her in that way, but I don't have the other pieces she has. I'm not book smart, and I don't have the ability to apply theory or rigor to that love. Some days I think I'd be better off just hanging with the street artists who ply their trade by the river. Some of their work isn't half bad. Like this young guy Max who sketches hilarious drawings of tourists on the steps outside the museum most afternoons.

My mother reaches inside her purse on the counter and roots around until she finds what she's looking for. "I almost forgot." She hands me a small white ceramic creature with brown spots. It's a calf, but a five-legged one. Renoir once said the idea of women painters was as ridiculous as five-legged calves. It's a shame that he was such an amazing artist but not exactly what you'd call an equal opportunist. "From the collectors. A gift for you."

I narrow my eyes at the calf. "That's weird. Why are they giving this to me?"

My mother shrugs. "I don't know, but I need to get to bed. I have an early meeting with the restorers. They're coming to look at that portrait, the one that had that little bit of sun damage. I need to get it fixed before it goes to the joint exhibit at the Louvre," she says, referring to a different Renoir, a picture of two young girls playing a piano that started to fade several weeks ago. I noticed the damage first and alerted my mother. The restorers are the best, though. I'm sure they'll fix it in time for the exhibit at our sister museum.

She returns to her room. I inspect the calf out of curiosity. The fifth leg—a shrunken baby leg hanging from its back—has a small cap for a hoof. I take the cap off and a bit of silvery powder with the consistency of confectionary sugar tumbles free.

I shake the calf more, but it's empty now.

Strange. Why would they want me to have a ceramic five-legged calf? Simply as an inside joke?

I place the cap back on and drop the calf into my backpack, then take out my notebook. I grab half a chicken sandwich from the refrigerator and eat as I flick through my drawings. I stop at the one I drew the night before, Olympia's cat. My sketch is technical and precise, worthy of nothing more than an entry in a cat guidebook someday. Veterinarians might even coo over its lifelike contours and shapes. I study it to see if I could maybe have drawn it a different way, a subtler way, to make the cat seem more . . . I don't know . . . enchanting. I run my index finger across the cat's head, but no ideas come to me. I close the notebook, tuck it into my backpack, and head to my room.

As I turn the doorknob I see strands of black hair on my hand. Sleek hair from a sleek cat.

CHAPTER 3

Chocolate-Plum Iris

I smell sheep at the top of the stairs. "It's like a petting zoo on that balcony."

My mother shushes me, then whispers, "That's their balcony."

"Well, I would think they'd want to know it stinks like sheep."

"I'm pretty sure it's not our place to point that out," my mother says as we arrive at the door to the collectors' home. The couple lives on the curving corner of a hilly street in Montmartre, a few bends and twists in the road above a onetime artists' residence made famous when Picasso joined the roster of live-ins. Notre Dame might be Point Zero in Paris, but Montmartre is the epicenter of painting. The cobbles are mortared with the colors of a palette, the streets have been touched by the soles of the greatest of great artists.

"Besides, how do you know what a sheep smells like?"

"Like wool. I'm betting a sheep smells like wool."

"Touché."

She smoothes her hands over her suit. "You should write a paper on this painting for your history class," my mother says before pressing the buzzer. "Since it has such a story behind it."

The Girl in the Garden was exhibited only once, at a gallery show in 1885, then it went missing. The story is that both Monet and Renoir were in love with the girl. Renoir painted her one day during a visit he made to Monet's garden, but then the girl's family hid the painting away to protect her reputation, so she wouldn't be known as *that girl* two married men were in love with.

"Are the collectors her family? The girl's family?"

She shakes her head.

"Do you think both artists were in love with her?"

"It's a story. A legend."

But legends can have a life all their own, and I can't help but wonder who she might have been, this girl whose likeness pulled off a disappearing act for more than a century, a feat to rival any magician's stage trick. Maybe she was a girl who lived in Montmartre, someone who went to school here, or waited tables, or did whatever girls my age did many years ago in Paris.

"Hello!" The voice comes through the buzzer. "Come in, come in."

I push open the heavy green door etched with curling ironwork panels and hold it for my mother. I let the door fall behind us as we walk down a stone path that funnels into a courtyard flanked by yellow tulips. I expect to see the couple. Instead we're greeted by a guy about my age. His head is shaved, but the odd thing is he's dressed like a woman, in tight jeans, purple flats, and some sort of sleeveless top that he might have raided from his mother's fall line. I'm caught off guard by the twist, but I know better than to let on.

"Bonheur," he says and holds out his hand to shake. For a moment, I think I've heard him wrong, that he's said *bonheur* instead of *bonjour*. Then I realize, Bonheur is his name. Or, more likely, it's the name he has given himself. The word means happiness, but considering how he's dressed, I suspect the name is an homage to Rosa Bonheur, the nineteenth-century painter who had to dress as a man to work on many of her pieces in public. Perhaps that's the twist.

"Such a pleasure to see you again," my mother says. "This is my son, Julien."

I shake his hand. "Good to meet you. Fan of Rosa, I take it?"

He beams. "But of course! And it's great to meet you. I've heard so much about you." He has a firm grip, and he doesn't let go of my hand right away. He beams at me and seems to study me like I'm an oddity.

"Thanks for the calf," I add, even though I'm not quite sure why he wanted me to have it. But I don't want to let on that I'm in the dark on that count.

"I make them myself. Come on in. My mom's inside." Bonheur leads us to an orange door at the end of the courtyard. We enter their home, a massive one for Montmartre standards. An elaborate security system is installed on the wall of the foyer, but beyond that the house is like a trip back in time, with old-fashioned carnival music playing on a phonograph in the living room and a small vintage carousel with a tiger and a zebra for riding that makes its home in a corner. Framed posters from the Moulin Rouge and a kaleidoscope of once-popular stage shows fill the walls.

Bonheur's mother calls out from the kitchen, "Ms. Garnier, I've just finished up the most divine clafoutis to share with you."

"Thank you, Ms. Clemenceau. And I've told you, please call me Marie-Amelie."

"Then, Marie-Amelie, you can't call me Ms. Clemenceau," the voice from the kitchen says in a playful manner. "Won't you join me in the kitchen?"

·As my mother walks away I notice the large oak table that's home to dozens of miniature ceramic calves. Like the one he gave me, each of these calves has a fifth leg. On a brown calf, a meaty extra back leg juts out of the cow's shoulder. On a black-and-white calf, a skinny front leg hangs from the rear haunches. A trio of black calves have fifth legs that descend from their bellies. "You work in ceramics?"

Bonheur gives a sheepish sort of shrug. "My little art form. What can I say? I've never been terribly good with a paintbrush, but I do what I can."

"Hey, don't knock it. I think these calves are cool. Kind of ironic."

"That's exactly what I was going for," Bonheur says with a bright smile. He reaches across the table for a black calf with pink polka dots, and a fifth leg where its tail should be. "This is my prize calf. In fact," he begins, then lowers his voice as he glances to the kitchen, "I'm giving it away at my surprise birthday party tomorrow night. My parents are going to Provence for the weekend."

I laugh quietly. "How is it a surprise if you know about it?"

"I hate surprises," he says, now intensely serious. "I abhor them within an inch of my soul. I read endings of books first, I look up spoilers of films in advance, and I always open my Christmas presents the second they arrive. Especially the ones I order for myself! So my friends and I are throwing an *un-surprise* party for my eighteenth birthday. We're going to act surprised about everything everyone says, and whoever pulls off the most authentic look of true surprise wins the prize calf."

"That does kind of sound like fun," I concede.

"You should come. Bring friends if you want. Just don't tell your mom, obviously, since I don't want her telling mine."

Before I can commit, our mothers emerge from the kitchen. Introductions are made, and we all sit down at the table with the calves to eat the baked dessert.

"I have the final paperwork," Bonheur's mother says, and they review his family's ownership of the Renoir through the years, the forensic and fingerprint reports my mother commissioned to verify the authenticity of the painting, and even a pigment analysis because Renoir used a particular mix of chromium salts and boric acid to sign all his works. He's said to have done this to ensure that fakes could never be made. As they continue on through the archival and forensic details that remind me far too much of school, I ask where the restroom is and Bonheur tells me it is down the hallway, the second door on the left.

"Be sure to check out the art on the walls. We have a Jasper Johns, a Monet, and a Valadon."

"Will do," I say and leave them behind.

In the hallway, I linger on the paintings and the way Monet has captured the cobalt-blue morning light on the pond near his home, his Japanese bridge arcing over the dreamscape of water beneath it. What must it be like to craft such beauty with your own hands? I only wish I could make something worth looking at.

I scan the rest of the walls for a Valadon, but I don't see one, so I open the second door.

It's not the bathroom. It's a modern room with bright-white walls, a long black leather couch, and a plasma screen hanging on the opposite wall. I look down to find a door in the middle of the floor. Perhaps a trapdoor to a basement? But how can there be a basement when they live on a steep hill? The door has a chain on it that is looped into an eyehook on the other side. A chalk drawing covers half the door. I step around to check it out right side up.

A woman in a pale-pink dress, so light it's the color of the inside of a seashell, dances with a man she looks away from. But the man's not here; he's not been rendered in chalk. It's half a reproduction. It's half of a Renoir, his *Dance at Bougival*. The dancing woman is Suzanne Valadon, who was an artist's model and an artist herself, not to mention the first female painter admitted into art school in France.

Is this chalk drawing what he meant by the Valadon he wanted me to see? Valadon and Renoir were contemporaries, both artists in Montmartre. But is there some greater connection Bonheur is trying to hint at?

I hear the voices down the hall. Methodical, detailed. They're still reviewing the documents.

I kneel down and unhook the latch, expecting a creak or a moan of hinges. But the door opens without a sound. Beneath it I see a set of stairs that wind round and round, until they descend into total darkness. There must be a cellar far below. I bet that's where Bonheur's family hid their art during the Nazi occupation to keep paintings safe from plundering. I close the door and shut the latch.

A chair's legs scratch across the living room floor.

Quickly, I leave this room and pop into the bathroom down the hall. I step in, turn on the water, turn it off, and head out as the cross-dressing teenage ceramist who uses a woman's surname as his first name walks by.

"Found it," I announce stupidly. I want to kick myself. Of course, I found the bathroom. But saying "found it" implies I stumbled across something else. Bonheur tips his forehead ever so slightly to the second door as he says, "Good."

He wanted me to see the trapdoor. He sent me to that chalk drawing. What's at the bottom of all those stairs?

"They're still talking about all that pigment, blah, blah, blah," Bonheur says and rolls his eyes in some sort of parents-are-so-dull gesture. "So my mom said I should just show you the painting."

I follow him to the white door at the end of the hall. He takes a key from his pocket, unlocks the door, turns the brass handle, and gestures to the painting hanging behind an imposing oak desk.

Forget trapdoors, forget five-legged calves and silvery dust.

Photo reproductions don't do this painting justice. Goose bumps rise on my arms, and my heart beats hard against my skin.

Her back is mostly to the painter, but she's twisting around, looking over her shoulder with a fierce stare, a sharp longing in her eyes, all the more unusual because Renoir never let his women look at the viewer. They always cast their eyes down or away. But this girl, her gaze is defiant, and her eyes are etched in pools of radiant blue, the same color as Monet's morning light. Long blond hair cascades down her back, and one hand is held up, as if she is trying to touch something or someone. She is surrounded on all sides by flowers, trapped almost by irises, in shades of violet, of royal purple, of a plum so dark it's nearly the color of chocolate.

A chocolate-plum iris.

And the girl? She is the most beautiful I have ever seen.

I turn to Bonheur. "About that invitation. I'll definitely be at your party."

CHAPTER 4

House History

Simon is obsessed with the history of Paris. But not the stuff we learn in textbooks. He prefers the tidbits he uncovers in rare bookshops and old, dusty libraries. Like how some Parisians turned to their own cats for sustenance during the Franco-Prussian War and found them quite tasty when served with olives and pimentos, or how Napoleon III's wife was rumored to sprinkle gold dust in her hair every morning.

But they don't teach us that sort of history here at Lycée d'Aile. They teach us boring history. And boring literature. And boring math. Because school is dull and dreadful, and truth be told, I can't tell you much about the approved curriculum, or whether this school will give me wings as the name promises, or even what I need to be studying for our end-of-year exams in a few weeks. My mission when it comes to high school is simple—to get by and get out. I suppose my problem with school is not just that it's boring. My brain doesn't seem to want to make the right connections between sophisticated math problems and, say, the proper method of solving them.

But there's that little matter of my mother holding my grades over my head, so I do my best to pay attention in literature and history and even in math the next day. The task is complicated when the teacher, Monsieur Douyard, fails to vary the intonation in his voice even once during the lecture on something having to do with negative numbers or negative squares or square numbers. I take notes the entire time, but my numbers seem to resemble the letters *SV*—Suzanne Valadon is on my mind—in an elaborate doodle rather than numerals. Too bad Douyard is calling on me for an answer.

"Um . . ." I have no idea what the question is. "One?" Every now and then in math you get lucky if you answer *one* or *zero*.

"If I were asking you to solve an equation, you'd have a chance of being correct. But seeing as I'm asking on which axis on a number plane you'd find this complex number, one is not correct. So, shall we try again?"

"Horizontal?" I say, hoping fifty-fifty luck lands on my side.

"No. The answer is vertical," he says with a cruel smirk. The girl in front of me snickers. Irène. She's always getting perfect grades on everything, and all the teachers love her and fawn all over her and have since the beginning of time. Red rushes to my cheeks. "We do have exams in this class, Monsieur Garnier. And I will expect you to be ready with all aspects of math, including imaginary numbers. Can anyone tell Monsieur Garnier what an imaginary number is?"

Irène waggles her hand high. He calls on her. Figures.

"The square root of a negative number," she pronounces.

He nods and returns to the board, and all I can think is, when will I ever need to know the square root of a negative number? Come to think of it, when will I ever need to know an imaginary number? Maybe if one of my imaginary friends at the museum wants to call or text me. I grin at the prospect of an imaginary phone chat.

When class ends a few minutes later, Simon informs me in a singsong voice that all I need to remember about negative numbers is this: "What goes up must come down, negative exponents turn around." He faux-pirouettes into the musty stone corridor, and I laugh.

"Pretty sure that was from about six years ago, which is probably where my level of math is these days anyway," I say.

"You can copy my work if you want." Simon does infinitely better in classes than I, something he pulls off with even less studying. We walk down the long hallway to the final class of the day, another one we share, and the only class I like: English. Thanks to working at the museum since I was able to walk, I've heard English and had to speak it every day of my life. I can even do flawless Australian, British, and American accents, including—step right up and take your pick—a range of California, Midwest, southern, and even Bostonian. I can drop my *R*s and turn my *A*s into "ahhs" like nobody's business. Unfortunately, my party tricks are as good as currency from the moon at this school. The teachers say we sound like we're making fun of other cultures when we try on accents. I want to say, have you ever heard anyone make fun of ze way ze French talk?

"I owe you," I say to Simon.

"You're coming up with those date plans for Lucy tonight. Don't forget."

"Social coordinator in exchange for math? Totally fair. Besides, I have something planned already. I'll tell you later," I say as we settle into class.

When school ends, Simon and I head through the square in the middle of the classrooms, down the stone steps and out onto the sidewalk into a crowd of classmates already forming their groups and heading to cafés or to homes. We don't have clubs or teams like most American schools do, so my after-the-bell activities can involve a little bit of legwork today.

"I am in need of your services," I tell Simon as we head out to the crowded avenue, unleashed into the freedom of a Friday afternoon. "And I don't just mean the copying."

"Ah, my dear Julien, I knew this day would finally come." He holds his arm out grandly. "Let me take you down to Pigalle and find a woman for you. How much money do you have? We can finally rid you of the *American Infection* once and for all."

"Yeah, not those services," I say, but this time I can laugh, because Jenny's fading even faster from my heart.

I met Jenny last fall on one of the tours I lead at the museum. She was wearing jean shorts, white sneakers, and a green T-shirt with a swirly slogan on it for a shoe brand. She asked me out for coffee, and I said yes, taken with both her big brown eyes and her directness. We went to the Café Montifaud around the corner from the museum for a café noisette and an île flottante, a kind of meringue that floats in a vanilla custard with caramel. She asked millions of questions. *Where were you born?* Here, in a hospital in the sixth arrondissement. *Have you lived here your whole life?* Yes. *What's it like to live in Paris?* It's like home. *This île flottante is so delicious. Can I get one in the States?* I shook my head and said, "You'll have to come back to Paris."

"I'm staying in France," she said, all cheery and bright because Jenny is one of those people for whom every day, everything is a grand adventure. "I'm starting boarding school here for my last two years of high school, but my French is terrible. Maybe you can tutor me?"

A flutter of the lashes, a soft hand on my arm, and I was hooked on her for the next six months. I must have been a great teacher too. Her French became so impressive she was able to hit it off in one night with the young French sculptor Christophe, who spoke no English.

C'est la vie.

But now there is a new girl, a painted one. I want to know more about her, and I can't exactly look her up on Facebook. "I need to do some research on a house. An address. I want to see how long it's been in someone's family," I say to Simon.

"Ah, thinking of going into the burglary business, are you? Now *that* I'm going to want a piece of."

"You want a piece of everything, Simon."

"So what's it for?"

"An artist I want to check out. Do you still know that hot chick who works at the Société?"

He speaks in a low voice as we cross the river. "Corinne. Of course. But don't say that so loudly. I don't want anyone to know about my geek side, hanging out in archives and whatnot."

"Right. With hot chicks. So geeky."

"So tell me you've thought of something incredibly adventuresome I can do with Lucy tonight? She's bringing Emilie along, so you're coming too, and I won't take no for an answer."

"'No'? What is that? Oh, right. It's a word you're not familiar with. Anyway, I'm going to a party tonight," I say, then tell Simon about Bonheur and his family's house full of oddities. Simon nods approvingly.

"I knew I could count on you for this."

"I have mad skills plotting your social life."

We arrive at the Grand Palais, an absolutely massive exhibition hall with a glass vaulted roof. Many steps lead up to an imposing entryway with tall brass doors. A security guard tells us the palace is closing in fifteen minutes, which translates to *go away now*.

"Fifteen minutes before closing might as well be closed. And it's a Friday. No one works late here," I say to Simon.

"Don't worry. It's cool," Simon says and we take the stairs quickly, then head down a long hallway to a room marked SOCIÉTÉ DES ARTISTES. "Corinne loves me because I make her laugh."

"What with your history-geek side and all."

Simon introduces me to Corinne, who is packing up. She's about twenty-one or twenty-two, has short red hair and muted green eyes. She is, as promised, totally hot. Simon explains I need to look up an artist.

"That's why everyone is here. To look up an artist," she says as she jams her phone into a gray purse. She doesn't look like she's going to laugh at all.

"Can you give him a few minutes? Pretty please." He places his palms together plaintively. "Besides, I really wanted your opinion on whether you think it would have made a big difference or a little difference if Jean Valjean had had a smartphone when he was down in the sewers?"

He bats his eyes, and she laughs instantly. "Little difference," she declares with a smile. "But you wait right here and I'll tell you why."

Simon dutifully sits on the edge of her desk, and I shoot him a quick thumbs-up. Corinne takes me to the slate cabinets that hold the records for 1894. That's when Valadon was admitted to art school, that's when she would have joined the Société as well. Corinne takes out the register, an old heavy book, the kind you'd find in a hotel with a guest list.

"Be careful," she instructs, and she leaves me alone at a desk with the dusty book. I cough as specks of the years gone by float into my nose. I turn the pages carefully, not wanting to damage this record that's seen more than a century of new years. I find the listing of members. I run my index finger down the page, then the next one, then the next one. I reach the *V*s.

Suzanne Valadon. Admitted 1894.

Then her residence. The same address as the house on the curving corner of the hilly street in Montmartre where *The Girl in the Garden* currently resides.

CHAPTER 5

And Music Is Her Scent

I keep trying to connect the dots between Bonheur's family, Valadon, and the painting by Renoir. I briefly consider that *The Girl in the Garden* might be a fake, or maybe a Valadon instead of a Renoir. But my mother is thorough and all the authenticity tests have checked out. The painting is undoubtedly from the hands of Renoir. Which means I don't know what to make of these disconnected links so I shift my focus to Emilie.

The party starts soon, so Emilie and I are near Bonheur's home, sitting outside at a crowded café with sleek metal tables and creaky wooden chairs, the perfect mix of old Paris and new Paris. Nearby in the square, a boys' choir sings under the direction of a rather stout older woman as passersby drop coins into a hat. Lucy and Simon are down the street, checking out Lucy's favorite American retro shop.

"Do you ever go to the ballet?" Emilie asks me.

"Sometimes. My parents are total fanatics. Season tickets and all," I say, and sure, guys aren't supposed to know much about the ballet, and that's why I generally keep my knowledge of dance close to the vest. But if there was ever a chance as a seventeen-year-old guy to admit that that you're familiar with this world, it would be with a ballerina.

"Cool. What was the last ballet you saw?"

"*Swan Lake.*"

"*Swan Lake*? Where was that being performed?"

I catch myself. Because of course the impromptu *Swan Lake* at the museum wasn't being performed anywhere anyone else could see. "Just a little indie theater, I think."

"Oh, how cool. What was it like? Good production?"

"It was just like a Degas."

"As all good dances should be," Emilie says, understanding what I have said perfectly, even though she has no idea I meant it literally. Emilie couldn't be anything but a dancer. When she and Lucy walked over to meet us a few minutes ago, I noticed Emilie's body first because it's impossible not to, especially when she looks as if she can bend in amazing ways. But she also moved like she was onstage, captivating an audience. "Though, I have to admit, I do kinda prefer modern ballet."

"Like Joffrey, or Martha Graham?" If I were keeping score I'd be earning some serious points right now for tossing out those names.

"Exactly. But honestly, I'd rather do Balanchine with maybe a streetwise type of dance."

I smile, thinking of the dancers in the museum the other night, and how I had hoped to rearrange them. "Like if *Swan Lake* had been danced to some sort of techno pop," I muse.

Her eyes light up. "Totally! Like Protracted Envy. Do you know that band?"

"Do I know that band? I love that band," I say, then we trade song recommendations. She says she's never heard of Retractable Eyes but they sound cool, and I tell her I've never heard of this Dr. Jade she likes so much, so I grab my phone and download some new music, and she grabs her iPod and does the same, telling me that I must check out Jane Black's new album too.

Since we're comrades-in-musical-arms evidently, she leans closer and whispers, "Can you keep a secret?"

"Of course. Keeping secrets is one of my specialties."

"What are your other specialties?"

"Accents," I say, sliding into one, which makes Emilie laugh, since one so rarely hears Australian-accented French. I like making her laugh. I move on to California drawl. "That and the tiniest bit of knowledge about ballet. But really, secrets. So tell me yours."

"I haven't told anyone yet, but I'm auditioning for the ballet next week." Emilie pushes a hand through her black hair that is straight as a blade and dark as the steel edge of the night.

"The Paris Ballet?"

"The one and only."

"I thought you were in high school. With Lucy."

"I am." Emilie looks side to side, as if she is sweeping the square for spies, before she whispers, "But I got an audition for this new summer program for high school students who are supposed to be promising or something."

"That's amazing."

"Don't tell anyone, though. Because there is *no way* I'm getting in, and then all my friends are going to be disappointed. I'm not good enough." Emilie's green eyes look defeated, and I hear music again. This time it's the faint sounds of *Giselle*. I turn to look at the choir and they're still singing, so the music must be coming from an apartment close by, drifting out an open window into the early June night.

"I seriously doubt the Paris Ballet gives auditions to dancers who aren't good enough."

"I'm sure it was totally a mistake that they let me even try out," she says with a forced laugh, and the music grows louder, as if the notes are swirling around Emilie, wrapping her in a cocoon of sweet sound.

"Oh, right. Of course. Just a little error the Paris Ballet made when sending out invites. Emilie, I suspect you're fantastic," I say, because she has to be. There's just no other way.

The violins from *Giselle* keep playing. "Is your iPod still on?"

She shows me her iPod. "See? Off. Why?"

Great. I'm not only seeing things, now I'm hearing things too. "I heard *Giselle*."

Her eyes widen. "You heard *Giselle*?"

I nod, feeling like a supreme idiot. I should know better than to let on that I'm hearing music no one's playing.

"Where is it coming from?"

"I don't know," I say, because how do I say, *It's kind of coming from you, and it's growing stronger?*

"That's my audition piece, Julien," she whispers.

"*Giselle?*"

She nods knowingly, holding another secret between us, and as she does an image flashes fully formed before my eyes—I can picture Emilie dancing on the stage of the Paris Opera House in front of thousands of people in their red upholstered chairs underneath the six-ton candelabra. The rising sounds of the ballet build toward a gorgeous finale, a dancer pirouetting, her head tipped back, giving in to the dance, giving in with abandon.

"You're going to blow them away, Emilie," I say, and I feel deeply compelled to tell her this, to share my certainty. "You're going to win a spot. I have no doubt you will be the newest member of the Paris Ballet next week." Once the words have been spoken, the music stops.

Emilie beams, the warmest smile I've ever seen. We're joined by Simon, Lucy, and a waiter bringing espressos. I thank him, and as he walks away, Lucy models a skirt with cheeseburger drawings on it.

"Just bought it. Isn't this the best?" Lucy gives a flamboyant twirl, then settles into a chair. It strikes me as funny that the non-dancer girl is the one bold enough to execute a 360 in a public square. Lucy seems to posses a natural showmanship, from the twirl to the skirt to the long brown hair with emerald streaks that frame her face.

"I think I want a shirt with french fries to go with it," Simon says. He takes a long swallow from his cup, as Lucy tells us her cheeseburger obsession stemmed from the year she lived in Chicago when she made it a mission to taste test the American favorite at nearly every diner in the city. We talk more about which cities in the US we most want to visit, and soon we finish our drinks. I notice Emilie looking at the choir in the square. She moves her foot up and down in time to the music. Her eyes have an intensity about them, and her shoulders are tight.

"You're thinking about how much you want to be dancing right now," I say to her.

"Is it that obvious?"

"Kind of."

"I just feel like I should be better prepared for next week," she says just to me.

"So go dance," I say, speaking in a low voice too.

She relaxes her shoulders. "Really? Because maybe I should take a class right now. Practice more."

"Do it," I say, and it's not that I want her to go. It's that I can tell she's already in love. With dancing.

"I need to go," Emilie says to all of us. "Sorry, Lucy. But I need to take a class."

"Emilie," Lucy says. "It's Friday night. C'mon. You're always taking ballet classes. Let's go to a party."

"What can I say? I'm inspired to go dance." Before she leaves she kisses me on the cheek and whispers in my ear, "Thank you."

I want to ask *for what*, but she's walking away.

CHAPTER 6

Voices in the Cellar

I was right about the sheep smell.

A sheep grazes on Bonheur's spacious balcony, nibbling on a patch of grass. The sheep keeps company with a goat. The sheep baas and the goat bleats and Simon cheers. "A party with farm animals. This is exactly what I needed for my Friday night."

We ring the buzzer on the green door with the iron gate. Bonheur lets us in. He was bald the first time we met, and now he's wearing a Marilyn Monroe–style wig.

"You have hair tonight," I remark.

"Sometimes I feel like a blonde," he says with a playful wink to our crew.

He's with a younger girl who's wearing jeans, black tap shoes, and a faded orange T-shirt with a unicorn leaping over a rainbow. Her brown hair is held back in a ponytail.

"This is my sister, Sophie," Bonheur says. "She's supposed to be doing her homework quietly in her room on the third floor."

"I surprised Bonheur by showing up," Sophie says, placing a hand on her hip.

"I surprised Sophie by pretending I'd let her stay for the whole party," Bonheur counters.

"Nice to meet you, Sophie," I say.

"Happy birthday," Lucy says to Bonheur and then compliments his looks, which include not just the pinup hair, but also a red dress with white polka dots.

"What's the story with the goat and sheep?" Simon asks as Bonheur guides us through the courtyard.

"They ward away bad spirits."

"What sort of spirits?" Lucy asks.

"The kind that thwart the artistic spirit," says the now-eighteen-year-old, who opens the door from the courtyard to the house.

Sophie darts in first and waves good-bye. "I'm going to tend to the flock," she says, then heads off for the balcony.

"She's just a farm girl at heart. I'm going to have to buy her overalls and a straw hat someday soon," Bonheur says.

Once we're inside, my eyes are drawn to the end of the hallway, but I force myself to return my focus to the living room. Bonheur's friends have all gotten the memo to wear bright colors too. They're decked out in swirling pinks and deep scarlets and swaths of blues and greens that mirror the sea. A sound system plays upbeat songs from pop superstars in America and England. No carnival music from a phonograph when the parents are out of town.

Lucy pulls me aside as Simon grabs drinks. "Do you not like Emilie?"

Talk about straightforward. "She was cool," I say, leaving out any comments on her fantastic body.

"Simon had told me all about you, and I thought you guys would be perfect for each other. You know—Ballet. Art."

"Right."

"So maybe we can all go out again?"

"Yeah. But you know, Emilie's pretty focused on that whole ballet thing, in case you hadn't noticed," I tease.

"I know." Lucy gives me a playful shove on my shoulder. "That's where you come in. I want her to do more fun stuff. Hang out! Go out!"

"Sure. But I think she'd rather be dancing." I want to addend that statement with something like "art is sacrifice" but that sounds cheesy, even though it's true. Besides, most of the thoughts I have about art I should keep to myself.

Simon rejoins us as a girl with dark eyeliner and slinky jeans emerges from the kitchen carrying a tray. "Time for candy!" she announces, and offers us soft candy cubes in pastel shades that are stacked on skewers, like pillow-candy shish kebabs. I take a raspberry-colored one, and as it melts I can feel each individual sugar crystal on my tongue.

Bonheur gives the eyeliner girl a kiss on the cheek, then a guy with broody eyes who's dressed all in black kisses Bonheur's other cheek. Maybe they're a threesome of sorts, or all just good friends. Bonheur's world is a little topsy-turvy, but then so is mine. I turn to say something to Simon and Lucy about trios and third wheels, but Lucy is riding the zebra on the carousel. She and Simon are laughing, and I have a feeling I've earned my keep as his social coordinator.

Bonheur circles by again offering drinks. Soda, a pale bubbly offering, and something green in a thimble-size cup. "It's absinthe."

"Just a soda," I say and take a can. Sophie pops up by my side. "One for the road," she says as she grabs a thimble, swallows the liquid, then dashes for the staircase and back to her room, I presume.

"Enjoy your absinthe, Sophie," Bonheur says, then turns to me. "She's such a good girl. Doing her homework on a Friday night."

My jaw drops, and I'm not faking any surprise right now because I can't believe Bonheur just let his little sister drink a hallucinogen. "How old is she?"

"Fourteen."

"And she just had absinthe?"

Bonheur smiles a wicked smile. "It's actually apple juice with green food coloring. See, did I get you there? With the surprise?"

"Maybe just a little. Do I get the five-legged calf?"

"I don't know. I kind of feel like I tricked you into surprise. Could you *act* totally surprised? Because everyone wants the prize pink polka-dotted calf, Julien. And it's worth it."

"Then everyone should compete for it."

"But can you look truly surprised?"

I have a hunch I'm being tested somehow for something, and I don't know what. But Bonheur has the painting and I don't, so I go along. I flash back to the night when the first Degas dancer in white burst through her frame, and call upon my best look of surprise.

"That is brilliant!"

I join in with the rest of his friends, and we all feign surprise and not surprise for several rounds until the pet sheep bleats from the balcony.

Bonheur smacks his palm against his forehead. "Oh, my sister forgot to feed Berthe again. Don't worry, Berthe. Carrots for you soon, love," Bonheur calls out to his ovine friend. Then to us: "I can't decide who to give the calf to. You're all too good at these games. You know what will help me decide?"

"Hot chocolate, obviously," says the broody boy in black.

"Clearly. Spiked and not spiked."

"Goes both ways," the boy adds. Bonheur laughs and ushers the guests into the kitchen.

I seize my chance and ask Lucy and Simon to cover for me. They station themselves outside the second door. I close the door quietly behind me. The room looks just the same as yesterday and the drawing, too, is unchanged. I pull the trapdoor and glance at the corkscrew stairs, long and dark. I take my phone from my pocket and press against the screen, so I have a faint glow as I descend the steps, one looping circle after another. I've made six or seven orbits down the staircase and the air is feeling mustier and heavier and the light from my phone only illuminates the steps right below my feet. Finally, after another dizzying round or two I arrive at the bottom. I point my phone downward to the stone basement cellar, then take several tentative steps in front of me. I reach a wall and sweep my phone up to light it. Empty. I do the same with the other walls; all are bare. There is nothing here in this cellar.

But voices.

The soft sound of voices.

They are not coming from above. They are coming from below. From underground.

I kneel down, press my ear to the floor. It's women's voices. But I can't make out the words. I guess you could say they are talking, but it sounds more like poetry, like they are speaking in sonnets, or rather that their voices make you feel the way a sonnet does. I have half a mind to lie down on the floor, one ear pressed against the cold all night, and listen to their siren song, though the rational part of my brain tells me that it is physically impossible for there to be voices underneath this rock. This home is built on a hill, on dirt, on bedrock. There should be nothing under me but concrete.

And yet I hear soft, gliding words, the sound of snowflakes floating down from a gaslit sky. Then laughter, like a bell, pure and bright. I press the heels of my hands against my eyes. This is how you lose your mind. This is the madwoman in the attic. The mad boy in the basement. Seeing art. Hearing voices. From the dancers in the Musée d'Orsay to *Giselle* in the square to these voices. Everything feels so unbearably real to me, even though I don't really know how any of it can be. I don't have a rational answer to how or why my world is tilting. But the voices aren't going away, so I hunt for the source of the sound, maybe a crack in the cellar floor. It's then that I see silver dust. Like the kind in the calf Bonheur gave me.

It's filled in a ridge in the floor in the shape of a rectangle, like desert sand outlining the edges of an archaeological dig. My phone gives off embers of light as I blow a stream of air into the dust so I can see what it's outlining. There's a small slot in the middle of one of the ridges. But the dust disintegrates with my breath, leaving only a shadow on the air—a reminder that it's clearly time for me to conduct my exodus too, and to get a grip on reality.

I take the steps two by two, spiraling higher, away from the voices. I near the top of this everlasting staircase. Light from the room floods the open trap door and I emerge, safe, into Bonheur's TV room. The door to the room is still shut. I pull it open, and two bodies fall in, catching themselves before they topple. Simon and Lucy untangle their arms and lips from each other.

"Just making sure no one came in," Simon says, grabbing for Lucy's waist to hold onto her.

"Thanks."

"Did you find what you were looking for?"

"I'm not sure," I say as we step into the hall. Simon doesn't ask what I was looking for. He gets that sometimes you just need to guard the door without knowing why.

"Are you having the time of your life?" It's Bonheur, and his red heels click loudly along the hardwood floors.

"I'm having the worst time. The absolute worst, most awful time of my life," Lucy says, pretending to cry.

Bonheur looks genuinely surprised.

"Gotcha!"

Bonheur wags a finger at Simon's new girl. "You did get me. Well done, well done. Now, why don't you two lovebirds head to the kitchen? You haven't had my hot chocolate yet. It's spiked with cayenne pepper. For *l'amour*!" He winks at Simon and Lucy, tipping his head to the festivities in the other room. Simon asks me with his eyes if it's okay to go, and I nod.

Bonheur cocks his head to the side and smiles. "The voices are lovely."

I do my best to act unsurprised. Does he hear them too? Is he crazy as well?

"Like a poem," he adds.

I have to know. I have to confirm I'm not the only one hearing things. "What are those voices?"

He beams, as if I have asked the one perfect question. "Muses."

I scoff. "Muses in your cellar?"

"Don't you believe in Muses?" he asks, as if Muses are the equivalent of the law of gravity. His certainty catches me off guard.

"I don't know," I say, stumbling through the words.

"Well, I do."

I'm not sure where to go next. I glance at the floor of his house, trying to gather my thoughts. His house. That's right. "Did this used to be Suzanne Valadon's house?"

"It did. She was my great-great-great-something. I lost track. But yes, she lived here." He assumes a dramatic pose, gesturing grandly as he continues, "Way back when she painted and partied and tempted the other artists in the heyday of Montmartre and the Moulin Rouge."

"Why would my mother not mention that you guys were related?"

He resumes his normal voice. "I have no idea. But Suzanne

had her own artistic politics and not everyone agreed with them. Not Renoir for sure. They didn't see eye to eye, but she loved that painting. *The Girl in the Garden.* She's the reason my family has it. She kept it safe. *We* have kept it safe for all these years." He grips my shoulder and turns me toward the white door at the end of the hall. "The painting is off limits to everyone." He lowers his voice to the barest whisper. "But would you like to see her again?"

I should say no. I should run far away from all these strange things—Muses, Valadon, his family guarding a prized painting.

But this is the real reason I'm not bothered that Emilie is off dancing. Because I'm off chasing a dream as well, and the hope that my reality isn't merely my illusion. "Why would you need to keep it safe?"

"It's not like other paintings, Julien. It needed more protection."

"Why? Who would want to hurt that painting?"

"It wouldn't have been hidden for so many years if there weren't people who wanted to hurt it."

Two artists in love with the same girl. Maybe the girl's family had been after it. Maybe they wanted to protect her reputation, as my mother said. My head spins with shadowy secrets of a girl who inspired love, aroused jealousy, needed protection.

Who is she?

"But you'll keep it safe at the museum, won't you?" Bonheur asks.

"Of course." I have so many more questions, but the closer I get to the door, the harder it is to put words into anything resembling a logical order. My own beating heart is leading me to that room.

Bonheur removes a key from a pocket in his dress and opens the door. He guides me inside. "Sit, stay. I'll leave you two alone."

The door clicks behind him, and I walk, like a patient hypnotized, to *The Girl in the Garden*.

Even with the space between us, I can feel a warmth coming from the canvas, a body heat radiating out. I study the girl, the way she looks back, the way her lips are parted ever so slightly. I want to trace a finger across those red lips. I want to know what she was saying when she posed for this painting. What would she say now if she could talk?

I stand close and watch her. She stays still and silent, but the room feels expectant, as if anticipation itself is wrapping around me like a long line of smoke drifting across an Arabian night. I stare so hard at the painting that I squint, and when I do, I see the faintest of lines surrounding her.

A shimmer of silver.

The canvas buckles near her hand. Then it's quiet again. I hold my breath, pleading for more. *This is real, this has to be real, please let this be more than an illusion.* There's a rustling then, and one slender, feminine finger pokes out. I feel a rush of blood to the head. I lick my lips briefly, hold my hands together, and I wait.

"Come out," I whisper. "Come out."

I move closer to the painting, inches away now. "Who are you?"

There's the gentlest swishing sound of a skirt from behind the frame.

"What is your name?"

Then a distant sound, like a far-off bell.

"What are your favorite things?"

Something like laughter, but it's not from the party. It's as if the canvas is echoing a sweet, inviting laugh.

I put my hands on the frame. This is as close as I have come to touching her. "What are you like, girl behind the paint?" I ask, and for a moment I can hear soft breath and the beating of a heart, and I'm sure neither one is coming from me.

The canvas is quiet the rest of the night, and when the sounds of the party die down, I'm one of the last to leave. Bonheur presses the pink polka-dotted calf into my hands and tells me I earned it.

"I want to see her again. Before she comes to the museum."

He smiles and programs his number into my cell. "Just think of me as your middleman. For *her*."

We're no longer calling her *The Girl in the Garden*. She's a she. She's a girl, and I want her to come out at night even if she is all in my mind.

CHAPTER 7

A Vision in Flames, Then Sizzles

I hand my mother my latest history assignment with a gleam of triumph. I have obtained a slightly above-average grade on it, and I want to gloat because it is my after-hours access.

"Ha. You didn't think I could do it."

She gives me a sharp look as she puts her glasses on. She won't believe I've accomplished anything academically until she verifies it with 20/20 vision. But it's amazing how an imaginary girl can motivate me. My mother peruses the pages, then gives an approving nod. She hands the paper back to me. "Well done. Now, do you think you could do me a favor and pay a visit to Claire at the Louvre to check out the *Interiors* exhibit? The Renoir with the sun damage has been repaired and is hung there, but I need your sharp eyes for a second look."

I sigh. "Seriously? Can I just have an afternoon off?" I need to check on a different Renoir.

"This is important. I need you. You were the first one to notice the fading, so I would just feel better if you could give it one final look. I don't want to have any problems."

"Okay," I say, giving in.

"And Julien?"

"Yes?"

"Don't let on that the piano girls had any sun damage at all. It's all better now, so the Louvre doesn't need to know."

"Of course," I say, tucking this latest secret safely away. Besides, sun damage happens. It's a standard part of the aging process, and it can also be reversed by a good restorer. No harm, no foul.

On my way out, I see the usual assortment of street artists who've set up shop along the river to draw tourists with pointy chins and oversize heads. Max is there, the guy who's the best of them all. He's sketching a gangly English boy who is fidgety and antsy, but the parents seem determined to capture their son as caricature. The too-long limbs remind me of a baby horse, and I say this to Max.

"You better hope they don't know '*poulain*' or I've lost ten euros," he says, but he's laughing.

"I'll cover you if they turn out to be bilingual equestrians."

❧

I'm not a religious person, and so I have to say I'm relieved that we have very few scenes of saints and martyrs, or crucifixions, for that matter, at the Musée d'Orsay. I'm not keen on interacting with anyone from the Old or New Testament when art comes alive after hours. Thankfully, we only have art painted after 1848, and most modern painters moved far away from the religious and historical scenes of the past.

But the Louvre is our sister museum, and it claims earlier works, including a seventeenth-century Georges de La Tour depicting Joseph in his workshop with a young Jesus. I'm glad it's daytime, so the father and son are staying put in their frames.

"It's ironic as an interior scene, don't you think? It was my idea too, because I do have years of practical work in the field."

The question, and the veiled insult about my age, comes from Claire. She's an assistant curator here at the Louvre and has been showing me how they're mingling the paintings for the joint exhibit opening soon on *Interiors through the Ages*. It's not the first question she asked me. The first was *Where is Marie-Amelie Garnier?* My response was simple: *She sent me instead, and I'd be honored if you'd show me the exhibit before it opens.* Then she huffed out an annoyed *Very well.*

Claire is one of those perfectly put-together people—sharp skirt, heels, proper blouse, and the kind of straight brown hair you see on TV hosts and anchors. Like many of them, she's also humorless.

"It definitely makes me think," I say, because I'm quite curious if any of these biblical characters hop out of their frames at night here in the Louvre. I've never been here when the museum's closed. Does the art make appearances for anyone when the doors are shut? I peer more closely at the brightly lit candle a young Jesus holds for his earthly father, as if the painting could reveal its nighttime secrets to me.

"Well, what does it make you think about?" Claire asks as if she's testing me, and I feel like I'm in school again.

I try to fashion an answer when a sharp and hot pain sears my hand. "Ow," I say, and I look at the source of the pain. Hot, burning candlelight has jumped from the painting into my hand. Nothing like this has ever happened during the day. The paintings I encounter are always quiet when the sun is up. "Fire. It makes me think of fire," I mutter, as I clasp my hand shut. I can't let on to Claire that her paintings are behaving strangely, so I keep my hand clenched until the flame dies out. When I open my hand, my palm is shaded a reddish-pink.

Claire turns to me and looks at my hand. "Oh dear. Your hand is all red."

I step back in shock. "You can see that?"

She narrows her eyebrows. "Yes, I can see your hand. What happened?"

"I don't know." I pull my hand away, but I'm flooded with equal parts relief and vindication. This isn't only in my mind. I half want to jump for joy to celebrate that I'm not nuts. But when I look at the La Tour again, I stumble. "Claire," I whisper.

"What is it?"

I point to the painting. The candle in it is almost burned out now. Is this because I snuffed out the fire in my hand rather than returned it to the canvas like I do with Cézanne's peaches and Olympia's cat? Prickles of fear run across my skin. Have I ruined a painting?

She gives me a funny look. "What do you mean?"

"The candle. The flame in the La Tour. It's gone."

She glances back at the painting and then to me, then laughs dryly. "Ah, you are so young and so funny. It looks the same to me. Perhaps next time you might want to bring along a more seasoned coworker."

The painting appears fine to Claire. But is it fine? Because when I look at it, it's blackened and dark. Only the smallest speck of white candlelight is left. The painting hasn't returned to normal like our paintings do after they come out and play. But I'm the only one who can see that it's changed, even though she definitely saw what the painting did to my hand.

"Sorry. I was just kidding," I say, trying to recover. *Marie-Amelie, thanks for sending your son. He's an idiot, but you knew that.* "But seriously, everything looks great. Just terrific. Fantastic. Stupendous, in fact."

"And the Renoir of the young girls at the piano looks amazing here. Please tell Marie-Amelie I'm so grateful for the loan."

I look at the piano girls. The painting is perfect, and the sun damage is completely gone. But when I lean in closer, I can see one of the keys that was brightened back to whiteness is turning pale once more. Claire's staring at the painting too, and my chest is tight with worry. Is the sun damage starting up again? Or is this painting afflicted with whatever weirdness has seized the La Tour?

"I love this one so much," Claire says and turns away. I realize she can't see this new sun damage on the keys, just like she couldn't see the bad behavior of the La Tour. But she could see the effect the La Tour had on my hands.

When I take my leave of Claire, I double back through the museum, popping into galleries, searching for any other signs of molting art.

I see none. Then I spot *Bathsheba*, Rembrandt's rendering of an Old Testament scene. Bathsheba has always been a round-bellied woman, but now her stomach is distended, like she's sick. I walk closer to the painting; bits of flesh are poking out of the frame.

This is my chance to fix things. I've always been fast. My reflexes are top-notch. When no one is looking, I make a quick move. I reach for the sagging section and try to push it back into the canvas. But the fleshy part won't budge. Soon a new group of tourists pours into this gallery, and I slink back among them.

I leave for the nearest restroom and splash cold water on my face. I stare into the mirror at my brown eyes that Jenny insisted were hazel the day we met, and I wish I saw the world as I did back then. Back when paintings weren't burning my hands and dribbling fleshy bits from frames that no one else can see.

"The piano girls are fine," I tell my mother. "Can't tell anything had been wrong with it."

The only thing wrong is with me.

"Wonderful."

There's no need to tell my mother the key on the piano is fading, since no one else can see it. Besides, she didn't tell me about Bonheur's connections to Valadon, so I see no reason to disclose every detail either. But I hunt through our galleries later, examining many works as if I'm a doctor with a stethoscope and a tongue depressor, doing a checkup to see if our art might have a temperature now too.

Everything here is in perfect shape. For now.

❧

"Dream, dreamt, dreamt."

My English teacher taps her pointer to the blackboard where she's written out the first set of irregular verbs in British English for class today. The tapping is our cue to write them down. I do, shoehorning the words next to yesterday's sentences with *feel, felt, felt*.

"And now a sentence please," she commands.

I dreamt the art was on fire, but it was only an illusion.

She calls on me.

"The other night, I dreamt the school was on fire, and it felt so real."

She nods approvingly, since I've not only used the word she asked for but yesterday's word too. She moves on to other verbs, and other students take their swings at *bring, brought, brought*, while I wonder what superheroes or secret agents would do if art was on fire. They'd fix it, they'd solve it, they'd save the day. But I'm no masked crusader.

I don't even know if any of this is real. But I know this—what happened yesterday at the Louvre didn't feel like a dream at all. It felt like life. And at the very least it's my life, so I need to figure it out. When the school day ends, I take the train to the Louvre, a criminal returning to the scene of the crime as guilt overcomes him. Whatever happened here yesterday is starting to spread. More keys on the piano are vanishing, a peacock feather droops from Ingres's *Grande Odalisque*, and the mirror inside a Titian has a hairline fracture.

Bathsheba looks worse too. There's a bruise now on the rolls of her stomach, black and blue.

The craziest thought occurs to me—did bringing that sun-damaged Renoir here, the one with the girls at the piano, infect the other art somehow? Are those piano girls patient zero in some sort of strange illness that's spreading? But the symptoms aren't quite the same. Because the Rembrandt, the Titian, the La Tour are all coughing and sputtering, while the Renoir simply seems to be fading again.

Either way, this much is clear—the art here isn't coming to life. More like the opposite.

I call Bonheur as soon as I leave. "Is the painting okay? Is she okay?"

"Of course. Why wouldn't it be?"

"I need to see it. I need to see her."

"My parents are back. It'll have to be late."

"Fine. Just text me when they're gone. I'll sneak out."

CHAPTER 8

Holding Hands

My mother and father are watching a TV show, of all things. They never watch TV. But tonight they feel the need to tune into a sitcom. They're on the couch cracking up. The indignity of parents. The annoying, irritating, vexatious indignity of parents staying up late when I need to slip out. I want to drop sleeping pills into their wineglasses or short out the tube. Instead, I'm at the dining room table doing my best approximation of studying for my exams.

But my brain is repelling math facts, and all I'm doing is tapping my foot, and checking my parents, and wishing they'd go to bed. Bonheur texted me a few minutes ago that the coast is clear at his home.

I switch to literature and try to read an analysis of Proust's *l'Éducation Sentimentale* that I found online, but the words are thick sludge. The details melt away from me because all I want is to see her. I tell myself it's crazy to feel this way about a work of art. That it's insane to want to see a painted girl so badly. But logic won't win this battle, so I stop pretending to absorb the analysis and I let my thoughts wander. I picture a girl in Montmartre in 1885, so clever and so beautiful that two of the greatest painters the world has ever known fell for her. But she held them off because she loved madly a boy her age who liked the same things, who liked music and food and days of doing everything and nothing.

After twenty more minutes of raucous laughter, my father rises from the couch and stretches.

"And on that note, I think I'll call it a night."

"Good night, Dad," I say, hoping my mom will join him. In slumber, that is.

"I better get to bed too. Final prep tomorrow for *The Girl in the Garden*. Very exciting, but very busy."

"Night, Mom," I say. *I have some final prep too.*

After the sound of water running and teeth being brushed turns into blissful silence, I walk quietly to the door, lift the latch in slow motion, and open it. I move into the hallway, sending a quiet wish that the hinges won't creak as I slide the door closed. Once I'm outside, I text Bonheur that I'm on my way. I walk quickly to the nearest Metro and hop onto the next train to Montmartre.

The subway only runs for another hour, so I need to be fast, and it's at least fifteen minutes to Montmartre. When the doors open at my stop, I head up the hundred looping spiral steps at the station and sprint the rest of the way to the house on the hilly street. Bonheur is waiting outside on the sidewalk, since I can't buzz at this hour. He's dressed down tonight in skinny purple pants and a white T-shirt. A red scarf circles his neck, but no wig, no makeup.

"What's wrong? You sounded freaked out on the phone earlier."

I flash back to Bonheur telling me the voices were Muses. To the way he clearly believes in them. To the fact that I've told no one my world has turned upside down since that late night in Oberkampf and it's as if I'm living inside a mirage. I haven't breathed a word to anyone about my untrustworthy brain, and now I've come here late at night to see if a painting is safe from a strange sickness only I can see. "Can I tell you something totally crazy?"

"Seeing as I have sheep on my balcony and a carousel in my living room, yes."

"I don't even know how to begin to say this—"

"Let me guess. The Degas ballerinas are dancing for you at night?"

I stare at him, dumbfounded. It's as if he's pulled back the curtain on a play, revealing the stagehands and the lights, revealing my secret—what I see in the galleries at night. Living, breathing, moving art. "They danced *Swan Lake* the other night," I tell him, like a confession. Then all the other strange secrets I keep pour out, all the ways I don't trust my own eyes. "And the other paintings too. The Cézannes, the Manets, the Matisses, they come to life. Olympia's cat breaks from her canvas and wanders around the galleries. The picnickers in a Monet brought their lunch out of the painting last week." I hold my hands up, an admission that I may be loony.

Bonheur has become his name right now. He is all grins and happiness. "I have to say, it sounds incredibly cool."

"Yeah. Admittedly, it *is* kind of cool. It's also kind of weird, don't you think? I mean, does your Monet come alive in the hall? Does *The Girl in the Garden* break free at night?"

"No. Of course not."

"See? That's my point." I tap my forehead. "I'm a mess. It's all in my head."

"Julien, I don't think it's in your head. It's where you are. It's the museum. Paintings only come alive at museums," Bonheur says with the same certainty he used when he informed me about the Muses below his house. "Not in a home, not in a private collection, not in a gallery."

"And how do you just happen to know that?"

"It's not what I know. It's what I've always believed. It's what I've always felt anytime I've been in a museum. That they *must* come alive at night. How could it be any other way? Only in museums because museums are sacred spaces for art. They're like holy places, don't you think?"

"But how do you know this if it's never happened for you?"

"You're asking me how I know of something I've never seen? I believe it. My sister, Sophie, believes it. My parents believe it. We all believe in the power of art even if we can't see paintings come to life. But some people can. People like you. The Muses have always told us that there are certain people who can actually see art come to life."

"The Muses told you this?"

He nods. "I'm kind of an emissary for them. Where do you think that silver dust comes from?"

"You're saying the silver dust in that five-legged calf you gave me is from a Muse?"

"Yes. And the one you won from the party too. They give it to me from time to time. The basement in my house isn't your average, ordinary cellar."

"It leads to Muses?"

"They live and work far beneath Montmartre. I talk to them. We talk about art. We talk about people who can see art come to life."

I hold up a hand. Maybe he's the crazy one. "And I thought I was going mad."

"Look, we can stand here on the street and debate Muses and madness and the magic of museums or you can come inside and see the girl you've kind of got a thing for."

I run a hand over my chin. "Is it that obvious?"

He positions his hands into a rectangle. "Let's just say it's as if you have a billboard on your face that says you've got it bad for the painted girl."

"Does she come out for you or anyone else here at your house?" I ask him, trying to hold back my jealousy, like it's a dog pulling hard on a leash, that she might spend time with others.

"No. I just told you—paintings can *only* come to life at museums. Now come on. Do you want to see the girl who's headed to your museum in a few more days?"

"Yes." The admission reverberates through my body, a note

held long and lasting on a guitar. There is nothing in the whole world I want more right now than such a visit.

We walk past the green door, through the courtyard, then he opens the orange door without making a sound. He taps a code into the security system and places his finger on his lips. "Shh . . ."

We pad quietly down the hallway, and I can feel heat rising in me. The whole house quivers, hazy and warped. There is a strumming in my body, and a whispering in the air that leads me on. Bonheur unlocks the door and lets me in.

It is just me and the room and this insanely gorgeous painting that I want to hold and touch, this painting that is perfect—no sun damage, no fading colors, no flowers wilting from the seams. When I am mere inches away, I lift my hand, but I am careful not to touch the frame, or even the canvas. The painting is still a painting.

But then it's not. There's a stretching. As if it's dawn and the first rays of a coral sunrise flare through windowpanes. A sound, a sweet morning yawn, delicate arms unfolding from the night. Eyelids fluttering open.

The tips of her fingers press against her walls, imploring the canvas to curve and arc with her. First slowly, then more quickly, the girl reaches her hand through the paint, spreading her fingers. I don't hesitate. I don't think. I reach for her, my fingers touching hers and then sliding into them. Her skin is warm and soft and radiant.

And confident.

There is a boldness in her touch that makes me feel that I can do everything better.

I can't help myself. I press my cheek to her hand. I feel her softness against my face. Her palm is so warm, so tender on my skin. I want her to come all the way out, to talk to me, to tell me who she is.

"I can't wait to meet you when you come to the museum," I say.

She whispers from beyond the canvas, "Me too."

CHAPTER 9

When Paint Becomes Body

At school I perfect the practice of fidgeting. I tap my pencil against the desk. I twirl it in circles, flipping it between my thumb and index finger. I lean forward in my chair. I scoot back in my chair. My instructors chide me, and I try to return to the task at hand. Somehow, I manage to finish the final exam of the year and am set loose for the rest of the summer.

I'm not far from the museum, and I'm tempted to run, but she won't come out until the sun sets, so I walk, popping into a bakery to grab a sandwich for later, since I don't intend to leave for a while. When I near the museum, I feel jittery nerves, like I'm ringing the buzzer at a girl's home for our first date. I walk along the side of the museum that houses the offices and slide my card key into an entrance that takes me to a set of stairs in the administrative wing. I grab the door of the nearest stairwell and take the steps two by two up to the first floor.

There are crowds everywhere, a platoon of visitors and tourists and residents packed around the entrance to her gallery. It's not quite like the crowds at the *Mona Lisa*, but it's close enough, and I feel like I'm at a concert, the revelers sweaty and shouting, angling to get closer to the rock star.

Then I see her.

My heart quickens, and my face feels flushed, and a part of me wants to push through the accumulation of people and run my hands across her painted body. But my heart settles down, a more peaceful rhythm now that the waiting is over, and the only question is whether she will like me too.

Which is, admittedly, a big unknown.

Eventually the museum closes, and as Gustave and another security guard keep watch, I wander through the galleries, always returning to the glass front doors to see if night is falling. The sun sets late in the summer, and I want so badly to tug it down faster on the horizon.

Soon enough, I'm greeted by a darkening sky that sends a thrill through me. My cells have become anticipation as I return to her gallery, where I hear the rustle of a dress. There she is, stepping out of her frame; so natural, so effortless, as if she does this every single night. Her long cream dress skims the floor, and she shakes out her blond curls, a Botticelli beauty emerging from a half shell. Her hair is long and luxurious, and it begs to be touched, and held, and kissed. She doesn't realize I'm here watching her, as her paint becomes body. Now she is flesh, and shape, and skin, and breath, and life.

She turns around, and her eyes are on me for the first time. They are the fierce blue of revolution, the color of a rallying cry.

Then she speaks. "I'm awfully hungry."

I slide into a conversation as if it were the next bend on a well-marked path in the woods. "It's probably been awhile since you had a bite to eat."

"More than a hundred and thirty years," she says, with a wry nod.

"I know where there's a great île flottante, but it's closed," I say, thinking of the nearby café that serves the floating meringue in caramel.

"Maybe you can bring one tomorrow?"

"Sure. It's the best in the city."

"I do love sweets."

"Fortunately, we have plenty of those here in Paris," I say, then I remember the sandwich from earlier. "I have half a sandwich in my bag." I pat my backpack.

"Would you mind terribly? I mean, may I have it?"

"Of course. Absolutely." I sit down on the wooden bench, and she sits next to me. I never take my eyes off her, not as I unzip the backpack, not as I unwrap the bread and cheese, not as I offer it to her. When the food reaches her lips, she rolls her eyes in pleasure.

"This hits the spot," she says.

"I can bring a sandwich tomorrow too if you like. Do you have a favorite?"

"Anything. Anything is good." Then she stops, holds up her index finger. "Actually, *everything* is good," she adds, and there's a ravenousness to her words, a hunger in her voice, and I don't think it's just for food.

"By the way, I'm Julien." I offer my hand to shake. Her touch is a confirmation of so many things, most of all that I'm not mad, because she is as real as I'd imagined. She's not a trick of the mind. She's atoms and elements, she is absolute, from the hair that falls past her shoulders to the folds of her dress to the slim silver bracelets she wears, each one the width of a few links of thread.

"You can call me Clio."

"Clio," I say. Then again, because her name is like a bell, clear and pure. "Clio."

"It's better like this, isn't it?"

"Yes, I would have to say it's better like this."

She sighs deeply. "I'm free. I'm finally free." Her voice breaks for a moment as if she might cry. But tears don't fall. "And it feels spectacular." She leans her head back, like she's on a beach letting the sun warm her face. "Ah, you have no idea what all those years inside a painting will do to a girl."

She stretches her arms up high, shifts her neck from side to side, then turns to me. Her gaze is a spark, a ride on a motorcycle after midnight, as her wild blue eyes light up as if she's about to suggest something naughty. "Would you like to show me this museum, Julien?"

Okay, maybe not *that* naughty. But it's the way she says it. Like nothing could be better than the two of us, nearly alone, in the Musée d'Orsay.

"I would love to show you this museum."

We wander through the galleries, and I show her the art. She trails her hand along the canvases, brushing her fingertips across pasteled bathers on beaches, bowls of peaches, and moonlit stars, then tracing them over petals of flowers, Tahitian women on islands, and cabarets in Montmartre. I don't tell her to stop, I don't say "keep your hands off" as I would to anyone else who tried to touch the paintings. There is a reverence to her touch, as if she'd never even dare think of hurting a painting, as if she could only think of loving them. When she reaches one of Monet's Rouen cathedrals she stops to consider it.

"I want to go there. I want to see the real cathedral. Have you been?"

"Yes. My father teaches art history. He took me to a lot of the places the artists here painted. Rouen, Arles, even Monet's garden."

Her eyes widen. "You've been to Monet's garden? The real one?"

I laugh once. "Yes, the real one. What other one would I go to?"

"What is it like now? Tell me."

"It's like this sensory paradise of colors and scents and sounds. It's like art made real. It's like walking through a field of inspiration," I say, then stop myself when I hear the words coming out of my mouth. "God, that sounds unbelievably pretentious, doesn't it?"

"No. It doesn't. It sounds . . ." Her voice trails off and she looks again at the Monet. She lays her hand along the doorway of the church. "It sounds like something I'd want."

The way she says "want" tugs on my heart. It's both wistful and painful, a wish from a girl who's been trapped for too long. Are the other people in the paintings trapped too? Something is different about Clio though. I've never talked to any of the other painted people this long. They've never said more than a few words, and none of them have ever seemed sad. She's not like them. I want to ask who she is, where she's from, but the moment is delicate and I don't want to break it.

"Do you want to see my favorite Van Gogh?"

"Yes," she says, and she's smiling again, sparkling again. "I definitely want to see your favorite Van Gogh, Julien."

The sound of my name on her lips makes me wants to touch her arm, to reach for her hand. I keep my hands to myself though— she wanted to come out of her frame, but I don't know if she wanted to come out for me or to be free of her painted chains.

I take her to the wing on the second floor that houses the Van Goghs and bring her to *Starry Night*. A couple walks along the River Rhône as starlight fills the night and sailboats bob in the water. Clio places a hand on her heart and closes her eyes briefly. When she opens her eyes, she reaches for the painting, her touch like a murmur on the waves.

"Have you been here?"

"Yes, Van Gogh painted this by the Rhône in Arles. But I don't remember going. I was too young when my dad took me there."

Neither one of us says anything as we admire the painting. Then her body shifts. She moves closer to me. We're not touching, but being so near to her is intoxicating. "We'll go together someday then," she says, and now she's looking at me.

A heady, swooping feeling races through me at the admission that maybe she likes me too. "Anytime, any day," I say, though I know it would be impossible. She may be real, but she's still painted.

"Show me more."

I do, and an hour or so later, she has seen haystacks and operas, mirrors and pheasants, doctors and patients. "You love them all," she says to me when we stop near her gallery. It's almost midnight, and I hate that I have to go home.

I nod. "Yes. I do."

She asks me another question. "You've been coming to see me, haven't you?"

"Did you see me? Could you see me?"

"You're the first thing I've been able to see or hear on the other side of the frame," she says with both frustration and relief in her voice. "I saw you in that room. You heard me, right?"

"Yes," I say, flashing back to Bonheur's house.

"I wanted to come out sooner." There is so much longing in her voice. Longing for what could have been? For the years she missed? She moves closer to me, so we're both leaning against the wall, inches apart. "As soon as I saw you, I tried to get out. It was the closest I've ever come to getting out until now."

"I'm glad you're able to come out now."

"Me too. You're so different from anyone I've ever met. You asked questions about me. You talked to me."

She is so straightforward, and it is an immense turn-on. Who was that Jenny from Pittsburgh? I don't remember. I don't care. There's never been another girl I've wanted as far as I can tell in this second.

" 'What are you like, girl behind the paint?' That's what you asked me."

"You remember," I say. I'm sure she's some sort of enchantress, and she has put me completely under her spell. "Who are you?"

"I told you my name. I'm just a sixteen-year-old girl."

"No. *Who* are you?"

Her gaze dances away and then back at me as she grins. "Julien, do you want me to tell you *everything* about me on our first..." Her voice trails off, as if she doesn't know the word. "What do you call it these days?"

"Um, date? First date?" I offer, hoping that maybe she sees it the same way.

"First date. Why, yes. I like the sound of that. And are visits to the museum good first dates?"

"I would have to say this particular visit to the museum has been my favorite date."

"And for me as well."

I feel wobbly, but I manage to hang on to ask another question. "Where have you been for the last century?"

She points to the gallery where her gilded frame rests. "On the other side of that painting."

We walk back. "What's on the other side?"

"Tulips and hollyhocks, pansies and irises." Her voice is pure, her French is impeccable, but she doesn't have the accent of a native.

"You don't sound like you're from here."

"You doubt my French?" She places a palm against her chest, as if I've offended her.

"Maybe a little."

"Do you think I'm French?"

"I don't know what you are. Or who you are. Tell me where you're from," I ask, seized by curiosity, by the thirst to know her more.

She shakes her head. "Come back tomorrow, please. Promise me?"

"I promise."

She walks back to her painting and steps into the frame, pulling up the gauzy hem of her skirts last, the lace edges brushing against the painted irises until she is immobile once more.

Then I do something I have never done before. I touch the art. Not with my hands, like Clio did. If the forensic experts dusted this painting for fingerprints they wouldn't find mine; they'd find the barest outline of my lips.

❧

I walk home in a hazy dream state, still feeling the faint traces of her so dangerously close to me, as if she's imprinted on my skin. And so I hardly notice, and I barely care, that there's a guy my age in jeans and a tattered sweatshirt sprawled out on the museum steps, watching me walk away.

CHAPTER 10

One of These Things Is Not Like the Others

Look! The sheet is messy on Olympia's bed." Clio points to the edge of the white satin sheet in Manet's *Olympia*. A small bit of white fabric is poking out of the canvas, hanging over the gilded frame.

I pretend to chide the painting. "I tell them to clean their rooms and put their toys away, but they don't listen to me. Ever."

"May I do it?" Clio asks.

"Be my guest."

She hands me the plastic takeout container with half of the île flottante still in it. The caramel had turned drizzly, and the meringue had sunk by the time Clio emerged. But still, she is digging the dessert. She gathers up the white folds of the sheet, and I tense for a second, hoping it doesn't remain stuck outside the canvas, like Bathsheba's belly. But the sheets take and Clio tucks them neatly back in. The art here behaves differently from the paintings at the

Louvre. The art here seems healthy. The art there didn't respond to my touch.

"There." Clio brushes one palm against the other.

"Now I finally have someone to help me get all the paintings back in order."

"Does this happen a lot?"

"The paintings are terribly lazy. They expect me to straighten up after them all the time."

"It's more like they're playing, though?"

I nod. That's exactly how the paintings here act at night. "Yes. They seem to be having fun."

"But you still pick up after them?"

"Of course. I always take care of the art."

"You are a caretaker," she says and takes another bite of the meringue, then offers some to me. I take the spoon from her and eat a piece. I don't like to be fed.

I hand the île flottante back to her, then look at my watch. I've got to be home by midnight. Darn curfew. "It's almost eleven. Do you want to go to the ballet?"

Clio raises her eyebrows. "The ballet? But I can't leave."

"I think I might be able to arrange for a special performance here."

"That sounds like a perfect, as you call it, second date."

Clio puts the empty takeout container on a wooden bench. We walk across the cavernous thoroughfare to visit my dancer friends. I tap twice near the frame. The girl in white squeezes her way out of the paint.

"I'm all better now," she announces. She points to her foot. "Thank you."

"Anytime. By the way, I'm Julien. And this is Clio."

"Oh. Hi, Julien and Clio," she says, giggling. "I'm Emmanuelle."

"Nice to meet you, Emmanuelle," I say, and it's the first time I've learned the name of one of Degas's dancers.

"Pleasure to meet you too," Clio says with a quick curtsy that reminds me once again of the time she's from.

Emmanuelle looks back at her frame and motions for her friend to join her. In a flutter of white tulle her friend springs free. Moments later, all the Degas girls are wriggling out of frames, encouraging the other dancers to make their getaways too. They jeté their way into the finale of *Swan Lake* as the dancers in pinks and whites and blues become the swans, with Emmanuelle as Odette. Her young friend plays the prince, still another girl assumes the role of the evil sorcerer. We watch them perform. When they're finished, Clio and I shout "brava" as the corps take their swanlike bows, then leap back into their frames.

As Emmanuelle goes still, I wonder what happens to her when she's inside the frame. If she pines for escape, trapped in some sort of bizarre eternity of paint, or if she is simply a shadow of the girl she once was.

Clio and I resume our walk through the galleries. "Clio, are you the girl Renoir painted? Or are you just, I don't know, a *version* of her now that lives on in the art?"

"You mean, am I like the other paintings? Paint coming to life at night?"

"Something like that. I don't entirely understand if it's really them who come out, or just some alternate version that exists solely in the art. But you seem different. Most of the paintings don't say much. More than a few words, at least, like with Emmanuelle. Are they ghosts?" I ask with a forced laugh.

She shakes her head. "But I've heard that the ghosts of great artists inhabit cafés."

"Really?" I can't tell if she's joking.

"Since that's where so many writers, artists, and poets hang out," she says with a teasing grin. "Though you'd think they might visit museums too."

"Please don't tell me we're going to be visited by a ghost of an artist."

She stops walking and faces me, her expression serious now. "When the paintings come out for you, it's what people have meant all along when they talk about artists being immortal. In a way, their work can live forever. When the art comes alive it's like the immortal version of the painting, like a little bit of the person painted has gotten to live forever. But the people, they aren't stuck inside the painting. They don't spend their days wandering beyond the frame. They aren't alive on the other side."

"You're not just paint when you go inside the frame?" I knew she was different. I knew she was a girl, and not just a shadow of the painting's subject. But I had no idea how real she was.

"That's why I asked about the real Monet's garden. Because I live in the painted one. All the time."

"You live in Monet's garden?"

"That's where I was when Renoir painted me. So when I go back in the frame, that's where I am, in a painted version. That's where I sleep. That's where I've been."

"That sounds beautiful and awful at the same time."

Her eyes are full of such sadness. "It is. It's gorgeous there, but it's lonely. I've been completely alone this whole time."

"Did he trap you? Renoir?"

She sighs and shakes her head, her beautiful blond curls moving gently, like a breeze. I can't even imagine what she's feeling. "There were things we didn't agree on. But, Julien," she says and places her hand on mine, "I don't actually want to talk about Renoir right now."

Maybe the story is true. Perhaps Renoir was in love with her, but she didn't feel the same. So he locked her away in a painted cage.

"Fair enough," I say, and I'm not sure where to go next. I want to ask her about her life before, about who she was and if she wants to go back. But maybe there is no back. Maybe there's just this, life inside and out of a painting.

"But you know what I do want to talk about?" she asks.

"What do you want to talk about?"

"You. Tell me about you." She reaches for my hand and slides her fingers into mine. "Tell me how you spend your days, Julien."

Right now, I spend them waiting for the night.

CHAPTER 11

The Gnarled Hands

I pass an art gallery where a Jack Russell terrier has camped out in the window, slumbering at the claw feet of a chair from years ago. I stop to say hi to the dog through the window, then I wave to Zola, the owner's daughter. Zola goes to school with me and helps out in her mother's gallery. Zola smiles and waves back, then points to the low neckline of her red-and-black dress.

I laugh and she pops outside. "Today's take," she says and removes a tiny pink-and-blue-china espresso cup from between her breasts. "I took it from Ladurée this morning. Their coffee is awful."

"Zola, how many times do I have to tell you? All the coffee in France is awful."

"And until the coffee improves, I will keep stealing coffee cups from all over Paris. I'm angling for one from the Red Café. Just opened a few days ago, and I hear the coffee is wretched."

Zola has amassed quite a collection of coffee cups in the last few years, tucking them between her breasts as she takes them from Les Deux Magots and Angelina as well as her neighborhood joints. She always brings them into school to show me her latest trophies. I don't discourage the hobby—it's entertaining to me, especially when she demonstrates exactly how she steals each one.

"Keep on then, my favorite thief."

"How is your Renoir doing?" In addition to running the gallery, Zola's mother is a renowned art authenticator and has verified paintings for museums around the world, including *The Girl in the Garden* for us.

"She's amazing," I say, feeling as if I have a wonderful secret, and I do.

Zola heads back into the store, and I turn the corner onto the museum's block, saying hello to a few of my mother's coworkers who are taking their lunchtime smoking breaks. I dart into a side door to the offices and snag my name tag.

"Julien." It's my mother, and her voice is crisp and too controlled, the way she talks when she's worried.

"What's going on?"

She tips her forehead to her office, and I follow her. She closes the door. "*The Boy with the Cat* has sun damage now too."

"What? It never even sees the sun." *The Boy with the Cat* is also a Renoir. Like the piano girls, it's always protected from the sun, so this shouldn't be happening.

"I know. But now it's fading too."

"When did this happen?"

"I saw it today when I was out on the floors."

"Are the restorers coming?"

"Yes. Right after they visit the Louvre." That can only mean one thing. I tense. "Claire called me today." My mother's jaw tightens and her coal eyes are hard. "The sun damage is back on the piano girls too."

"Where's the sun damage on the piano girls?" I ask carefully.

"The keys. On the piano keys." She holds out her hands, as if she's looking for an answer to fall into them. "I have no idea what is happening. Why are our Renoirs getting sun damage?"

"I don't know," I say, even though I'm pretty sure she was asking rhetorically. I do know there seems to be two different things happening to the art—there's the simple fading of the Renoirs, then the stranger shedding of the others, like *Bathsheba*.

"Maybe sunlight is getting into one of the rooms where it's not supposed to," she says, grasping for an answer.

"Of course. That's probably it. What about *The Girl in the Garden*, though?"

She smiles, and her shoulders relax. "Perfect. Thank God."

"Are any other Renoirs fading?"

"I checked each and every one. They're all fine, so let's hope it's just contained to those two, and when the museum closes I'll have the crews do a thorough check of the room to see if sunlight could be sneaking in."

I head to the main floor, where I find my tour group for the day. I guide them through the galleries, stopping at the usual paintings before I bring them to one of Renoir's portraits of a woman,

Gabrielle with a Rose. She is half-dressed, holding a rose near her ear. One breast is exposed and the woman's chest is luminous, the shawl over her shoulders looks like the inside of an oyster shell. I scan quickly for any sun damage. My heart catches when I see that the corner of the shawl, a tiny sliver of painted fabric, has turned pale.

I flash back to the piano girls. I was the first one to notice the sun damage in that work several weeks ago, and then my mother could see it. When the damage returned I was the first one to notice it at the Louvre, then a few days later Claire could see it. For some reason, I can see the sun damage before anyone else can.

My chest tightens with the knowledge that any day now my mother, and everyone else, will be able to see what's happening to *Gabrielle.* A fuse has been lit, slow and quiet.

I force myself to focus on the tour group.

"Renoir painted until late in his life, and this is one of the last masterpieces he created. What's particularly interesting about this work is he was crippled with arthritis when he painted it," I tell them and hold out my hands, turning them into claws. "He strapped the paintbrushes to his wrists and painted like that because his fingers were too gnarled to hold the brushes anymore. And yet, even with his damaged hands, he still crafted such works of beauty."

I take a step back and let them admire the painting, especially since this may be one of the last times anyone can enjoy it in its proper state.

A woman with short hair and glasses clears her throat and speaks. "I've noticed that you have a lot of paintings by men. But the only women you seem to have here are the painted ones." Her tone is challenging, like a student in a graduate class. She's not the first person to make this observation though, so I have a response ready.

"We have paintings by Berthe Morisot and Mary Cassatt."

The woman scoffs. "Isn't that kind of like saying, 'Oh, I have a black friend'?"

I hold up my palms to her, a sign that I'm not fighting. "They were amazing painters too. Their work isn't here as some sort of quota."

"But you have mostly male painters on your walls."

"Unfortunately, most artists have been men. In France, women weren't even admitted to art school until 1894, when Suzanne Valadon was the first. But things are starting to change."

"Maybe your walls can change then," she says, holding her chin up high.

"Perhaps they will. I personally think anyone can create art. Girl, guy, educated, self-taught. Art is for everyone."

"I disagree."

There's a guy's voice now, and I'm feeling a bit ganged up on. I look for the voice, and I'm surprised to see someone I know. It's Max, who draws caricatures by the river. "You have to be great to make art that matters," he says.

I give him a look like he can't be serious. I don't know Max well, but this doesn't sound like the guy who joked about horses the other day. The other visitors start to look away and shuffle their feet.

"Well, one of the things to remember about great art is it can cost a lot," I say, going for humor to ease my way out of this awkward attack from different angles. I guide them to the nearby Van Gogh, his *Portrait of Dr. Gachet*. "This is the physician who treated Van Gogh in the final months of his life. The artist produced only two authenticated paintings of Dr. Gachet. One of them is here on our walls," I say, pointing to the red-and-blue image of a man who looks as depressed as his patient was. I'm glad he's never popped out of his frame at night. "The other sold for $82.5 million at auction."

There are gasps from the crowd at the price tag. "Enjoy the rest of your visit at the Musée d'Orsay."

I quickly thank today's group, and as they scatter I pull Max aside.

"Hey, Max. What's the story? You seem a little—"

He cuts me off. "Your painting is a fake."

"I'm sorry?"

"Your *Girl in the Garden*. It belongs to my family," he says as he stares at me with unflinching eyes. A thick curl of dark hair slides onto his forehead. "To my parents."

"Whoa. I don't think so." I want to ask how he could even own a Renoir, but for all I know his family could be recluse millionaires, collectors who live in a castle and bid anonymously at auctions the world over. Still, with the ratty sweatshirt and its worn cuffs hanging down to his fingernails, he hardly has the trappings of someone whose family traffics in priceless paintings.

Sweatshirt. My mind returns to the other night. The guy on the steps I barely noticed, but noticed enough to see his sweatshirt. That was Max. Why is he watching me?

"I have the papers," Max says as he taps a black leather folder.

"And how come you never mentioned this all the times I saw you by the river? It's just coming up now?"

"It was not part of our conversations," he says, and his voice is off, like it doesn't quite fit him.

"You'd think that's the sort of thing that might come up though."

"It's coming up now. And I came to you first since you've always liked my art. My great art." It's as if Max is prodding me, poking me in a hunt for soft spots. Pointing out that I've been nice to him, then twisting his own words about great art back on himself. "And I thought you might want to introduce me to your mother so I can resolve the matter with her."

My mother is focused on the sun-damaged Renoirs right now, so if I bring Max to her with some spurious claim, she'll have a fit. She'll berate me for not having done the legwork myself. I walk to the stairwell and motion for Max to follow me. "Show me the papers first," I say, hoping I come across as tough and steady. But inside a queasiness sets in. I don't want him to take her away. I don't want Clio to leave, and even though I hardly believe the painting is his, I can't take any chances.

"It was ours. It was stolen during the Nazi occupation in 1942, and we've been searching for it since then."

Provenance.

I curse silently. To be sold, shown, or exhibited a painting must have a traceable history and the owners must also prove its whereabouts during the Nazi era, when hundreds of thousands of paintings were looted. My mother conducted a thorough vetting on *The Girl in the Garden* already, but all provenance claims are taken seriously. Max reaches inside the folder. Using only the tips of his fingers to handle them, he shows me a series of papers claiming his family bought the painting from Bonheur's family before the Second World War. He leans closer to me and his breath smells like heavy rose perfume. He smells like what I imagine the girls at their vanities in those Renoirs smell like. "She, the girl, was my great-great-grandmother. We bought the painting to protect her virtue."

"That's just a story," I say, shaking my head and repeating the words my mother said to me. But the story of two artists in love with the girl—with Clio—feels more true every night.

"I would like to show Ms. Garnier the documents."

I don't want to believe him, but the documents look as real as any others I've seen. Since I'm not one to authenticate records, I take Max to my mother's office, where he introduces himself as Maximillian Broussard and makes an impassioned case for his family's ownership of *The Girl in the Garden*. "As you can see, we still feel a great responsibility to guard her reputation, even now."

"Mr. Broussard, we have researched this painting's ownership thoroughly, but we treat provenance claims quite seriously and I will certainly look into this," my mother says, a cool veneer masking what must be a roiling sea inside. He leaves copies of the documents with my mother, and she tells him she will reach back out to him tomorrow after she confers with her board. "Julien, can you show Mr. Broussard out?"

I guide him upstairs, out to the floors and to the exits. "I am sorry to be the bearer of such bad news, but I am sure you understand family obligations of this sort," he says.

I say nothing as the crowds move by.

He leans closer and speaks in a low voice, the cloying rose perfume hanging heavily near me. "But some girls can just be trouble, and they shouldn't be let out."

It's as if all the sound were vacuumed up, as if all the visitors became clay figures, stuck in an animated pose, and it's just Max and me. This guy who seems to know more about a painting than he should. A guy who's been watching me and watching her.

I'm stuck for a moment, the soles of my boots trapped by my own shock, as I watch him walk away from the museum. But when he heads across the street, I follow him. He settles back onto the green-slatted chair in front of his easel, pushes up the cuffs on his sleeves.

When I see his hands I nearly gasp. His fingers are curled inward, the nails scratching his palms, bent up and seized.

Like Renoir's.

Then he cracks his knuckles, and turns his TEN EUROS sign around. His hands are back to normal. Young, flexible Max's hands.

Clio's words about the ghosts of great artists ring through me. *Though you'd think they might visit museums too.* What if she wasn't joking? Maybe the ghost of Renoir is inhabiting Max the street artist?

I walk over to Max as he reaches for his pencils. I turn the other green chair around, the one his caricature subjects sit in when drawn. I plunk myself down.

"Dude, you're going to have your picture drawn?" he asks, and he sounds like Max again, like the guy who draws exaggerated sketches of tourists.

"What was the deal with that back there?"

"What back where?"

"Hello? In the museum?"

"I've been here the whole time. What are you talking about?"

"You were just on my tour. You had all those documents from the painting."

"I don't know what you've been smoking, but can I have some of it?" Max laughs. The dour boy he was a few minutes ago has vanished.

I stand up and run a hand through my hair. I mutter something about needing to leave, then walk across the bridge, trying to make sense of this newest wrinkle. Just when I settle into the idea that living art is my life, I learn that ghosts might be real too. The rose perfume smell, the hands—are those signs of ghostly possession? My phone rings, and Bonheur's name flashes on the screen.

I answer, and am about to launch into the story of Max because I have a hunch Bonheur believes in ghosts.

But he goes first. "I literally just finished my final test for the *bac*, when I picked up Sophie's message."

"Congrats on finishing your exam," I say, needing to skip past details like *le bac* and his quirky sister. "Listen, this guy I know showed up today on my tour trying to claim—"

"Weird curl on his forehead?"

I stop walking. "You know him?" I duck into the doorway of pharmacy that promises to cure all manner of headaches.

"I saw him walking up and down our block the other afternoon. Seemed fishy. Since Sophie finished classes before I did, she's been keeping tabs on him during the days. He's mostly outside the museum, but she found where he forged the papers earlier today."

I pump a fist in the air. "Yes! I knew they had to be fake. I can't believe you guys saw him do it."

Color me impressed. I didn't know Bonheur or his sister had a penchant for spying. The thought crosses my mind briefly that Bonheur could be tricking me. But I trust him. I tell him what Max said at the museum.

"I didn't think he'd get to the museum so quickly, but he moves fast," Bonheur says. "Let me see if Sophie's still there, where he doctored those papers. Hold on just a sec."

My head is swimming as this painting becomes a ripple in a pond that won't stop. Each movement it makes spreads. When Bonheur comes back on the line, he gives me an address.

"Sophie will meet you there in twenty minutes. I can be there in forty-five. And listen, bring that calf you won at the party."

"Why?"

"You never know when Muse dust might come in handy."

CHAPTER 12

The Appearance of a Key

I text my mother that I'll miss my final tour of the day and that she'll need to have someone fill in for me, and I exit the Metro in the Marais to find Sophie. The address Bonheur gave me is on rue des Rosiers. I pass familiar shoe shops selling short boots with high heels, stores hawking expensive tailored shirts for men, and the Jewish deli housed in an old dress store that still has the sign *LES JOLIES JUPES* in blue mosaic tiles above windows now full of rugelach and challah bread. At a corner where three roads converge, people crisscross and lean away from the tires of tiny cars shoehorning their way through the narrow lane.

I walk past a falafel shop. It's where Simon spends many evenings, holding court at one of the red-vinyl booths as friends come and go. I scan the open front, looking for his familiar shock of dark blond hair and slouched-back leisurely command of a patch of this eatery, but he's not here. As I walk and look at addresses, I send him a quick text to see if he'll be around later.

I reach my destination, checking the number above the door against the one on the paper I'm still holding. They match. I've arrived at a vintage shop, the kind with a pastiche of vendors peddling black lace skirts alongside silver tea sets next to sky-blue vanities and lemon-yellow dressers. I pull on the handle, but the door is locked, and the sign says BE BACK IN FIFTEEN MINUTES. I'm about to call Bonheur when the door is pushed open.

"Shh." It's Sophie.

I step inside.

"Want a bite?" Sophie holds out a falafel sandwich wrapped in wax paper. The pita pouch is stuffed with tomatoes, purple cabbage, cucumbers, and fried chickpea patties. Tahini threatens to slide down the bread. "Messy, I know," she says. "But so freaking delish."

"Not hungry, but thanks."

"Seriously." She thrusts the sandwich at me, but I decline. "Have you had them? You will never have anything better in your life." She takes another bite, tearing off a hunk of the falafel sandwich, then wipes off her hand on a napkin and offers to shake.

She seems calm and steady, and I feel unmoored. "Did you break into this shop?"

She shifts her free hand back and forth in a so-so gesture. "I hid behind a dresser when they put the rugelach out." Sophie points to the Jewish deli. "Cass can't resist rugelach, so she took off. She won't be back for another ten minutes, prob."

"Cass who?"

"Cass Middleton."

"Did you just say Middleton?"

"Duh."

"As in *the* Middletons?"

"Double duh."

Oliver and Cass Middleton are notorious, the father and teenage daughter pair of British forgers who conned the art world a few years ago, pulling off magnificent fakes. They fooled art historians, curators, and gallery owners across continents and far into the vaunted halls of auction houses in London and New York, of collectors in Stuttgart and Kyoto, and of museums in St. Petersburg, Boston, Madrid, and here in Paris too. They were very nearly caught in a scandal involving a fake Gauguin a year ago, but there wasn't enough evidence so the case was dropped. It had been widely rumored that they'd resurfaced in France, but this is the first I've heard of where they landed, here in a vintage shop in the Marais.

"Great. So we've just broken into the Middletons' shop and you're eating falafel."

"Well technically, Julien, *I'm* the one who broke in. But c'mon. Let's go to the back." She wraps the remaining bits of her sandwich into the wax paper, balling it up in her hand and tossing it into a trash can by the counter.

The store is large and haphazardly laid out with meandering paths through the goods, like a maze for rats. We walk and the store stretches back, offering up jewelry boxes stacked on bureaus with gilded mirrors, next to hats in pastel hatboxes and retro purses arranged on velvet couches.

Sophie points to a coffee-colored door, marked with peeling

paint and a long scratch near the keyhole. "See that door? It's locked. But that's where the guy was dummying up the papers. Trying to claim that painting was his when it's been in our family the whole time."

Sophie snorts, and she sounds so indignant.

"Why is this so important to you?" I ask her. "I mean, I know it's your family's painting. But is that all there is to it? Why do you care so much, Sophie?" I'm not averse to snooping in a back room for evidence of forgery; I can't stand forgers, but I know why the painting matters to me personally. I want to know the raison d'être for Sophie and her family, and since the painting was a gift to the museum, it's not about money. "You're asking me to break into a room. Tell me why this is so important to you."

She rolls her eyes. "Sheesh. Now, Julien? You want to go through all my reasons now?"

"Yes. Now."

She counts off on her index finger. "One. Because of Suzanne Valadon. My great-great-great-however-many-greats. She always believed anyone could make art. And I believe that too. So that's why Bonheur and I call ourselves the Avant-Garde, like an art society, to keep that idea alive."

"Fine," I say, because I'm cool with art societies. The history of art is sprinkled with groups of artists banding together around an ideology or a goal, from architects evangelizing new ways of building to painters trying to resurrect the past. "Her *artistic politics* as Bonheur said. Gotcha. What else?"

She adds in the middle finger to the count. "Two. Because she asked our family to keep that painting safe because of the curse on it."

"Wait. There's a curse on the painting?" I ask, but perhaps that's why Clio is trapped—because the painting is cursed.

"Obviously. Suzanne said there was a girl in it. That's why we had to keep it away from Renoir's family all these years. To keep the girl safe."

Valadon and Renoir. Once contemporaries, then enemies. That's the connection I was seeking when I researched Bonheur's home. "Why would they be enemies?"

"Because Renoir believed art and inspiration was only for great artists. Valadon didn't, and the Muses don't either. They believed that one day there would be an age of great artistic creation and expression. For everyone." Sophie holds her arms out wide, as if she were parting the artistic seas.

"So there's a curse on that painting because Valadon had some inclusive view of art and Renoir was an elitist? Well, that's all I need to know. Let me just get out the crowbar I keep in my backpack to break into this room."

"There's one other little teensy, tiny detail." She points exaggeratedly to me. "That would be the inspiration part of the whole shebang. The whole human muse thingamajig. Muses have always been eternal, but when the first human muse arrived on the scene—humans, who live, love and die and so on—that would mark the start of this great age of artistic expression." She taps me now with that index finger. "You, doofus. You."

"Me?"

"Yes. Didn't my brother tell you all this? The paintings come alive for you. You dance with them at night or whatever. What did you think, you were hallucinating? The Muses have always told us a human muse would eventually appear, and I guess they saw you hanging out with the Degas dancers some night and figured out that you're the first human muse. There are Eternal Muses and now there are human muses. Now, let's go into that room," she says, so offhand, so matter-of-fact that she could be telling me about her geometry lesson or giving me directions to Notre Dame from here. Turn down this road, cross this bridge, and there you are. Muses. Human muses.

"Oh, sure. Human muses. That makes sense. And naturally, I'm one. Me. Of course," I say, feeling like a pawn in some cat-and-mouse game cooked up by Bonheur and his wacky little sister. "I think maybe I'll just leave this whole idea of curses and Muses behind, and let the experts do the actual authentication instead of an art society consisting of two people who believe in Muses."

"You don't believe me?"

"No, I don't. I think that all sounds ridiculous." I'm about to walk away when I think of Clio's eyes. How she's not like the other art. How she's just a girl trapped in a painting for all those years. How I'm the only one who can see her. I can't just stop. I have to help, even though the idea of human muses is ludicrous.

"Julien," Sophie says in a quiet plea. Her face transforms to a kind of reverence. "I'm not putting you on. I swear. You're not the only one who loves art. You're not the only one who believes in its power. I do too. So does my brother. But you are the only one who can do this. You're a human muse. You're the only one who can keep that painting safe." Her expression is tinged with desperation, with the kind of yearning an art society can stoke. She believes this so deeply, but I just don't know how to take this news. I thought Muses were all women. I thought Muses were a closed club that wasn't taking any new members. I also once thought peaches and cats and dancers stayed put in their frames.

"Why me?" I ask.

"Why not you?"

Because I'm not a scholar, not a genius, not even a terribly talented artist, I want to say. Because I'm just a boy who loves art—all art. "How do you want to get in the room?" I ask, pointing out the practical problem. "You said the door was locked. You'll have to find another way in."

"*You're* the other way."

"I'm the other way?"

"You brought the calf, right? With the Muse dust in it?"

"Yes."

"Then let me prove it to you. That you have a talent we don't have. That we need you."

I hardly know what to make of Sophie's conviction, but my world has become so topsy-turvy that anything seems possible, even something as absurd as what Sophie's suggesting. I take the pink polka-dotted calf I won at the party from my backpack and hand it to Sophie. As crazy as the idea of human muses is, it would also explain all the things I see. It would mean I'm not losing my mind.

Sophie takes off the cap from the calf's fifth leg and taps some of the silvery dust into her palm. "See? Draw a key and touch it with the silver in here."

She closes her fist around the dust.

I could not feel stupider right now. I could not be more certain the joke is on me. But then I remember the cat's hair, how a piece of it materialized where I had drawn her, when I rubbed my silver-coated hand across the page. This can't be. But what if? I want to know if maybe I can do something with my second-rate talent with a pencil and paper. Something that matters. Something that makes a difference.

Sophie reaches into her pocket, takes out a sheet of paper, and thrusts it at me. She turns around and bends her back so she's fashioned her body into a drafting table. I take the pencil from my backpack, hoping against hope, praying against prayer. I glance at the lock; it's the kind that'll happily let in an old-fashioned skeleton key. I shake my head, wanting to believe but knowing better, and yet still I draw. A precise, pristine skeleton key.

Sophie straightens and opens her hand. She pinches some dust and sprinkles it on the drawing. Nothing happens. "Now you do it," Sophie instructs.

I'm convinced now that I'm crazy, but I do it anyway, tracing the outline of the key with the silver dust that remains on my fingers. Here, in my hand, as Sophie promised, a skeleton key appears.

CHAPTER 13

Rubies Found

It's *Harold and the Purple Crayon*," I say in wonderment at the key that has weight and shape and even scent. I bring it to my nose, and I smell rusty metal. I want to laugh out loud. I want to cackle with amazement. I have officially blown my own mind. Maybe Sophie is right about me.

But Sophie is Miss Practical. She pulls me to the door, takes the key from my hand, and unlocks the entrance to a dark back room. She inches the door closed. She jams the key at me, and I tuck it into my pocket. The room is the size of a large closet, and it's faintly lit by a desk lamp encased in green glowing plastic, a vintage number that could easily be sold in the store. There's a large ornate wooden desk against one wall, standing proud on carved and imposing legs. A cabinet is wedged along another wall, meeting the desk in the corner.

"You could be a cat burglar," I say, but Sophie is already off and running, foraging through papers, through wax seals from various art galleries, through stationery from state-run museums, through invoices of sales. All the tricks of the forging trade are here.

"He was here earlier today, so there must be something. Some evidence. Some slip of paper." She stops rooting around. "Hello? We don't have all day. Try the trash can."

I kneel down and look through trash, and the thought flashes through my mind that seconds ago I drew a key that became manifest, and now I'm picking through litter. "Nothing here but a few apple cores and some rubber bands."

"There has to be something. Those hands. Those claw hands. He has to have dropped something. He can't have gotten it right the first time."

I place my palm on Sophie's arm. "You saw his hands?"

She nods and turns her hands into something broken—knotty, ragged claws.

More proof I'm not insane.

I rifle faster through the papers on the desk, then papers on the file cabinet, then papers in drawers. Nothing.

Then I see a glint, like the shine of a jewel if I were looking for rubies or diamonds. A handful of pages have slipped into the steep valley between the desk and the file cabinet. I slide my hand along the desk legs, grab the pages, and pull them out. They're rough copies of fakes, first attempts at forged documents. My heart springs against my chest, a jack-in-the-box boinging and bouncing. Maybe I could be a detective. Maybe that is my true calling. I could be pretty good at this cloak-and-dagger, backroom spying stuff, especially with my newfound magical drawing skill.

Because this is the evidence, the proof that Max, the street artist and host to Renoir it seems, *was* here at the headquarters of the art world's greatest forgers. This shop is vintage all right, it's retro in the most ironic way, because they're still doing what they did years ago. Only the shop is just a cover.

"Hide them. Put them in your pants or something," Sophie hisses. She tilts her head to the side, like she's heard something.

"Are you crazy?"

"Just do it."

I fold the pages in half, then in quarters, then tuck them down the front of my jeans.

"I hope you're a good liar because you need to come up with a cover for us," she says and yanks the door open. I follow, leaving the secret lair from which, I presume, a new reign of art forgeries has begun. I click the door shut behind me, then walk past old phonographs and stiff ballet slippers into the main section of the store, where I am face-to-face with one of the most cunning art forgers in the world.

CHAPTER 14

An Accent Is Worth a Thousand Words

Cass Middleton is wide eyed and broad shouldered; we're the same age, but I have a hunch she could take me easily in a fight. She looks like a rugby player, and she reminds me of a tree trunk. Her blond hair is pulled high in a ponytail and she has cinnamon crumbs on the corner of her lips. The cinnamon rugelach across the street *are* the best in town. She probably burns them off beating up opponents on the field.

"Are you looking for something in particular?" Her voice is warm as she speaks to us in French, but her gray eyes are sharp and piercing, and she smells a thief, or two, since Sophie is right next to me.

I don't have a plan. I don't have a strategy. But in the span of two seconds I arrive at two conclusions. The first is *don't run*. The second is *be an American tourist*.

I adopt a doe-eyed clueless look, as if I couldn't possibly have understood what she said to me. I immediately shift into my best midwestern accent, an American kid here on vacation with his family, checking out the Marais, the most happening, hippest 'hood in Paris, as all the guidebooks say.

"Sorry, I don't know French," I say in English. I'm just a boy from Nebraska, without even a single French phrase to call upon. I don't need her connecting any dots between the teenage boy in front of her and the curator's son at the Musée d'Orsay, where the target of the store's latest forging pursuits resides.

Being British, Cass Middleton obviously speaks perfect English, so she segues naturally into the new direction of the conversation with the hapless tourist. She repeats the question. "Were you looking for something in particular? Our store was closed for a few minutes, so I didn't expect to see anyone in here."

I let the lightbulb go off in my temporarily Nebraskan brain, and I laugh, like we have a shared joke, and point to the door, that naughty, tricky door. "I didn't realize the store was closed. And I thought I might find even more treasures in there, but it's obviously an office, so sorry about that too." I press my hands together and start riffing, making it up as I go. I can still feel the outline of the key in my front pocket, and it shifts around in that moment. I do my best to ignore it, as I spy the price tag on a purple hat perched atop a nearby lamp. The hat doesn't cost much. "But yeah, so, I think we'll take that hat. My sister and I were looking for a gift for our mom and we were just saying this hat is exactly what she'd want. Right, sis?"

Sophie nods but doesn't speak.

"It's a lovely hat," Cass says. "Shall I wrap it for you?"

"Yes. That would be great."

"Did you find anything else you wanted?" She shifts her attention to the door; her eyes like razors, her gaze drilling the lock. "Were you looking for something *there*?"

"There? No." I hold up my hands. The key wiggles more in my pocket. I hope she doesn't notice. I hope the key doesn't burst from my jeans. That would be all sorts of awkward. "I got turned around, honestly. This store, it's a little, well, kind of like a maze. Sorry. But that's great, really. I mean that as a compliment. We don't have cool stores like this back home in Nebraska. It's all big-box beasts, you know. With nothing special on the shelves."

Cass appraises me from top to bottom with her stone-gray eyes, hunting for evidence of my thievery. I brace myself as the key jiggles around, tickling the top of my thigh. I try not to move or laugh because this key is now bumping and squirming inside my pocket. "I'm so glad you like our shop better than a Walmart. My dad will be delighted to hear that. We pride ourselves on all the, as you say, special items. So would you like a necklace to go with that special hat?" She says, goading me. She may not know exactly what I did, but her radar is up even as she plays the role of helpful employee.

I answer quickly, because there is only one answer. "I'm sure my mother would love one. Something to match, s'il vous plaît."

See? I'm such a thoughtful American tourist.

"Perhaps a bracelet too?"

I mentally picture my wallet, and the money I've earned from my tours. The hat and necklace aren't expensive, but I don't think I can cover more than those two items.

"She's not a big bracelet person. Says they're always getting in the way."

"What about gloves then?"

I don't answer immediately, because I can feel the key shorten and shrink. Then, as quickly as it arrived on the scene, the key is gone. My pocket is empty again. "She says her hands are naturally warm, so I think I'll just go with the necklace and hat."

"Very well," Cass says as she heads to the register and rings me up. I join her, and thrum my fingers against the counter, watching as she wraps up the fake gifts, purchased by a fake thief, from a preeminent fake artist of the last few years. "Where did you say you were from? Nebraska?"

"Yes, ma'am. Nebraska."

"What part of Nebraska?"

Heck if I know. I do accents, not geography. I haven't a clue about any cities in Nebraska. "Topeka," I offer, hoping it's in Nebraska.

"Oh, I bet it's lovely there in Topeka, Nebraska. All that space," she says, then she hands me the newly swaddled gifts. "Come back," she says, and I escape, many euros lighter, two unnecessary accessories heavier, but with the proof in my pants.

"You do know that Topeka is in Kansas, not Nebraska, right?" Sophie points out after we leave.

"Evidently, I didn't know that. Nor did Cass Middleton. But there's your brother. Why don't we ask him if he knows geography as well as he knows magical secrets he keeps to himself?"

Bonheur is walking toward us on the sidewalk. "Did you find them? The fake papers?"

"We did," I say. "And a big thanks for letting me know you thought I was the first human muse."

"Julien, you're not seriously mad, are you?"

I shrug. I'm more irritated than mad. "It would have been nice if you said something, especially that night we were talking on your block."

"Would you have believed me? If I said something then, would you truly have believed me?"

"I don't know," I answer truthfully.

"You were just starting to come to terms with seeing art come alive. I thought you would have just walked away if I dumped all these things on you."

"So how did you know? Did your Muse friends tell you?"

"Yes. They alerted us. One of them saw you watching the dancers one night at the museum and knew then you were a human muse."

"Great. So the Muses are spies too."

"Not exactly," Bonheur says as my phone rings.

I take it from my pocket. It's Simon calling. Someone who isn't doling out bits and pieces of my secret life to me like kibble for a dog.

I answer.

"I have decided to grant you an audience right now at my falafel castle."

"Be right there." I hang up, then turn to Bonheur. "Listen, I'm going to get something to eat and then give these papers to my mom. I'll catch you later."

"Julien," he starts, and I can tell he's about to try to explain himself again. But he seems to realize that now's not the time. "Have fun tonight at the museum, okay?"

Bonheur fancies himself a bit of a matchmaker for Clio and me. It's hard to stay mad at him.

"I will. See you," I say and walk away from Bonheur and Sophie.

I pull the papers out of my jeans and look them over once more.

"Hands in your pants again, Garnier?"

Simon calls out to me from his command post in the falafel shop.

"Some days I just can't help myself," I say, as I slide into the booth across from him, dropping the bag with the hat next to me. Simon is with Lucy, and she's snug against him, like they're two jigsaw pieces and she keeps lining herself up, making sure the interlocking edges fit just so.

"What have you got there?" Simon asks, a tip of the forehead to the papers in my hand.

"It's complicated."

"But is it interesting?" Lucy's voice is a purr, and her green eyes are the perfect complement to the emerald streaks that curve like streams down her cascade of dark hair. "Complicated can be dull. Or complicated can be fascinating."

"I would have to say this falls more on the *fascinating* side of complicated."

Simon slaps a hand on the table, then holds out a big palm, the king of the shop waiting to be entertained with a story.

"Um . . . ," I begin, then trail off, as I try to assemble the clues.

Muses. Dust. Paintings that come alive. The voices I heard in Bonheur's cellar were women's voices and they sounded like poetry, like history, like music, like art. Like Muses. *The* Muses. But now, there's a human one too.

"Do you believe in Muses?" I ask my friend and his new girl.

Simon pulls Lucy closer to him so they're sealed airtight. "I think Lucy is my Muse," he says, then winks and leans in for a quick kiss.

"And what does she inspire you to do?" I ask.

"To order falafels. Want one?" Simon asks.

"Sure."

He raises a hand, and the waiter appears. Waiters never move that quickly. Simon must be magic in this place.

Magic. The word rolls through my brain, like a marble in a Rube Goldberg machine, jumping, darting, doubling back. There is magic somewhere in Paris. There is clearly magic in art, magic in dust, magic in my hands. I can't help myself. I grin, big and wide, and surely crazily. Because I'm *not* crazy, and maybe Bonheur was right to wait to tell me. I had to see it—the way I drew the key—to believe it. These things are real, and they're magic, and they're happening to me.

The only problem is there are curses, and art getting sick at the Louvre, and Renoirs fading from the sun. Good magic, bad magic, maybe?

After we order, Simon returns to the question. "So, Muses. You mean the nine ladies who inspire artists, writers, musicians, and so on?"

"Yes. Those Muses."

"Sure, I believe in them."

"As you should. Muses are powerful women," Lucy offers, and I chuckle silently because not all Muses are women. "Goddesses, even."

"I like goddesses," Simon says.

"I *love* goddesses," I say.

"I *worship* goddesses," he adds.

"So here's the story," I say, then I slide into the truth. Well, some of it. I have to tell somebody something, because the people I encounter don't tell me enough, and because my world is becoming stranger. "So there's this guy who's trying to claim he owns the Renoir painting we just hung, when he clearly doesn't. So I followed him out of the museum and I found these documents, which are the copies of the fake papers he showed us earlier today about the painting."

"You're a detective now," Simon says, as if he's proud of my cunning.

"And a burglar too. Don't forget that. I've got plenty of skills. Speaking of, can you look into someone for me? Research a name?"

"Sure."

I give him Max's full name and ask him to research his family, where they lived, what they've done.

"Do you want us to follow him too?" Lucy asks, and her eyes light up, mischief in full bloom. She turns to Simon. "Wouldn't that be fun?"

"What I did for my summer vacation," Simon quips, narrowing his eyes. "Espionage."

"You know, that's not a bad idea." If Bonheur and Sophie can do their own legwork, there's no reason I shouldn't have my people on it either. "That would be great if you would."

The waiter brings our food and we eat. Then I remember the hat and the jewelry. "Lucy, would you like a purple hat?"

"I would love a purple hat," she says and then coos when I show her the hat. She models it, tilting her head just so.

"That hat is turning me on," Simon says and dives in for a kiss. My cue to go. I place some euros on the table.

Simon waves them away. "I'm like the mayor. I never let my people pay. Go on your way."

I thank him, then leave the falafel shop, walking back across the city, rehearsing a slightly more detailed version of the half fact, half fable story of my discovery of these papers. I'm not going to let Max take *The Girl in the Garden* away from me. Christophe may have won over Jenny, but Clio stays with me.

⁊

My mother is in her office. She's eating roast chicken with small potatoes from the *traiteur* around the corner.

"If you thought my history paper was impressive, wait till you see what I have."

She raises an eyebrow. I grab a slice of the chicken and stuff it in my mouth.

"In fact," I continue, "I'm pretty sure you'll never give me a hard time about school again." I show her the papers I *found*. I leave out certain details—the possibility that Renoir's ghost is sharing Broussard's body, that I broke into the back room of a vintage shop courtesy of a key I drew, and that, evidently, I'm a human muse. The gist of my account for my mother is this—I followed Broussard all the way to the Marais, into a shop where I found these copies on the floor. Oh, did I mention the shop appears to be owned by Oliver Middleton and run by his prodigy teenage forger of a daughter?

"The art world is full of thieves and scam artists," my mother says, seething. "The nerve of Broussard. And that trumped-up tale of protecting the girl. I bet that story was all a lie anyway. It's just a painting. She's just a model."

I wince. Because Clio's not just a model. But who is she? Perhaps I can find out tonight.

My mother stands up and waves the papers victoriously. "I'm going to show these to Stefane," she adds, referring to her colleague, the vice curator or something who works with the museum's board on all provenance claims. "This is the proof we need to keep that forger out of our museum."

She walks away, then pops back in seconds later. "And, Julien. You can come and go as you please."

Good-bye, midnight curfew.

CHAPTER 15

Invisible Girl with Real Lips

I spread the desserts out on a bench in one of the galleries. Monet's picnickers watch us, their eyes shifting back and forth, their lips curved in smiles. But they stay inside their frame, as Clio and I sit on the floor with the bench as our table, and I show her what I've brought.

"This apricot tart is pretty much the best thing I've ever had. There's a bakery down the street that I got it from, and one of the first times I went there, an American mom was there with her young daughter. The mom was trying to order yogurt, so she said *un abricot yaourt,* but it sounded like *abricot tarte,* so the baker gave her the tart. She shrugged happily and sat down outside with her daughter to eat the tart. It looked good to me, so I ditched my bread order and went for an apricot tart too."

Clio takes a forkful and tastes it. "I'd never go back to yogurt either. Then again, I'd never order yogurt at a bakery, because I can't resist sweets."

She hands me the fork, and I take a bite too. Next, I show her the fruit crumble with blackberries, raspberries, strawberries, and blueberries. "You know what the best part of a berry crumble is?"

"No. What's the best part?"

"You eat that and you've got your five-fruits-a-day requirement in. Done. Well, four fruits. But close enough."

She smiles and tries the crumble. "I feel so healthy right now."

I point to the *macaron* I picked up at Pierre Hermé. "Now, this guy is one of those rock-star pastry chefs."

She raises an eyebrow. "What does that mean? Rock-star chef?"

I'm reminded there were neither famous chefs nor rock stars in her day. "He's written books, his stores have lines out the door, tourists flock to him, and he mixes absurd flavors together, but everyone loves them. So I got you a grapefruit-wasabi *macaron*. I kind of went out on a limb here, but I figured you had probably never tried that combo before."

She takes a bite and her eyes go wide from the burn of the wasabi. "My nose is on fire."

"Maybe they skimped on the grapefruit and just put wasabi in."

"Oh, there's grapefruit flavor in there too. It's all tarty and citrusy."

"We could totally do food reviews."

She laughs. "What's your favorite food?"

"Me? I like everything. But you can never go wrong with pizza. Or fries. Or chicken. Or roasted potatoes. Or sandwiches. I can pretty much eat all day."

She laughs, then leans closer to pinch my stomach. "But you hardly seem like you eat all day."

I think I might be blushing. I like her hands on me. "I walk a lot." Then I add. "Walked a lot today. All over the city. Crazy day."

"Why? What happened?"

"Everything, it seemed. For starters, this guy showed up trying to claim he owns your painting." Clio raises an eyebrow. "But my friends had been tailing him, so they knew he'd been forging the documents. And we found the fake papers, so that's not an issue anymore. But they—my friends—think there's a curse on your painting."

"A curse. Interesting," she says, and she's veiled again, enigmatic.

"Oh, wait. I forgot one really cool thing that happened today," I say. "Turns out I can draw things and they come to life."

Her voice rises with excitement and her eyes brighten. "Show me. Show me now."

"Really?"

"You think I don't want to see that?"

"Okay, what do you want me to draw for you?" I reach into my backpack for my notebook, pencils, and the pink polka-dotted calf. I stretch out across the hardwood floors and prop up on my elbows.

"Hmm. Flowers are a no. I've seen plenty of those. And clearly, you already excel in the food department, so we don't need chocolates."

"A necklace?" I offer.

She looks sharply at her bracelets, one on each wrist. There's barely any space between the metal and her skin, and I don't see a clasp on them. "I detest jewelry."

"So that's a no on flowers, jewelry, and drawn chocolate for you."

"Wait. I've got it. You know what I desperately want?"

"Tell me."

"A new pair of shoes." She pulls up the hem of her long skirt, revealing a pair of form-fitting beige slippers. "I want something fun. But I have no idea what's in style today. Do you?"

I laugh and shake my head. "No, I don't follow shoe fashion. Or any fashion for that matter." Then I vaguely remember seeing shoes in a store window in the Marais this afternoon. I snap a finger. "Wait. Short boots."

Clio claps once. "Yes, boots! What color?"

"That's going to have to be up to you."

"I like green. Lime green. Would lime-green ankle boots be weird?"

"Let's find out." I start to draw. "I have to warn you though. They'll only last for a few minutes."

"I will take whatever I can get."

I sketch out a pair of shoes, with Clio giving directions along the way. Greener, higher, and not such a pointy toe. "There?"

"Perfect."

"Here goes." I tap out a sprinkling of Muse dust onto the drawing and trace the shoes with my fingertips. Seconds later, they become three-dimensional. Clio brings her palm to her mouth. "That's amazing." She takes off the slippers and pulls on the boots, then stands and twirls, holding up her skirt to show me the shoes.

"What do you think?"

I stand up and pretend I'm appraising the ensemble, though I'm really just enjoying the view of her. "A pair of jeans, a tank, and I say you're ready to go clubbing with me in Oberkampf."

"I do like dancing," she says and then reaches for my hand and assumes the start of a ballroom dance pose. She stumbles once, then catches herself. "I never said I was any good at dancing though. I've always been better with painting. Or at least, having an eye for paintings. Like that one."

She points to a Monet, an image of a street in Paris in celebration in the late 1870s. "I remember when it was first exhibited."

I quickly do the math. Clio's sixteen, so she must have been nine when she saw this painting. "What was it like? Seeing this for the first time? Before Monet became, well, Monet as we know him today."

"It was heaven." Her lips are parted, she's about to say something, maybe more about the painting. But she stops. "What did they tell you about this curse?"

"Not much. My friends—they're related to Suzanne Valadon, great-great-great-grandkids or something—just said Renoir cursed your painting. I don't even know if artists can curse a painting," I say with a shrug.

She looks at the calf, then back to her shoes, but doesn't say anything.

"Is there a curse on your painting, Clio? Is that why you're trapped?"

"My shoes are starting to disappear."

I take her elbow so she doesn't trip again as the shoes dissolve into dust, then vanish. Her feet are bare now. She wiggles her toes. "I miss my shoes. I'll have to ask you for a new pair every night."

"I'll be at your service."

She's quiet again as she laces up her slippers. But I still want to know about her. "If you're different than the others, can you just leave now that you're in a museum? Now that you're alive again, can you just walk out the doors?"

"I think I probably could. In fact, I bet *you* could open the door, hold it for me, and I'd be on my way," she says, and I hate everything about that idea. "But I don't think I actually want to leave right now. I don't want to go back."

I breathe a sigh of relief. "So what's back? Where are you from?"

She waves a hand as if she's dismissing the question.

"Do you have a family?"

"I was very close with all my sisters. But we worked all the time."

"What kind of work?"

"This and that," she says in that evasive way she has. "That's why I don't want to go back just yet. I'd just have to work again. I got tired of working."

I wonder if she'd truly have to work if she went back. But it seems too cruel to point out that there isn't likely any *back* for her to go to all these years later. That her sisters probably aren't waiting around for her to pick up the household chores.

"Besides," she says, and her blue eyes are playful now. "The other reason I don't want to leave is I rather like this boy who visits me in the museum."

"Oh, you do, do you?"

"I do. I do like him. He brings me sweets and he takes me to the ballet and he makes me shoes, and he even let me touch his stomach." She says the last part as if it's the most scandalous thing in the world, and all I can think right now is how much I want to kiss her.

Then I hear footsteps. Gustave pops into the gallery. He holds a bit of wire and some fake gems in his hands, fiddling with them. "Hey, Julien, want to hear something crazy?"

"Sure," I say nervously. But he doesn't acknowledge Clio, only me. Clio steps forward, forming a shield between Gustave and me, but he can't see her, and she just whispers, "This will be fun," so close to my ear that I have to resist pulling her against me with all the restraint I possess.

"So, I just talked to my buddy who runs the night shift at the Louvre. Says he saw a lemon fall out of a de Heem over in one of the galleries a few minutes ago. They were adjusting it for that *Interiors* exhibit or something," he says, and now my frequency tunes into every word Gustave says. Could the security guard be a human muse too?

"Really?" I say to Gustave.

Gustave shakes his head. "Can you believe that? What a loon. I think he must have had one too many hits to the head back in the day."

"That's crazy," I say, even though it's not the least bit crazy, and I'd like to know who he is and why lemons are falling for him too. I try not to look at Clio's fingers, grabbing lightly for my

T-shirt, tapping on my stomach. I force myself to stay still in front of Gustave. "What did he do with the lemon?"

"Threw it out," Gustave says, and my heart lurches. "Said it was stinking the whole joint up."

Now I'm sure the guy isn't a muse. That's just not what you do with art. My mind twists back to the Louvre, to when the fire leaped into my hand, to Bathsheba's drooping belly, and now to a lemon gone rancid. It's as if the art is throwing itself overboard, walking the plank of its own canvases. I only wish I knew why the art over there is going lemming, while the Renoirs here are simply fading. I hope Clio's painting doesn't give out.

"Bizarre," I say to Gustave.

"You're telling me," he says, looking down at a smooth slice of copper wire and a fake ruby. "I just can't figure out how to make this look right. And I wanted to enter it in a subway art contest."

In a flash, I picture where the wire should go, how the piece would look edgy but clever at the same time.

"Just bend the wire through the ruby." I demonstrate by miming how to move the pieces. Gustave looks at the wire, then the miniature sculpture, then something seems to click for him. He nods several times. He does as I suggested, then holds the piece of art proudly in front of him. "That does look good. Thanks, Julien. I'm going to call it *Crazy Like a Lemon*. See ya," he says and wanders back to his post near the front doors.

I turn to Clio and am about to ask what she thinks is going on at the Louvre. But she speaks first, grinning the whole time. "You're the muse."

"Yeah, I guess you could say that. That's the other part of my crazy day. I learned I'm the first human muse. Go figure," I say, and it doesn't feel strange to tell Clio. Everything about this—*us*—already exists on its own weird frequency.

"I thought you might be."

"A human muse? You thought that?"

"It crossed my mind. I mean, how else would you be the only one to see the other paintings and me?"

"What about the guy Gustave mentioned? The lemon at the Louvre."

She shakes her head. "Forget the Louvre right now. Forget lemons," she says, trailing a finger down my arm that sends heat to every point in my body. If a lemon fell from the sky, or shot up through the earth to land in my hand, I'd toss it over my shoulder without looking back.

"Gone. Lemons are wiped from my brain."

"Good."

Clio backs up then, my hand in hers. She leans between two Monets, the gardens at Giverny on one side, a sailboat on a shimmery, sunlit Seine on the other. Her hips jut out slightly underneath the gauzy fabric of her dress, and she waits, expectantly, for me. This I have dreamed of. This I have imagined since I first saw her painted likeness on the wall at Bonheur's carnival of a home.

"You know what you said a few minutes ago? About the boy you like at the museum?"

She nods.

"I like you too," I say. "I like you a lot."

"You should really kiss me then."

Her lips part slightly, and she seems nervous, but like she wants this as much as I do. I move closer, touching her hair first. Her golden-blond curls are like the softest cat's fur against my skin. I run my fingers through her hair, then kiss her for the first time. She tastes like a song, like a perfect summer day. She shivers as I touch her. It's so sweet and so sexy at the same time. I kiss her more deeply, and she answers me by looping her hands around my back and pressing against me.

I lose myself in her kisses. If anyone walked by, they'd see me kissing air, but I don't care, because she's not invisible to me. She's more alive and more wonderful than anything I've touched, and I'm sure the world is rotating around this moment, and this moment *is* the world.

We slow down, but we don't stop. We linger on each other with soft hints and mere whispers of kisses, until she says, "More," and crushes her lips against mine in a feast of kissing, hungry and ravenous.

At some point we pull apart for breath. "Tomorrow I want you to come to my place."

"The gardens?"

She nods wryly, like she has a trick up her sleeve, and I start counting down the hours.

CHAPTER 16

Degas Dancer, to the Fifth

I have only one tour today, and it's a morning one. I see a familiar face in my group—Emilie. She gives a small wave, acknowledging me, then a quick smile. I want to ask if she's heard from the Paris Ballet. She'd look at home on its stage, with the powerful and graceful way she moves, like a swan mingled with a leopard to make her. When we stop at the Degas I've gotten to know, I do a double take. Emilie is a photocopy of Emmanuelle, just a few years older. Black hair, milky skin.

Someone else notices the likeness too.

"You look just like her," says a round woman standing next to Emilie. The group turns their eyes on the flesh-and-blood girl. Emilie's ears flame red. "Maybe you're related to her."

"You never know," Emilie says, looking away. I sense some discomfort in her, so I jump in and guide the group to another painting and another topic altogether.

When the tour ends and the group disperses, she waits behind at the Van Gogh, standing next to Dr. Gachet's royal-blue coat.

"So? Are you dancing under the chandelier now?"

She nods slowly, then shares a big, beaming smile. "And hanging out with the Phantom in the underground lake. But he hasn't crashed the chandelier yet."

"I knew you'd get in. That's amazing. Congratulations!"

"Thank you." Then there's a pause, and during that beat, Emilie seems to draw in all her courage, because the next words fly out of her mouth, as if she's released a fleet of hummingbirds. "Doyouwantogogetacoffeerightnow?"

I glance down the hall, wondering if Clio can hear, if Clio would be jealous. But coffee is just coffee. "That would be great."

We leave and walk through a crowd of people lounging on our steps, stretched out in the warm June sun. I tense when I see Max on the sidewalk. But he's sketching a young couple, moving his pencil quickly across the paper. His hands are normal, pliable hands. I take that as a good sign that Renoir's ghostly reclamation project might have ended now that we've thwarted his forgery efforts. We walk past him, and I say hello.

"Hey, Julien," he calls out. "Guess what?"

"What?"

"I'm going to be teaching a class on caricature at an after-school program. Just found out this morning. Applied for the gig a few weeks ago. I'm totally psyched."

"That's great."

"Pretty soon, a whole generation of French youth will be drawing pointy chins and big noses," he says and laughs.

I laugh too. Mostly because it seems that Max has regained sole proprietorship of his own body.

Emilie and I pop into a café and order coffee. Like all French coffee, it'll be horrid, and yet I'll still drink it.

"So that Degas. You want to know the reason I got so red when that woman made the comment?"

"Red? I hadn't noticed," I say playfully.

She pretends to swat at my hand. "I'm sure you saw my ears. They're like beets when I get embarrassed."

"Why would that embarrass you, what she said?"

She taps her long fingers against the table. Everything about Emilie is long and lean. Her legs go on endlessly. Her arms could hold wings. Her fingers are slender and elegant. "You're going to laugh when I tell you. You probably won't believe me."

The waiter brings us coffees, and Emily stirs sugar into hers. "Try me," I say. "You'd be surprised at all the things I believe and believe in."

"I'm like the great-great-great-something of some Degas dancer," she says in a rush, the words a traffic pileup. "That's what my mother has always told me at least. It sounds crazy, doesn't it?"

Her crazy is nothing compared to *my* crazy. "Emilie, that doesn't sound the least bit crazy. That you're related to one of Degas's models actually seems one of the more normal things I've heard or seen these days."

"Whew," she says, and wipes her hand across her forehead. There's a nervousness to her still, but it's mixed with a touch of boldness too. She seems to shuffle between the two, like she's at war inside with who she wants to be. "So she was supposedly this amazing dancer. Her name was—"

"Emmanuelle." We say it in unison, and Emilie looks shocked. "How did you know her name?"

"She dances in the galleries. Makes a beautiful Odette," I say casually, then I realize my mistake.

"Dances in the galleries?"

I wave a hand to dismiss my gaffe, and now I'm the one whose ears are probably turning red. "After a while, the art seems to come alive," I say, as if it's just one of life's many made-up things. "You spend a lot of time in one place, and, well, you know how it goes."

She nods thoughtfully and takes another sip. Then she returns to the issue. "So really, Julien. How did you know her name?"

I improvise. "It must have been in one of the catalogues. The descriptions of the art, you know?"

"Sure." My answer makes perfect sense, more sense than the truth.

"Sometimes I wish I wasn't related to her," she says, and I hear the faintest notes of music again, like the time we were at the café in Montmartre. I glance around, looking for the sound.

"Why?"

"It's too much pressure. I'll never live up to it."

"Do you hear that?"

"Hear what?"

"It sounds like flutes. You haven't heard them at all?" I point in the general direction of the ceiling, even though the music is, more precisely, surrounding Emilie.

"No, but is the music pretty at least?" She sounds amused.

"Very much so. Why do you think you won't live up to her?" I ask, and now the music starts to form a score I recognize from the many times my parents have played it. It's *Sleeping Beauty*. I could hunt for the source of the music, but I'm pretty sure I'll never find it, because Emilie is the source. "Because I'm awful. I'm rehearsing right now for—"

"*Sleeping Beauty*," I answer, and as if lightning struck the sky, I understand why I hear music with her. It's like last night when I saw how Gustave could finish his piece. That's what he needed—a final touch of inspiration. With Emilie, she seems to need confidence. I only hear the music when she's feeling insecure. Like the day I met her in Montmartre, my words of encouragement seem to be what she needs. They're her inspiration. This must be how I *work* as a human muse. It's a heady thought and a humbling one too.

"How did you do that again? How did you know?"

"Just a guess," I say.

"Really?" She narrows her eyes, in a faux inspectorly way, then wags a finger at me. "Or did you just know that's the next ballet on our calendar?"

"That must have been it. I'm sure I read it somewhere. I'd love to come see it. I bet you'll even win a solo," I say, and the flutes stroll away.

"I'm trying out for one." Emilie's shoulders relax, and she smiles. "And thank you for saying that. For some reason, I always feel so much better about my dancing after I talk to you."

"I'm glad. You should feel good about your dancing."

"Will you come to the performance?"

"Name the time. I'm there."

She gives me a time and a date a few weeks from now. We finish our coffee and say good-bye. On the way back to the museum my phone rings. I answer, and Bonheur says hello in a cheery voice.

"Hey. What's going on?"

"Now, don't shoot the messenger here, but I'm only calling because the Muses want to know how everything is going with *The Girl in the Garden*."

I scoff. "Really? The Muses want to know? Did they send you an e-mail? Or hire a skywriter?"

"I wish it were either of those options. But it's terribly prosaic. They just write on paper and leave it in the basement."

"Oh, well of course," I say as I head up the steps to the museum.

"So, the girl in it," Bonheur presses on. "They want to know how she is."

"Tell them she's fine," I say as I wave to the guard at the reserved entrance. He lowers the ropes and lets me through. "Tell them she's great. Oh, and Bonheur?"

"Yes?"

"Tell them I appreciate their concern," I say with a smile, because I'm getting a wicked kick out of the the things the Muses tell Bonheur and his sister.

I bound down the steps to the main floor, but then stop short when I smell that rose perfume, thick and heavy. I turn around, and I see Max walking to the door, slightly out of sync, as if he's hijacked his own body. I get a good look at his hands; they're curled up again into the cuffs of a long-sleeved shirt. My chest tightens. I know the museum is open to the public, I know anyone can come in if he pays for a ticket, but I don't take any comfort in that knowledge. I doubt he is here to admire the art. He must have been casing the joint.

But I have no idea why.

꧁

My mother pulls the door to her office closed. She has tears in her eyes. She'll never let on in front of her coworkers that she cries. "It's Gabrielle. The sun damage. Her painting has it now too."

My heart falls at the news.

"Her shawl," she continues, a hitch in her throat. "And it's not just us now. The piano girls are fading even more at the Louvre. And I heard from Boston today. *Dance at Bougival* is having problems too. It's like the Renoirs are turning into faded knockoff prints hanging in malls."

I wish I could say something calming, I wish I knew how to solve the problem with the art. I'm a muse. I should know what to do. But I haven't a clue. Could the curse on Clio's painting have brought this into the museum? I hope not. I can't stand the thought of losing her if her painting is somehow infecting others. But that can't be the case. The Renoirs started to fade several weeks ago, well before Clio arrived here. She can't be making the art sick, not the Renoirs, nor the pictures at the Louvre.

"You really didn't notice anything in *Gabrielle*?"

I take a deep breath and opt for the truth. "I thought the shawl looked pale yesterday, but then Max came by with the claims about *The Girl in the Garden* and I honestly forgot about it. I'm sorry."

She purses her lips together and nods, as if she's forgiving me for the slipup.

"I understand. But I need your eyes, Julien. I need you to conduct a thorough investigation of all the Renoirs now. You're the one who first noticed the problem with the piano girls several weeks ago, so please let me know if you see anything else like this in our other paintings."

"I will," I tell her, and head off on my latest mission, taking little comfort in finally understanding why I can see the outbreak before anyone else does. After I've combed the floors, I've found trouble brewing in another Renoir, and I alert my mother that another one of our masterpieces may be the next one to fade away.

She groans and drops her head into hands. I feel bad too, but mostly I feel selfish that I'm glad it's not happening to Clio's painting yet.

I'm free for the rest of the day, so I take off for the Louvre to see what's up with that lemon.

CHAPTER 17

For Everyone's Eyes

It is June, so there are crowds everywhere, and visitors are ogling the usual suspects, the Venus de Milo, works by Italian Renaissance Old Masters, and of course, the most popular resident of any museum anywhere. The *Mona Lisa*. It is a zoo every hour of every day by her frame. Flocks of visitors hold their phones high over their heads to take pictures of the woman behind the glass, the photographic evidence like some kind of hunting trophy to show their friends online that they were at the Louvre.

Truth be told, I'm not even a fan of that painting. It's small and it's ordinary and it's much ado about nothing. But none of those works are on my agenda. I head straight for the *Interiors* exhibit to check out the vanishing act conducted by de Heem's lemon.

Quickly, I locate the small frame that spit up its insides last night.

If you didn't know what you were looking for, you might miss it in this pint-size postcard of a painting. But what I'm looking for is indeed gone, as advertised by Gustave's buddy. The lemon that's usually perched near the edge of a table, with a rind half peeled and the insides glistening tartly, is missing. It's as if it were never there at all, and now that space has been filled in by a blackish-brown paint, the same shade as the table.

The true test comes next.

I turn to an American pair of travelers standing next to me. Two sisters, I surmise, in their fifties or sixties. I shift to English. "Excuse me. This may seem like a strange question, but do you see a lemon right there?" I point to the spot the lemon used to occupy.

One of the ladies laughs. "Is that a trick question? There's no lemon in that painting at all."

Something has changed in the last few days. I'm no longer the only one who can see the shifts in the art here. But I'm the only one who can see Clio; I'm the only one who can see any of the art coming alive at the Musée d'Orsay. So why can others now see these paintings here in their newer, stranger state, as well as the fading Renoirs?

I hurry to the other galleries. I find the Ingres first. The drooping feathers in the odalisque's peacock fan aren't hanging over the canvas anymore. Most are missing, like a rat burrowed into the feathers and gobbled some up, leaving behind a fan half the size. I locate the Titian next; the woman inside is checking out her reflection in a mirror that's cracked down the middle. The tiny fissure has now stretched its way across the entire mirror. I strike up a casual conversation with a couple next to me.

The woman has crazy, curly hair and I think she might be that singer Emilie told me about.

"Funny, how she's looking at herself in a cracked mirror, isn't it?" I say.

I hold my breath as I wait for a response. The woman cocks her head to the side. "You know, that *is* ironic, isn't it?" She grabs the guy's arm and shows him the mirror. "Look at that."

I'm about to leave, but I have to ask. "Jane Black, right?"

She smiles and nods.

"Love your music." Then I'm off.

Bathsheba is next on my itinerary, and she's morphed too. No longer is her belly pooching out over the frame. Instead, her stomach is smaller, as if a plastic surgeon stopped by and gave the fleshy figure a nip tuck.

"That's one sexy biblical figure." The remark comes from a young German guy ogling the Rembrandt. "I don't remember her being such a babe, but she's got a rocking bod."

I run both my hands through my hair, pushing my palms hard against my scalp. Bathsheba has a rocking bod?

Sure, most people aren't aware that the paintings are morphing, but for the first time, others can see what I see. The trouble is, we're gazing at art that's on the cusp of turning ill.

I start to leave when I spot a tiny Band-Aid on the floor of the gallery underneath Bathsheba's frame. I bend down to pick it up so I can toss it out, but I nearly recoil at its touch. It's not a Band-Aid. It's a sliver of dried flesh, a hardened bit from the belly of a work of art.

I suck in my breath and get the hell out.

CHAPTER 18

Coffee Cup Thief

When I'm mayor of this fine, fetid city someday, I'm going to pass an ordinance so there are dog bags on every corner," Simon says as we sidestep a pile the owner of the miniature poodle in front of us should have cleaned up. It's later in the afternoon, and he's got his first field report.

"I'm totally voting for you. For that reason alone."

"Really? You don't care about my economic or social platform? And all my great reforms planned?"

"Nah. You had me at dog bags. What else does a politician need to impress his constituents?"

We're walking down a narrow stretch of sidewalk, bound on one side by a boarded-up old bakery and on another by a store with red lights and black windows that's only open at night. This is Pigalle. The overly optimistic say it's an up-and-coming neighborhood. The realistic say it's trashy. All I care about is what

Simon says, and that's that Pigalle is where Max Broussard lives.

"So listen, Lucy keeps asking me about Emilie. She has this fantasy we're all going to be a foursome or something."

"Ooh, a fantasy foursome. Hold me back."

"You know how girls are. She wants us all to do something."

"Maybe she just doesn't want to hang out with you alone."

Simon stops and turns around. "You know, I think I'd be content to not show you where Broussard lives."

"I'm kidding." We keep walking. "Anyway, Emilie stopped by my tour this morning. Invited me to a performance."

"See! I knew it. She's into you too. Lucy's going to be so happy."

"Yeah, but it's not like that."

"Why not? She's a dancer. You need to be all over that."

Call me crazy, but for some reason I don't think telling Simon *she's only into me because I inspire her to dance* is going to fly.

"There's kind of someone else I'm into," I admit.

"Really?" Simon raises an eyebrow as we cross an unevenly cobbled patch of street. He points to take a right. We turn and this street is even narrower. The dilapidated buildings tilt inward the slightest bit, closing in on you as you walk down curving streets and along structures that whisper of the past, of candlelit nights and hooves on streets. And of a Paris without modern plumbing too, come to think of it. "What's the story?"

My phone buzzes with a text. I check the screen. *Sophie and I are tracking Dear Old Cass. She's up to something, going in and out of a church near her shop in the afternoons. Will stake her out tomorrow this time and alert you, OK?*

I punch in a return message to Bonheur—*The drama never ends. I'll be at the ready*—then tuck my phone back into my pocket.

"It's complicated," I say to Simon.

"Oh well, don't tell me because my little pea brain can't handle it."

"It's just that it's early."

"So how do you know her?"

"She hangs out at the museum."

"Have you talked to her? Asked her out?"

"Not exactly out."

"Do you need me to come by and do it for you?"

"Ha. Hardly."

Soon we reach a quiet side street wedged between two brick buildings. Ugly squiggles of graffiti line one building. On the other building there are smudged floor-to-ceiling windows that look into a shabby sort of studio space. The place is a mess, stacked with smocks and pottery wheels, kilns and sculptor's tools, sketch-pads and pencils. "This is where he lives?"

"Nope. He lives there." Simon points to the connecting flat. "I looked up the address in a real estate guide, of all things. It's like a closet. I think it's ten square meters and a total dive, from what I can tell. The chick who runs the studio let me into the building— I used my Simon charm, of course."

"Are they connected? The studio and his apartment?"

"He lives with some other chick who rents space in the studio. He gets his studio space for free, and his apartment has been handed down from his grandparents. There is no way that dude *ever* owned any expensive art. Not in his lifetime. Not in his parents' or grandparents' lifetimes. Where would he hang it? Above the sink? And before you say he could have a country home in Normandy, I looked into that. Nothing. He owns nothing. He's an orphan too. Parents died years ago in a car crash. He is the classic struggling young artist."

Simon points to an easel in the studio. There's a sketchpad on it, and a drawing of a dog with floppy ears. "That's where he draws. He's totally like your Impressionists before they hit it big. Living hand to mouth, barely making ends meet, just trying to rub a few centimes together."

The big question, though, is why did Renoir choose this young artist to inhabit when Max isn't even a painter? Was there a rhyme or a reason to the possession?

"But he's hardly ever here. Lucy talked to him."

"She talked to him?"

"Of course. She's quite an amazing secret agent. She had him do her caricature across from the museum this morning," Simon says. Lucy must have been talking to Max while I was at the Louvre, and Max must have been himself if he was able to hold a pencil well enough to draw. "She got all sorts of details. He was telling her about the class he's going to be teaching. How he thinks cartooning or what have you is a fun way for kids to express themselves. Seemed really excited about it, she said."

"The caricature class. He mentioned it to me this morning too."

"She also chatted him up about where he hangs out. He said he spends most of his time outside the Musée d'Orsay."

"Right, that's where I've seen him and talked to him," I say, then things click.

Location, location, location.

Renoir must have picked Max for his proximity to the Musée d'Orsay. But is Renoir trying to stay close to one of the largest collections of his own works? Or to Clio, the girl he was supposedly once in love with.

Simon unfolds a piece of paper from his back pocket and shows me the caricature Max drew of Lucy. It's cute—he made her green streaks look like they're wings in her hair.

I press my forehead to the window of the studio. The place is a cluttered mess. At the floor of the easel are papers, sketches, and comic book drawings of cats and dogs with oversize heads and snouts. I notice a number at the bottom of one of the sketches: *19.* I try to make out the words that follow. *Rue de* something . . . but the marks are scratchy, scraped on by an unsteady hand. I peer closer until I can see the first three letters of the street name. The address is for the shop with the Jack Russell in the window.

The same one that verified the painting Clio's in right now.

⁂

We race up the Metro steps and dash by a café with late-afternoon coffee drinkers lingering over half-drained cups. A guy tosses some bills onto the round table by his espresso cup, then leaves. I double back. The cup is red. I look up at the sign. It's the Red Café.

"What do you think this cup costs?" I ask Simon. "The cup itself."

"Don't know. Five euros? Ten euros at the most?"

I grab a ten from my pocket and toss it on the table, then wipe the last bits of coffee dredge with a napkin before the waiter can make it over. I drop the cup carefully in the front pocket of my backpack as we keep going.

"I'm all for thievery, but might you consider something a bit racier than coffee cups?"

"Currency," I say. "For Zola."

"Ah. But of course."

We reach Zola's mom's gallery and head inside. Zola is talking to a customer who's considering a pink painted canvas with a miniature metal skateboard sticking out of it. Modern art, for sure. Zola smiles at us and holds up one finger to indicate she'll be done soon. She's wearing an electric-blue dress with ruffles below the knees. Simon and I walk around as she finishes. There's an ornate armoire with gold trim and about one thousand drawers in it. The price tag is in the five figures.

"I'm getting that for my mom for her birthday," Simon jokes. "She totally needs a new bureau."

"She'll love it. But, you know, be sure to check online. You might find it cheaper," I say, keeping up the volley, though, of course, neither one of us is a shopper.

"Great. We'll see you back tomorrow to pick it up," Zola says and shows the customer the door, waving good-bye.

"Ring it up! That'll be ten new dresses," Zola says as she waltzes back into the store, pumping her first.

I raise an eyebrow in question.

Zola points at herself with her thumbs. "Commission. This girl gets paid in commission."

"Sweet. That beats the heck out of my hourly," I say, as Zola sweeps by to bestow a kiss on each cheek.

"And to what do I owe the pleasure of a visit?" she asks, as if she's a grand old dame entertaining guests at her country home. "And from double-the-trouble boys, no less."

"Always trouble," Simon says, planting quick kisses on Zola's cheeks.

I reach inside my backpack and present her with the coffee cup. "First, from the Red Café around the street."

"Oh, look. My favorite color. How was the coffee? Was it horrid?"

"Can't say. I just snagged the cup from a table as I walked past."

Her eyes widen, and she pushes my shoulder. "I'm so proud of you."

"I tried to get him to put it in his shirt like you do, but he wouldn't go there," Simon says.

Zola laughs. "Well, he needs proper training from the master, but we can get him there."

"And he'll need a bustier too."

"So listen," I say. "I hear there was a guy here today—" I crunch up my hands.

"I remember him," Zola says. "He had a wheeled shopping bag with an art crate in it because he had trouble with his hands."

"Why was he here? What was in the crate?"

She motions for us to step closer. "He had what he claimed was a Renoir. My mom's off at an appointment now, but she was here and he showed it to her. He was certain—we're talking adamant— that he had the original *Girl in the Garden*."

"Is that what was in the crate?" I ask, a ribbon of fear running through me, even though I know rationally he can't have had Clio's painting.

She nods. "Or so he thought. He kept insisting that Renoir himself had specified that the painting be left with his family. That it not leave his family's hands at all. Never be shown, never be exhibited, never even be touched by anyone."

Never even be touched. "Why would he want a painting to never be touched?" I ask, but all I can figure is the legend has to be true. Maybe that's why his ghost is skulking around. Maybe he wants to be near her again. Or maybe he doesn't want anyone else to have her?

"It's strange, isn't it?" Zola says, but she doesn't have any idea either.

Something doesn't add up though. "If Renoir was dead-set on hiding the painting away, how did it leave his family's hands then?"

"That's the funny thing. Because the painting he brought in

today was a near-perfect replica. But it lacked his signature pigment."

I turn to Simon. "Renoir had this special pigment for his signature. Supposedly so fakes could never be made. So Renoirs would always be verifiable and unique for all time."

Simon nods. "Got it."

"But this one was a copy obviously," I say to Zola.

"Yes, from long ago. The canvas was more than a hundred and thirty years old. It was the same type of canvas Renoir's contemporaries used in the 1880s. In fact," Zola says, placing her hands on her hips and tilting her head just so, "it was identical to the canvases Suzanne Valadon used."

A lightbulb flicks on in a darkened room and it all makes sense. "That's what he brought you and he didn't know it! Valadon must have made a fake. After he made the original, she made a fake and tricked him. She switched out the paintings and kept the original. That's brilliant. That's how she kept the painting safe for all those years without him knowing. Because he thought he had the real one, but she really did, and she asked her family to keep the girl safe."

If I were the type of guy who danced jigs, that's what I'd be doing. Because I get it now. Suzanne Valadon knew Renoir had trapped Clio and wanted to protect her.

Except there's that nagging detail of *why* Renoir's painting are fading now. There's more going on than a bait-and-switch. I flick back on his words to me the first time Max showed up—*some girls can just be trouble and they shouldn't be let out.* Why would Clio be trouble for him?

"Thank you, Zola. I will be bringing you coffee cups every day for the rest of my life," I say.

"Anytime, Julien."

Simon and I leave. "So, want to let me in on what's really going on?"

I turn to Simon in front of the Jack Russell in the window. "Do you believe in ghosts?"

"Should I believe in ghosts?" he asks as we keep walking.

He doesn't say much, just nods as I take him through my Ghost of a Great Artist Come Back to Preserve his Legacy theory as we pass more antique shops and art galleries that line the street by the river.

"And so Renoir's taken up cohabitation with this street artist Lucy and I have been tailing?" Simon asks.

"Yes. And a bunch of Renoir's paintings at the Musée d'Orsay, the Louvre, the museum in Boston, probably other museums and collections, are fading. It's like there's something bad going down with his art and that has to be why he's around. And somehow whatever is happening to his paintings has got to be related to *The Girl in the Garden*."

Simon shakes his head and claps me on the back. "It is truly never a dull moment with you, Garnier."

I stop walking. "You don't believe me?"

"Does it matter if I believe you? I'm your friend and I'm going to do whatever you need me to do. I'm all in, whether I believe in ghosts or not."

"All right, whenever Bonheur figures out what's going on with Cass, you're coming with me then, okay?"

"As if I'd miss it."

"I better get back to the museum."

"For your complicated girl."

I give him a sheepish shrug, an admission of sorts.

CHAPTER 19

Irises in Hand

"Touch my painting."

I lift an eyebrow. "I thought you'd never ask."

Clio swats my arm.

"Sorry. But you kind of walked into that one."

"I know," she says and rolls her eyes.

"But I want you to touch the flowers first. So you know you can go through the painting without freaking out."

"Whoever said I was going to freak out?"

She gives me a sideways look. "Right. Not me. But just in case, I want you to get those irises."

"So I should just reach in there with my hands?"

"This from the guy who kissed a painting the other night."

I blush. She knows.

"I'm not going to hurt the art though?" I ask, thinking of the other Renoirs. I don't want to add to the list.

"You're a muse. You can't hurt a painting." Her voice softens and she dips her fingers into mine. "Your hands are no ordinary hands. Your eyes are not like the eyes of others. You see things other people can't see. You can touch things other people can't touch."

She uncurls my fingers one by one, kissing the tip of each softly. I want to do so much more with her hands. But I let myself exist in this one achingly magnificent moment, with her velvet-soft lips against my skin.

"Now," she instructs. "Reach inside."

I take a breath, fighting back all the instincts that tell me I could damage the art. But I do it anyway, like I'm petting a nervous animal, or maybe *I'm* the nervous animal. The canvas feels crackly, the petals on the irises chipped. "More. You can't hurt it, Julien."

I press harder against the canvas, but it's still flat and dry, and I feel stupid. I'm standing here trying to grab the guts of a painting, like a twisted medicine man stretching his hand into a chest to retrieve a beating heart. I pull my hands back, stuffing them into my pockets.

"I feel like an idiot. I can't do this."

"It's okay," she whispers in my ear, her voice pure poetry. "Close your eyes and just feel."

There's something about Clio that makes me believe I can be better than I ever have before. So I do as I'm told, letting her words be my guide. I close my eyes, take my hands out of my pockets, and reach forward. Everything is dark now, and I am blind by choice, but I can touch. This time the canvas bends back. Like a dance partner letting me dip her, the surface stretches and invites my hands in. Against the blurry black of my closed lids, I see a momentary flash of silver, and in my palm I can feel the softest flutter of a petal, smooth and real. I grasp, tenderly but firmly, a bouquet of irises. I open my eyes.

"I told you so," she teases.

"Holy blue irises in my hands."

"Now put them back."

I do the reverse, and the flowers are lapped back into the frame.

"And now, perhaps you'd like to come on inside and see 'my house,'" she says and sketches air quotes. "Just don't take anything with you except the clothes on your back."

I take a quick look at her painting—odd without her in it. The space where she resides is empty, but not blank white. It's filled in by other colors, but as if the colors have spilled into the middle. I reach my hand through and the midsection of the painting expands inward, creating a weird and warped sort of tunnel. There's a rushing sound far away, like wind is whipping a secret passageway open.

"Oh, this is definitely a ladies-first situation."

She steps inside the painting, and I follow her. The canvas folds in and closes up, calm again, quiet again, and I am on the other side.

CHAPTER 20

Inside the Cage

I have been to Monet's garden before. An hour west of Paris, it's a popular destination for many visitors to France. You feel transported, like you've been swished back in time to the late 1800s when Monet painted so many of his masterpieces.

But this. This is more than the real thing. This is like a high-definition version of the gardens, with orange dahlias that blaze like the sun and pink poppies the color of a seashell. All the flowers are in bloom. In front of me lies a blanket of pale-blue forget-me-nots that look like the Impressionist paintings they inspired because they *are* the Impressionist paintings they inspired. All the colors are more vibrant than any palette I've seen on the other side. They are a new color wheel, like someone spun all the colors in the world faster and faster, and made them vibrate, and now they've become more electrifying versions of themselves, like the notes played by a virtuoso violinist.

"We're not in Giverny," I say, in a daze.

"No, we're not."

We are someplace else entirely. Someplace that doesn't exist for anyone else, anywhere else. Someplace that exists only beyond a painting. The flowers, the pond, and the trees are fully alive, but also slightly gauzy, slightly surreal.

"Do you want to see the bridge that Monet painted over and over?"

"Heck yeah."

Clio points past some purple tulips that edge the pond. Hovering over the glassy-blue surface is the green bridge from Monet's backyard. We walk along the pond, and I watch the water lilies, hazy and quivering in the water. We duck under weeping willows that brush our backs, and when I stand up straight again I step onto the Japanese bridge.

"Do you hate it here, Clio?" I ask, because even though it's a strange and wondrous place, it's also her cell.

"Sometimes, yes. I used to pretend there was a door at the end of this bridge. A plain, simple wooden door with an old-fashioned ring handle. Dark metal. You pull it open"—she demonstrates opening an invisible door, pulling easily—"and there. The other side." She stays frozen like that, in her mimed pose. "I'm finally on the other side."

She turns back to me, and my heart aches for her for being stuck for so many years. "But this is escape too. With you," she says, letting her voice trail off as her lips zero in on mine. She presses lightly at first, grazing my lips, and I let her lead, like she seems to want to. She could take me anywhere, and she has. I push my hands through her soft, golden hair, letting the strands form waterfalls through my fingers. She leans into my hands, like a cat, and lets out a small sigh.

This is an escape, and like most it's both lovely and temporary. I know this thing between us can't last. She'll either want to or need to leave soon enough, or her painting will fade from existence if the damage keeps spreading.

"Why don't you leave then?" I ask when we pull apart. But even if she left, what would she have? Where would—or could—she go? It's as if she's slipped through time.

"I told you last night. Do you want me to just keep saying it over and over? Because of you."

I laugh. "It doesn't really get old to know an awesome girl is into you." I lie down with her on the bridge. The overhead sun warms us. "Even if I'm the only boy you've seen in more than a century."

"Oh. So I'm just a desperate girl then?" Her voice hardens. She has a tough edge.

"I don't mean it like that."

"How do you mean it, then?"

I run my hands through my hair. "I just mean you're beautiful and funny and smart and sweet and you could have anyone."

She scoffs at the last part, but all the things I feel when I draw adequately and turn in assignments adequately rise up. "It's just, I'm hardly ever good enough. I'm like this interloper. I want to be an artist, but my drawings aren't special, so I lead tours instead. And my parents are these hyper-overachievers—scholar and curator—and I can barely keep it together in school. And you come along, and I just think, *why me?*"

"Because, really, I was looking for a scholar?"

I manage a laugh. But I wonder if I should have shared all that. If I should have let the girl I'm falling for see my stupid insecurities.

"Actually, I think I want a scientist," she says, pretending to be deep in thought. "Someone who works in a lab and wears a lab coat. Oh wait. Not that. A banker. That would be great. Or how about an athlete? Since I just love sports so much. But no, instead, I like someone who likes the same things and who cares about me." She touches my wrist as she talks and runs a finger across my palm. My worries slink away. I plant a soft kiss on the inside of her hand. "So I thought I would finally tell you who I am."

I prop myself up on one elbow, all eager and then some. "I want to know."

"You do?"

"Yes."

"Everything?"

"Yes."

"Like about my family?"

"Yes."

"And where I'm from?"

"Tell me everything." I lace my fingers through hers. She squeezes back.

She props herself on her elbow, mirroring me. "I have eight sisters," she says. "*Eight.*"

She says the number as if it's the answer to a riddle, and I have to figure out the question. It lingers between us—*eight*—and I picture a swirling figure, two intertwined circles.

"I'm like you," she continues. "Only eternal."

It's as if there were a few notes playing in your head and then someone turns up the radio and the song is blasting at full volume, and you know all the lyrics. "Do you have a sister named Calliope?" I ask, in a hushed breath.

She nods happily, like she enjoys revealing this secret.

"And another named Thalia?"

A grin spreads across her face. "Yes. Though Thalia is more like a mom to me."

"I don't remember the names of the others," I admit, and I feel stupid for not remembering that Clio's the name of one of the nine Muses. Which means Clio isn't just a sixteen-year-old girl from Montmartre. She's so much more. No wonder her painting needed so much protection. No wonder Suzanne Valadon made a fake to trick Renoir.

"Erato, Euterpe, Melpomene, Polyhymnia, Terpischore, and Urania," she says, rattling off the names of the other Muses from myth.

"You're a Muse? Like a real Muse? Not just like a human muse? But the Muses from forever and ever?"

"As I live and breathe, I'm a Muse. An Eternal Muse. Thalia made me. She made all of us."

"Made you?"

"Well, we weren't just born from human moms. We were made to be Muses."

The sky could fall, the earth could split open, the garden could tear into two, and I wouldn't notice. I am inside a painting with a Muse, and I know this second is just a mirage, or maybe it is hazier than that, a reflection of a mirage, a dream within a hallucination. If I was amazed at paintings coming to life, if I was astonished to learn why I can see them, that's nothing compared to learning this. That the girl I'm seeing secretly at night, in the museum, inside a painting, the girl no one else can see, is a Muse.

She flicks her fingers, and a spray of silver dust lands on me.

"Holy crap. You're like Spiderman."

She shoots me a curious look. "Who's that?"

I forget that our cultural touchstones are not the same. That while we may be able to talk about classic art and music and literature, she won't know much about modern creations—comic book characters, pop music, hit movies. "He's this superhero who makes webs, super-strong spiderwebs, from his fingers."

"Sounds—how do you say it these days?—hot?"

"Maybe to the girls," I add, and it occurs to me that in some ways I am dating a foreigner once again. The difference is she's not from another country; she's from another time altogether. She is from *all time*.

I touch her bracelets. They should be wispy, since they're hairsbreadth thin, but they are as solid as a bank vault. "Is that where you keep the silver?"

She laughs and shakes her head. "No. Our bracelets are our marks. They mark us as Muses. And I'm the Muse of painting."

"I thought Clio was the Muse of history or something?"

"I was, but when painting became big during the Renaissance I switched."

"Switched," I say, then laugh. "Like a mid-career change."

"Exactly."

"What do you do with that silver dust?"

"It's for inspiration."

"Oh, sure. No biggie." I pretend to flick my fingers. "*Hey, here's my silver dust. Want to be inspired?*"

She pushes my shoulder and laughs. "You're the one who drew shoes with it, silly."

"Why can't I make silver dust with my fingers?"

"Ooh, are you jealous of my Eternal Muse skills?"

"Maybe a tiny bit. But what I really want to know is how on earth one of the nine Muses has been inside a painting since 1885?"

"I told you. Renoir trapped me," she says, and it all starts coming together why everyone has wanted her painting. The legend of two artists smitten with a girl was just that indeed. A story, cooked up to shield an even more valuable secret, the one of a Muse caught in a web she couldn't escape from. "That's why I didn't tell you right away who I am. The last person—the last *human* I saw—essentially put me in a cage. I have a tiny bit of trust issues," she says and holds her thumb and forefinger together to make light of the statement, but it's a heavy one nevertheless. Of course she'd have trust issues. "But I felt that you were different from the first time I met you. I wanted to make sure. I wanted to tell you when I knew I could trust you."

"You can totally trust me, Clio. I would never do anything to hurt you. But why did he trap you?"

"Oddly enough, it had to do with human muses."

"What?"

"We used to talk, Renoir and Monet and Valadon and I. I was the Muse for all of them, and we had many discussions about the nature of art. So one day, Renoir and Valadon and I were in Monet's garden and he was working on a painting, and the three of us were talking about what separates the good from the great. Valadon believed strongly that art could be for anyone and by anyone. But Renoir had firm beliefs that only great artists like himself should make art, be inspired, be known around the world. And I didn't agree with him."

"What did you say?"

"I told him—I stood there in the garden, and I said, 'I believe it's my destiny to guide art and artists to a more open age where anyone can make art and anyone can show it.' Things were different then, Julien. During his time. Art was very closed."

I nod. "I know. It's changing. It's starting to be different now. There's public art, and graffiti art, and videos, and cartoons, and experimental music, and a million ways to express yourself."

"And that's what I always believed would happen. That anyone could create art, that anyone could consume it. And I told him that. I said, 'I know you will have a great role in this, and that humans, not just Muses, would do more of the work of inspiration.' And let me tell you, he did not like that idea whatsoever. He said to me, 'Only men and only great artists can make great art.' Suzanne was shocked that he'd say that. She started to berate him, but then he trapped me."

"How? Did he stuff you into his canvas?"

"He took my powers of inspiration and twisted them. Muse dust is very limited but very powerful, and binding. He had been painting the gardens, and said he wanted to show me what he'd done so far, so when I looked at his canvas, he took me by the wrists and flicked my fingertips onto the painting. And I went in it. It's like a reversal, the way he used the dust on me. The last words I heard were, 'Let's see if a human muse can free you someday.'"

Every part of me aches for her. For the bitterness, for the pain. For having everything you love, everything you believe, turned against you.

"I'm so sorry that happened to you, Clio," I say, but how do you even begin to comfort someone who's been caged for so long, even if the bars are beautiful?

She holds out her hands as if to say *c'est la vie*. "I've gotten used to it, I suppose."

"So he did curse your painting. He cursed it with your own powers. That is sick and twisted. It's a self-fulfilling prophecy."

"Kind of. It's ironic in a way because the thing I believed wholeheartedly in, the thing he didn't want to happen at all, he sort of made it happen. He put it all into motion through his arrogance."

"But here's the thing. He's still after the painting," I say, and I feel terrible for telling her that Renoir is back, but I can't keep it from her. I tell her about the haunting of Max, and then what I learned today about Valadon swapping a fake. There's no point in hiding it. Whatever we're in, we're in it together. "It's like he's trying to get you back. I mean, you're safe here. You're totally safe at the museum. But why now? What is he so worried about?"

"I don't know. I was cut off from everything after the moment he trapped me."

"Besides, he didn't know he had the fake. He didn't know Suzanne swapped them out, so if he was crazed enough to trap you, you'd think he'd have—" I stop talking.

"Destroyed the painting? Destroyed the fake that he thought was the real me?" she offers, finishing the thought I didn't want to voice.

"Well, yeah."

"He wasn't violent. He was, oddly enough, a gentleman. And he never would do that to one of his creations. He loved his art more than anything in the world."

"Art can be a stupid, jealous thing."

"In a way, I kind of know how he felt. I used to love art more than anything. But then I started thinking more about how art was created and it never made sense to me why it was only the nine of us Muses who could bring about true and great inspiration. It didn't feel right to me. And my beliefs started changing about making art, but also about what I wanted. The only problem is you can't really *want* as an Eternal Muse. You just *do*. You just do the work."

"So let me free you then," I say, because it's the least I can do for her. "I mean, that's what this curse or prophecy or whatever is about, right? *Let a human muse free you.* Let me free you from your painting. You said all I had to do was open the doors of the museum and let you out."

She looks at me and lays a soft hand on my cheek. "If you did, I'd just have to go back. I'd have to work. The painting is what binds me to the museum, and the museum is what lets me come out at night. Once I leave the museum, I'll be bound again—to being a Muse all the time," she says, and it's such cruel beauty, the way these traps contain her. "I miss my sisters, but I know what it's like being a Muse. We are always being called upon. We are always working. I used to love working all the time. But being in that painting for so many years, I'm not the same. I don't know what I want anymore."

I circle back to the call with Bonheur from this morning. "Clio," I say tentatively. "This is going to sound weird, or maybe it's not. But my friend called earlier today and said the Muses were asking about you. They wanted to know if you were okay."

She smiles. "And what did you tell him?"

"I said you were fine."

Another smile. "Good answer, Julien."

"Do you want to see them? Do they need you back?"

"I'd like to see them at some point, but I'm rather enjoying where I am this second. Besides, my sisters obviously filled in for me all those years. Just look at the walls here. I didn't inspire Toulouse-Lautrec or Seurat. The later Cézannes aren't mine, and the later Monets aren't either, not the water lilies, not the Rouen Cathedral. Even your favorite Van Gogh was made without me. So my sisters must have filled in for me."

"Muse sick day," I joke.

"Extended leave of absence," she adds.

"So you're going to take a few more days off?"

"They got by this long without me. So I think I'll play hooky a little longer," she says. "That is, if you'll keep having me?"

"Is that a serious question?"

She nods, and she looks so nervous.

"Yes. Whatever you want, Clio," I say, even though my heart is heavy inside because whatever we are will inevitably unwind. It will never be more than an escape into a garden that isn't real.

She brushes her lips against mine, and I melt into her. Then she turns shy and says in a quiet voice, "It's always just been us girls, you know."

"Your world with your sisters? It's just the nine of you?"

She nods, and I sense what she's trying to tell me. "Have you ever been involved with an artist though? The artists you inspire? I would think Muses and artists would be items a lot of the time. I mean, writers and singers are always talking about their muses."

"Never. Never wanted to. Never interested. Never even thought about it."

"Not even the tiniest idea? Like, 'Oh, that Rembrandt is so hot.'"

She laughs. "One, he's not. Two, not even the flicker of a thought."

"So I'm your first kiss?"

She nods and blushes. "Am I bad at it?"

"No, you're amazing. But to be sure, we should really kiss more."

"Just to test things, of course," she says.

"Lots of testing."

We kiss with the sun warming us, lying on the green slats of Monet's surreal bridge. As I kiss her neck I tell her all the places I want to kiss her more, the visits I'd make on the treasure map of her body. *X* marks this spot on her shoulder, then this delicious one on her wrist, then this divine location at the hollow of her throat, as she shudders and pulls me closer with each touch, an intrepid explorer uncovering a new land of kisses. I am only too happy to be her guide, even if time is ticking on the other side.

CHAPTER 21

The Masters

I should go. I have no clue what time it is, but I bet it's the middle of the night and I have to get home at some point."

"What a bummer to have a curfew, even a middle-of-the-night one," she teases.

We're still on the bridge, and we both stand up to make our way to the blue irises where the painting opens up. But Clio stumbles at the edge of the bridge, and I reach out for her hand to keep her from falling.

"I'm a bit clumsy sometimes," she says, laughing, and our clasped hands are on the railing at the same time. "Can't even get back to the Musée d'Orsay without tripping." But when she's got her footing, we've stepped onto another bridge, a mirror of the first, though the light is different. It's brighter and greener here.

We've somehow walked into another painting in the Musée d'Orsay. We're in *Waterlily Pond: Green Harmony*, one of Monet's many versions of his Japanese bridge. We step off the bridge and into the museum, but we're nowhere near Clio's painting.

We both look at each other, as if the other one has an answer. "Did you know you could do that?" I ask her.

She shakes her head several times. "I had no idea. And trust me, I searched every corner of my painting. The bridge never went anywhere except across the pond. I don't think it connected until we touched it at the same time."

"Two muses touching it together?"

"It must be," she says, but she's as surprised as I am. It's as if we've found a hidden tunnel.

"Convenient, you might say, that the Impressionists painted so many versions of that bridge." The remark comes from Dr. Gachet, Van Gogh's doctor and the subject of one of our most famous portraits. He speaks in a low, sonorous voice as he points lazily at the image behind me. It's the first time I've seen him corporeal.

"They connect? The bridges all connect?"

He holds his hands out wide. "I'm not the one jumping in and out of paintings. I was simply making an educated guess."

Then he wanders down the hall, and when he turns the corner I see Olympia alive for the first time too, waving flirtatiously at him. They link hands and walk off.

Clio whispers. "Olympia and Dr. Gachet have a little something going on."

"Paintings hook up. Bridges connect. Girls and boys are muses. Just another night at the museum. You know, we should go to the

Hermitage sometime. We have another one of the bridges over there right now as part of a Monet exhibit."

"We'll have to make it a date," she says.

I walk her back to her canvas. Before she reenters, I ask her something that's been tugging at the back of my mind. "Clio, I know you said he loves his art more than anything, but if Renoir wound up cursing you to keep you from ushering in this new art age or something, do you think he'd go to any lengths to stop it from happening now?"

"He locked me in a painting for more than a century, so I'm sure he'd want to stop it but I don't know how he could. Why are you asking?"

"Just thinking about every angle."

Only I'm not at all sure if he's after her or me.

⚜

Simon works on his bike tricks, and I lounge on the steps in Saint-Germain-des-Prés across from two packed cafés the next afternoon, eating an egg-and-cheese crepe. We don't say much, because he's practicing some kind of midair twist, and I'm trying to solve the mystery of Renoir's return. His motive for trapping Clio in the first place was to somehow prevent the arrival of a human muse, but he's done nothing to hurt me. So I don't think I'm the one he's after. He seems to want Clio back, but the question is, what lengths will he go to to get her?

Simon executes a bizarre half-flip on his bike and lands on two wheels just as my phone buzzes.

It's Bonheur.

"What's going on? Another message from the Muses?" I joke, but I suppose I understand now why they've been wanting to hear from their missing sister.

"Well, I told you to be at the ready, so if I were you I'd get over to the Marais as fast as you can. Cass has been spending a lot of time in the church behind her store. With paints. With easels. And with canvases."

"She's forging again?"

"Evidently she's relapsed."

"Do you know what she's making?"

"No, but she just came out of the church, so now might be a good time to see what's inside the house of worship."

⁊

Bonheur fits in well in the Marais. He wears black leggings, a bright-pink satin apron tied around his waist, and a long brunette wig. His shoes are black flats. Smart guy. They're probably more comfortable on the cobblestones in this neighborhood.

"Been cooking?"

"No, I'm trying to bring back aprons as an accessory," he says as Simon and I greet him. "Let me show you where Cass has been cavorting."

We pass the vintage shop and turn at the end of the block, then turn again, so we're in an alley that runs along the backside of the shop. The alley is filled with boxes, trash cans, and other garbage from the stores and restaurants. But across from the back door of the shop is a pair of arched brown doors. Bonheur yanks them open. The doors lead down a narrow stone path, and at the end of the path is a church. We walk into the church, musty, cold, and quiet inside. A few candles flicker by the altar, and a pair of painted Madonnas hang high above us, watching over.

"This is where she's been coming and going. Maybe she's making them in another room or a basement?"

Simon heads for the altar. I grab Bonheur and talk in a low voice. "Do you know why Suzanne Valadon asked your family to keep the painting safe? Do you know what's in it?"

He shakes his head and his eyes look so earnest. "No. She only said there was a girl. Why?"

"She never said anything about a—" I stop myself before I say Muse. If Valadon never even told her family who Renoir had painted, I'm not going to reveal Clio's identity.

"She didn't leave a ton of specifics. She just said Renoir had given it to her and the painting should be kept incredibly safe until the Muses alerted us that a human muse was here," Bonheur says. "That the girl in the painting was cursed until a human muse came along."

That's what he and Sophie have been passionate about—the idea of human muses, the new age of art. But he doesn't know there's an Eternal Muse stuck in the painting. It's as if everyone has a little piece of the puzzle, but there's no one who knows everything. Clio doesn't know what happened to her painting after Renoir's famous last words to her. Nor does Bonheur. All I'm doing is assembling the clues, and they don't add up yet.

"All right, let's look around."

Bonheur and I fan out, hunting across this tiny church, its handful of pews, its vestibule and the nave for an entrance to the basement. Simon, however, leans against the altar, looking amused.

I don't find a door, nor does Bonheur. I hold up my hands. "Now what?"

"Maybe you could draw a door," Bonheur offers with a shrug.

Laughter booms across the church. "Seriously. I'm all for magic. But not everything is magic. Some things *are* real," Simon says, tapping the altar. "You won't find this in any history book, but I've learned that some of these old, alleyway churches hid the secret doors to the basement beneath the altar."

"Watch this," he says, then leans his shoulder against the lecternlike altar, pushing it as a quarryman would a rock blocking the entrance to a cave. The altar groans as Simon shoves it over a few inches to reveal, as promised, a door in the floor.

"Voilà."

"I bow down before you," Bonheur says, doffing an imaginary top hat.

Simon holds up a hand. "It's nothing. But I will gladly accept applause and adulation, and I also insist on being the first one to go down." Then he gestures to me. "You, my man, are coming along."

"Obviously," I say. Then to Bonheur, "Can you stand guard?"

He gives a crisp salute, and I think he's happy that we're all good again.

I follow Simon down a loop of uneven stone steps. The stairs are short, and we reach the basement immediately. There are lamps here, so I pull a chain on one and it illuminates a breath-taking and chilling sight.

Two easels. Two paintings in progress.

A coldness seeps into my bones as I walk around the easels, considering the fresh canvases from all angles.

The start of the piano girls is on one canvas, and the beginning of *The Boy with the Cat* is on the other. Two of the paintings that are sun damaged are being remade.

I'm filled with icy dread because now I know why Renoir's ghost came back. To protect his legacy, even if it means remaking his legacy. Renoir wasn't merely working with Cass to fake the papers and try to get the painting back. He's working with her to re-create his art, starting with the first two that are fading away before everyone's eyes. Because Renoir couldn't remake his art in Max's body, not when he's cursed with those gnarled hands. He needed Cass and her quick, young hands. I can picture the scene perfectly—Renoir overseeing Cass, giving her direction and guiding her just like in the days of old when master artists would watch over apprentices making copies. This was how young painters learned to paint, by reproducing the work of their teachers.

I shake my head, because it's so subversive to twist a teaching technique and use it to make fakes.

I scan the basement and see stacks of blank canvases. They must be planning to re-create each work that fades away. I return to Clio's words—*Muse dust is very limited, but very powerful.* When he trapped her, could the Muse dust have backfired on his paintings to make their colors leak away?

But there's one thing missing from his copies. The special chemical brew that makes every Renoir a Renoir. I hunt around this impromptu workshop, but I don't see his signature pigment anywhere. Unless he is hiding it someplace else. No one—not a museum, not a private collector—would show or buy a Renoir without the pigment.

"He's rebuilding his collection," I say to Simon. "The ones that are fading away. He's remaking them."

"For what? To sell?"

"No. The museums are all keeping track of which Renoirs are damaged. I think he's just trying to *save* them," I say, because I'm betting this forgery shop has more to do with preserving what he loves most in the world than with making money. His art, his legacy.

A door slams above us. Simon and I look at the old musty ceiling at the same time. I've never been a fan of lengthy underground stays. "Let's get out of here," I say, and we rush up the steps.

"I told you you should be a detective," Simon says as we reach the altar. "Screw the magic. You can put two and two together like nobody's business."

"Nobody's business, indeed," says a warm British voice.

A fist knocks me on the chin, and I spin and crumple to the ground. I'm winded from the surprise attack. Then hands are on the neck of my T-shirt, twisting it against my skin, and my breath feels tight. "Shouldn't you be back in Nebraska by now? Or is your French just so good from your little vacation with Mummy and Sissy that you're staying behind?"

My jaw is throbbing, and all my instincts tell me to land one on her, but I manage to resist because she's a girl. A brute, yes, but still a girl. Cass wipes me of any more thoughts when she reconnects with my cheekbone in a sharp blow. My face stings and my brain feels as if it's rattling. Simon grabs her by the wrist, but she swings a heavy arm in his direction, her elbow smacking him dangerously near the groin.

Simon doubles over and groans. I glance around for Bonheur because I could sure use some help.

"Looking for your other friend? I tied him up by his apron strings." Cass straddles my stomach with her barrel of a body, pinning me, and now I have no chance of smacking her back. "Now listen, pretty boy. I don't come around and mess with your business. You don't mess with mine."

"You're a forger. That's not a business. It's a crime."

"Oh, is that the pot calling the kettle black? Because I have a feeling the boy from Topeka wasn't just wandering around my daddy's store getting lost. Nicked some papers the other day, didn't you?" She breathes heavily on me, and I can smell cinnamon on her breath.

I smile and she tilts her head, curiosity taking its hold on her.

"Those cinnamon rugelach are the best in town, aren't they?" I say.

She gives me a look, disarmed by my comment in the midst of a fight. It's enough for me to wriggle out from under her. I grab Simon by the arm and bolt. I push open the door, and Bonheur's on the other side, his wrists pinned behind him, his hands tied tightly to the door handle by the apron strings.

Cass made some serious knots, so it takes a minute to undo

them and there are red marks on Bonheur's skin from trying to slip out. When he's free, I tie the door handle closed with the strings from his mangled accessory.

"I'm so pissed. This was my favorite apron," he says in a huff.

"Guess we need to go shopping now and get you a new one."

CHAPTER 22

Falling in Moonlight

Clio is waiting for me in the corner of the gallery. She's reading a book. I'm pretty sure it's from a Cézanne; I've seen it on the table in one of his paintings.

"This is a good book. I'll return it later. But it kept me—" She stops talking when she sees the cut on my cheek. She rises and reaches her hand to my face but doesn't touch. "What happened? Are you okay?"

"I've been getting reacquainted with aspirin. And ice too."

"Your cheek is all bruised, Julien."

"You should see the other guy," I joke. "Actually, it was a girl, and she's fine. I just have the mother of all headaches now."

She places her hands in my hair and kisses me tenderly on the forehead. I close my eyes and sway toward her.

"Better now?"

"Not yet. I need another."

I feel her soft lips on my eyelids. "Does that help?"

"Only a little."

There's a flutter against my bruised cheek.

"More please."

She kisses my jaw where Cass first whacked me. Soon, her lips find mine and she gives me the sweetest kiss I could ever hope to have in my life. Her lips taste like cherries, and all I want is to stop time with her right now.

"Clio," I say softly.

"What is it, Julien?"

"Nothing. I just like saying your name."

I can feel her smiling, and I open my eyes.

"Let's get you out of here," she says.

"How?"

"Come with me. Second floor. You said *Starry Night* was your favorite Van Gogh."

"Right," I say, not sure where she's going with this. When we reach the painting, she holds out a hand, and I take hers in mine.

"I had no idea we could go in other paintings." It is a dream in here, lush blues drip over the water, and banana-yellow stars sparkle in the night sky. They cast long rays of moonlight like gas lamps glimmering across the Rhône.

"Being a Muse comes with certain privileges," she says.

I wince as we hop into one of the sailboats on the water.

"Lie back," Clio says, letting me rest my aching head in her lap.

"This is much better," I say as she rows out into the Rhône.

"So what happened to you?"

I recount my afternoon for her, sharing all the details of the forgery den, the works being re-created, and how a strapping English rugby player knocked me around. "What I really want to know is what's happening to Renoir's paintings. It's like they're cursed and he knows it, Clio. And it's spreading. It's as if all the colors are bleeding out," I say, explaining to her what's been happening to the Renoirs for the first time. I've never thought to mention it to her before. But now that I know she's a Muse, I give her all the details. "Have you ever seen anything like that happen? I mean, you've seen pretty much all the art in the world, right?"

She laughs once. "Yes, pretty much. And I've never seen anything like this happen."

"You said Muse dust was very powerful though, right? Could it be used for a curse? Renoir used it to trap you—that's like a curse," I ask, looking up at her.

She stops rowing. We float lazily over exaggerated ultramarine as she strokes my hair. "That kind of damage to paintings has never happened before. But technically, I suppose it's possible because Muse dust is the only thing powerful enough to have such great effect. Because art magic is highly specific. It's for inspiration and creation. It doesn't work for other things. It's not like I can snap my fingers and fend off an enemy with Muse dust. Or make a sketchbook appear out of thin air. But it's also the only thing that can *change* art. That can transform kernels of ideas into fully realized masterpieces."

"Okay, so here's a crazy thought," I say, twisting around to look up at her. "I know this might seem like the last thing you want to hear since Renoir is probably not on your list of favorite people, but why don't we see if *you* can fix the Renoirs with your Muse dust? Maybe we could get him off our backs at least."

She tilts her head, considering. "That's not a bad idea."

"Or does that just feel wrong, considering what he did?" I ask carefully.

She shakes her head. "No, we need to try it. I don't want him to do anything more to you, my human muse." She brushes her fingers against my face. "Or that brute of an English rugby player either," she says in a whispering tease.

I smile at her. "She's a terror, let me tell you."

"And, I have to say, despite everything he did, I still do love his paintings," she says with a guilty sigh. "I hate admitting that, but it's the truth. Is it terrible to feel that way?"

"No. That's the thing about art. You can learn that an actor is a total jerk or whatever, but he's still amazing and it's like this gnawing in your chest. You want to hate him completely, but the work is so good you can't."

"Exactly. So when we leave this painting we'll try."

I toss out another theory. "Do you think the other Muses have cursed him?"

She holds up her hands. "We don't curse paintings, Julien. We are lovers of art. Our inspiration is for the art, not the artist. The job of an Eternal Muse is to coax out the idea and then to keep the art alive. To hold it up for all time with our love for it."

I demonstrate holding my arms up in the sky, like I'm Atlas holding the world. "Like that? You hold art?"

"Sort of. Our magic and our love helps keep the memories of art and literature and beauty alive through the years."

"So how does it work? Being a Muse? Do you just appear before an artist or something?" I ask as I look at the sky. The golden stars bathe the night in a warm glow, as shimmery water laps the boat. The sound of sweet waves is as gentle as Clio's hands in my hair. She seems to want to take care of me, and it almost makes me want to get beaten up again.

"It's like Homer's *Odyssey*. Literally," she says, then quotes the opening lines from the epic poem. "*Sing in me, Muse, and through me tell the story.* Our home connects anywhere in the world, so when poets, writers, painters, dancers, actors, musicians need us, we go. They don't even have to call us by name. We just *know* that they need us," she says, tapping her chest. "We each have an area of the arts that we specialize in. Mine being painting, as you know."

"Tell me who else you've inspired."

"Pretty much all of painting," she says playfully.

"I know that. Who are your favorites?"

"J. M. W. Turner. English painter," she says. "I like him a lot."

"Him or his works?"

"Jealous? His works, silly. I also adore Ingres and Géricault, especially *The Raft of the Medusa*. That was such a hard one for him because it was so emotional. I put so much love into that painting to help him realize its potential," she says, and I love hearing her talk like this. I close my eyes and listen to her stories. "And I like Francisco Goya a lot. His *paintings*," she adds and runs her finger along the neck of my T-shirt. I relax into her touch, to how completely different it feels from Cass's earlier today in the church. "Vermeer and Rembrandt, too. The Dutch masters are so amazing. De Heem too. I love his still lifes."

"His is one of the paintings that's all weird at the Louvre," I say and open my eyes. It crosses my mind that the paintings might be acting up because Clio's missing. Could that be why the art is molting across town? If it's her job to keep art alive, then is the art behaving badly in her absence?

But I dismiss the idea. She's been gone so long, it can't be because of her.

"Da Vinci was mine too," she continues. "You want to know the real story behind the *Mona Lisa*?"

"Sure."

"People are always wondering what she was thinking or doing. What is that enigmatic expression for, they want to know."

"Right."

"Well, she—Lisa del Gioconda, the subject of the painting—had been hosting a dinner party with her husband. Leonardo was there too. Lisa told a dirty joke, and that was her expression at the punchline."

I laugh so hard that painted water sloshes on me. "That's the story behind the *Mona Lisa*? She told a dirty joke at a dinner party?"

Clio nods. "That's the truth, the whole truth, and nothing but the truth."

"Hey, I have a question for you. If you inspire all these artists, you must be able to speak every language. So you can talk to them, right? That's why you speak perfect French but you don't have the accent of someone who was born here."

"I do speak all languages," she says proudly. "Impressed, are you?"

"Yeah, and I thought it was a good party trick that I do accents. So how do you say in Dutch, *Oh, Mr. Rembrandt, I think you need a bit more brown in this self-portrait?*"

She answers immediately.

"You know I have no idea what you really said."

"Oh, I'm just faking you out, Julien. With my fake Dutch."

"How do you say in Italian, *Leonardo, I think the* Mona Lisa *is lame?*"

She laughs and rattles off a quick Italian phrase.

"All right, I have a good one. How do you say in Spanish, *Mr. Goya, your paintings are so beautiful they remind me of the most amazing girl I've ever met?*"

She blushes and lowers her face, then repeats Spanish words back to me. Even though the pain shoots across my jaw, I sit up in the boat so I'm looking at her.

"How do you say in English, *I can't imagine being without her?*"

She looks at me. Her eyes don't let me go. "I feel the same."

I take her hand. Run my index finger along hers. Feel her skin warm to my touch. "Clio." I breathe her name into the painted world we float on. I cup her face in my hands, my palms on her cheeks, holding her soft and close as golden starlight streaks across the night. All my nerves fly up my throat as I ask the next question. "How do you say in French, *Clio, I'm falling in love with you*?"

She loops her fingers through mine, lacing them tightly. "Julien, I'm falling in love with you too."

CHAPTER 23

The Flooding

Streaks of pale-pink morning light filter through the windows at the front of the museum. The sun rises early in the summer; it's only five in the morning.

I catch a glimpse of Renoir's *The Swing* that hangs next to *Gabrielle*. The dress the woman on the swing wears now looks as if it's been washed a few too many times. I stop and stare more closely at the fading colors. I touch the dress gently with my palm, as if I'm saying good-bye to *The Swing*. Clio tried to repair *Gabrielle* when we left *Starry Night*, but Renoir's art is lurching closer to colorless.

When I reach the front doors, Gustave motions for me to come over. "Hey, Julien, remember my sculpture from the other night? Got it in the subway art contest just in time and now I'm going to be doing a few pieces in one of the Metro stations on the Balard line. Just heard from the project coordinator."

"That's fantastic."

"You helped me figure it out. So thank you," he says and tips his chin, looking proud of his accomplishment. Then it hits me— I'm more than something of a muse to him. I must be *his* muse, helping him along to realize his potential.

I point both index fingers at him. "You are a rock star."

I push open the door to head into the dawn but double back. "Hey, Gustave. Can I ask you for a favor? Can you keep an eye out for a guy about my age—weird curl on his forehead, and very old-looking hands?"

"Sure. Why?"

"Just something about him. I don't trust him near the art, know what I mean?"

"I hear you. I'll pass on the word to the day shift too." His phone rings. "My buddy at the Louvre," he says in an offhand way, then answers. The guy who spotted the lemon. I freeze, then make a split-second decision to pretend to check my phone so I have a reason to listen to their conversation.

"Trickle of water? You don't say?" Gustave looks at me and twirls a finger near his ear. He pauses as his friend speaks. I swipe the screen to keep busy.

"Just mop it up."

Another pause as I scan my text messages without reading them.

"Yep. See you Sunday for cards."

He hangs up, shaking his head in amusement. "He's losing it. Seeing things again."

"What's he seeing?" I ask, doing my best to remain cool and calm, but inside I'm frayed thin with nerves.

"Says when he was in room 77, he heard a trickle from the big Géricault. Turned around and saw a drop of water on the floor. Told you he was a loon."

"Yeah, sounds like it," I say, but it's as if I've been punched by Cass again, this time in the gut.

⌇

The Louvre doesn't open for another four hours. I go home and manage a bit of fitful sleep. But inside I am yanked in so many directions I might as well shred all my limbs and let loose my stuffing. I finally wake up, shower, down a coffee, and leave after my parents have both gone to work. I grab the Metro and exit a few stops later at the Louvre, where I line up early so I can be one of the first inside. I know exactly where to find *The Raft of the Medusa*, one of the most famous icons of early eighteenth-century painting that depicts the aftermath of a French naval wreck in a storming sea. I take the marble steps two by two as a woman with flaming red hair nearly collides into me as she heads the other way. I say sorry, but she's already gone.

My heart is pounding so fast I feel like a rookie in the police department heading to his first crime scene. Eager but terrified. I turn the corner and stop in my tracks. I'm paralyzed at the sight, as if I'm witnessing a horrific car accident unfolding in slow motion. *The Raft of the Medusa* is gushing. Like a fire hydrant on a summer day, water pours out of the massive canvas from the rocky waves Géricault painted, the ones Clio helped him to create.

This is no mere trickle on the floor. The painting has sprung a leak.

A young man in a gray jumpsuit—a janitor, I take it—races in with a mop and a bucket. Seconds later, he is joined by an older man with black slacks, a striped dress shirt, and a silk tie. He's probably on the curatorial staff, but I don't recognize him. I back up as he runs into the gallery, frantic as he shouts instructions and obscenities.

"It was just kind of dripping a little while ago," the janitor explains. "Then, bam! The water just shot out like a hose."

The man in the suit rolls up his sleeves, like he's a handyman ready to do damage control. But he doesn't have a clue what to do. No one does. The janitor mops feverishly, and the man starts shooing away crowds and then shouts to an assistant who rushes in, "Close this gallery. Close this gallery now!"

I race into the next gallery as crowds crane their necks for a view of the flooding. I need to check out the others.

First, I find the Ingres. I recoil when I see the painting is eating itself. The blue cushions have folded over the concubine and all that's left of her is one eye that stares out desperately at me, as the cushions squeeze and strangle her.

Then the La Tour. The tiny trace of candlelight left in the painting has turned into a red-hot flame as fire licks the canvas.

Next, the Titian. I run into its gallery and step back instantly. The mirror in the painting wobbles precariously, hanging inches out of its canvas. Time freezes as it hovers, then speeds up as it clatters to the floor with a deafening crash, shattering into broken shards that send frightened visitors scrambling for cover.

I grab for my phone, dialing my mother.

"Are the paintings okay? Besides the fading Renoirs. Are all the others okay?"

"I think so. Why?"

"I'll be there soon to explain." I hang up and run to Rembrandt's Bathsheba, only to find her shriveled up into tiny little hardened pieces on the floor, like pork rinds.

I call Bonheur as I run out of the Louvre, telling him he needs to take me to the Muses now.

CHAPTER 24

Layer Cake Paris

Sophie's outside holding open the iron gate to the green door. She has on her red sparkly tap shoes, her toe plate smacking the cobbled sidewalk in a jazzy, impatient rhythm. It briefly occurs to me that Clio would probably like a pair of red sparkly shoes.

"I heard about the Louvre. It's awful," she says. "Does anyone know what's going on?"

"They don't have a clue." We race through the courtyard. "Where's your mom?"

"Went to some fashion show over on the Champs," Sophie says and mimes gagging as she yanks open the orange door. I take it Sophie's not a fan of her mom's haute couture empire. "Then she's leaving for Milan for the week. But it's not as if she minds that you're going to see the Muses."

"She knows everything?"

"What? Did you think my brother and I run a secret

clandestine basement operation without our parents knowing a thing?"

Seeing as my own mom isn't the wiser about what happens on the other side of her frames at the Musée d'Orsay, yes I did. I don't answer.

"Besides, we're not the only ones," she says as we head down the hall to the TV room, passing the Jasper Johns and Monet's bridge.

"Only ones what?"

"With access."

"To the Muses?"

"Yeah. Lots of families all over the world can get in touch with them. There are many patrons of the arts, Julien," Sophie says and rolls her eyes as she pulls on the trap door. I love being talked to as if I'm a dolt for not knowing how Muse access works.

"And many of them need to be in touch with the Muses," she continues. "Hence, the Avant-Garde. Like I told you."

"Well, take me to your leader, Sophie."

She descends into the dark, her tap shoes leading the way. We loop round and round, the air growing heavier, like a dense fog. At last we reach the basement, the one I sneaked into a few weeks ago at Bonheur's party. I hear the voices again, and they sound like bells. The sound pierces me in a new way, reminding me of Clio and her pure, sweet voice. She's one of them, and the home down below is where she used to spend her days.

Bonheur is here in the cellar, and he's waving a sheet of paper. He's smiling, but businesslike. He hands me what looks like the kind of stationery you'd use for an invitation to a fancy tea party.

Julien—I'm working at La Belle Vie today. Fastest way to get there is to take the third door on the right. —T

I look at Bonheur.

"T?"

He nods. "T."

"For Thalia, I assume."

"Yes."

I rub a palm across my face. "This is a note? From the head of the Muses?"

Another nod, this one longer.

"Like we're in high school and she's telling me where to meet her when classes end?"

"She gave it to me, and I'm giving it to you," he says, his voice clipped with urgency.

"She gave it to you?"

"Yes, Julien, yes. She has crazy red hair and she smells like pomegranates."

"And she's working at La Belle Vie?"

"Yes, yes, yes," he repeats, spreading his arms in frustration.

"The head of the Muses is writing you notes." I can't help but feel that I'm losing it again.

"And you're in love with a girl who's trapped in a painting. So there."

Sophie huffs. "Guys! You're both being idiots. There's art exploding at the Louvre." Sophie sticks her chin out at me and points downward. "Go."

I'm in too deep to stop believing. "I'm guessing we get there through this door in the floor thing?" I point to the rectangular outline, edged by silver Muse dust.

"I've never been down there, Julien," Bonheur says in a soft voice. "This is as far as Sophie and I can go."

I'm alone in this. I have to rely on the person I've never put much faith in. Me. But it's always been just me. Now, it *has* to be just me; there's no other way.

"See?" Sophie demonstrates, pressing her hands against the stone slab edged by silver dust. Nothing happens to the slab. "It's a one-way door for us. When they need it, they open it. We talk in here, in our basement. Otherwise, we just leave each other letters," she says, tipping her forehead to the side of the slab with the mail slot for Muses.

Bonheur follows suit, showing me as well that his hands can't open the slab.

A brief gust of anger rips through me, but I don't even know who I'm mad at. I'm ticked at the Muses for never telling Bonheur and his family the whole truth about the painting, I'm angry at Renoir for trapping Clio, and I'm enraged at myself for not knowing how to save the sick art. "I swear, if I get stuck underground in Paris for the rest of my days, I will come back as a badass ghost and haunt you both forever."

Bonheur laughs and holds up his hands. "Duly noted, and I will consider myself now fully prepared for your ghostly vengeance."

I kneel outside the line of sparkling shimmery dust. I place my palms on the stone slab, and it's a chemical reaction at my touch, baking soda and vinegar making a volcanic concoction. The slab slides open, like a door at a department store. I half expect to tumble into a magical underground world, where the sky is endlessly blue and the hills are sunlit green. But I have no such luck. Instead, I'm in the catacombs.

I don't understand why anyone gets a kick out of subterranean trips through the intestines of Paris and its dank, musty tunnels far below the streets. This city is a layer cake, with houses built on top of cellars, built on top of tombs, and you never know where the bowels will take you. I never know because I've never gone into the catacombs.

It's creepy dark down here, an infernal burrow that pinches my lungs with its airlessness. I don't move for a moment, as I try to orient myself and let my eyes adjust. The third door on the right, the note said. I look up at the slab above me and turn right, but it's so black I can barely see in this narrow, twisty cave. Then I remember—I've got a light on me, thanks to modern technology. I reach for my phone from my back pocket and swipe the screen. Simon's friend Corinne at the archives was wrong—it would have made a big difference if Jean Valjean had had a smartphone when he was down in the sewers. My phone guides the way, and I find the door quickly, turning an old rusty handle that opens to a set of stairs. The steps take me up to another door and into the backroom of La Belle Vie, a famous perfume shop on the rue de Rivoli not far from the bridge with all the padlocks. This is a layer of Paris I never expected to unearth.

I walk into the shop.

La Belle Vie sells only flacons, not the scents themselves. The bottles are beautiful things—the sort of gift you'd buy your mom and she'd be thrilled to spritz a little something on her wrist from the old-fashioned bottles complete with puffy atomizers. The bottles are all hand painted, some with delicate purple flowers, others with flowing red vines. They are things no one ever needs. Beauty without reason. It's the perfect location for a Muse to do her work.

The sign on the front of the shop has been turned around, letting customers know the store is closed. The curtains are drawn. A woman is bent over the counter, with sheets of flaming red hair surrounding her. She wears laboratory goggles, holds a miniature pair of tweezers in one hand, and stares hard at the pages full of musical staffs and notes spread on the counter in front of her. She flicks the tiniest bit of silver dust from her fingertips to the paper. Then, like a surgeon, she lowers the tweezers with pinpoint precision over a line of complicated-looking orchestrations.

I wait, not wanting to disturb her project. She seems to grab something from the paper, but when she peers closely at the tweezers, she sighs at them with disdain, then drops them on the counter.

"Hi there," I say carefully.

She jumps, then shakes her head. "I'm so sorry. I was trying to get these lost notes."

"Excuse me?"

She stands and offers a hand. She wears a thin silver bracelet on each wrist, just like Clio. "I'm Thalia." She has high cheekbones and soft skin that does indeed smell like pomegranates, but her hazel eyes look tired. "The Roques, who own this shop, are music lovers. They found a lost symphony from Mahler, but some of the notes are missing. I was trying to see if I could coax them out."

"Okay," I say, as if that's the sort of thing I hear every day. "And the Roques are like Bonheur and Sophie, I take it? More emissaries?"

"Yes, they let me work in here when I need to. That's why I had you meet me here, since I knew I'd be working on this symphony for a while," she says, and Clio was right—it is all work as a Muse. I'm being squeezed into Thalia's schedule as she multitasks. "That's part of my job. I handle a lot of the problems and complications with art, literature, and music."

"Like an ombudswoman in a department store? Someone who looks into complaints?"

"Kind of, yes. I do some inspiration work myself, but lately my tasks are centered more on the things that go wrong."

"Do these catacombs go everywhere? Like around the world? So you can handle whatever . . . goes wrong?"

"They do. Well, you can only open these doors if you're a Muse—human or Eternal. But yes, that's what gives us access to wherever we're called on to work. We don't get to spend much time together down there." She points.

"In the catacombs?"

She laughs. "No, far below. Where we actually live in a gorgeous house in a lovely field. It's beautiful and peaceful. But we're working most of the time, so we're rarely home. Which is why we're glad to have some help from humans, and you're the first."

"Well, I actually need *your* help. Because we have a serious problem with the art. Just a little Géricault flooding, and a Titian breaking, and an Ingres being strangled with cushions. I think it all started with the Renoirs and spread from there. But the Renoirs are the least of it now. They're only fading and the rest of the art— well, it's pretty much having a massive meltdown. I have no idea what's going on, so I hope to God you do and can help me stop it."

She purses her lips and looks away. I watch her closely. Her eyes are stony, but there is something a bit like guilt in the way her jaw is set and then in how she exhales. Heavily, with shame.

Oh.

Oh my.

I know what happened.

I stumble, stepping back, as a wave of understanding clobbers me. I grab the edge of a shelf full of green etched bottles with antique gold caps to steady myself. I didn't want to be right about this, because it feels so wrong.

"You did this, didn't you?" I say, my voice so low it can barely register the shock. "You cursed the Renoirs."

She swallows tightly, then turns back to me. Her eyes are wet but hard. "I love Clio. I love all my Muses. They are all I know, and when he took her from me," she says and a deep breath seems to expand through her chest and into her shoulders, a breath of righteousness, as her words turn into the serrated edge of a knife, "I was furious."

She walks close to me, her steps controlled and crisp. "I tried to free her myself. When Suzanne switched out the paintings and brought the real one to me with Clio in it, I did everything I possibly could to free her. I used dust on it to try to reverse what he did. I tried every tool in my tool kit to bring her out. I took her canvas with me to museums around the world. To London, to Florence, to the Louvre. I hid inside the museums until night fell and tried to free her then with the magic of a museum. But Muse dust is powerful, and he'd cursed her until a human muse came around. It was binding, and there was nothing I could do. I was helpless and I was livid." As she recounts the story her eyes fill with fury, with the kind of anger that must have engulfed her then. "I did the thing I never thought in a million years a Muse would do. I hurt art. I cursed beauty."

The confirmation of what I'd thought to be possible all along. That the Renoir damage was never from the sun. That it was a curse, the most powerful kind a painting could ever have on it— a curse from the ultimate lover of art. I can picture Thalia trying to free Clio but coming up empty, a wail of rage echoing through her. I was disgusted moments ago, but I understand why she did it. I might have even done the same. "You really loved Clio," I say.

"Of course I did. Of course I do. My Muses are the only ones I've ever loved. And I went, quite simply, ballistic. I cursed every last painting of his but hers."

My heart floods with relief at the last part. "What was the curse, though, and why is it happening now? Why not kill off his art back then?"

Thalia's shoulders drop. She bites her bottom lip, then looks at me. Her eyes are tired. Being an Eternal Muse seems exhausting. "When he took what I loved, I wanted to hurt him. So I cursed his art to fade away . . . starting when a human muse appeared. It seemed the fitting punishment given what their disagreement was over."

But I can barely hear what she's saying because there's a ringing in my ears, and a slowing of blood in my veins. My vision blurs and everything in me stalls. "So it's because of me that his art is fading?"

"No, Julien," she says quickly. "No. Absolutely not."

"But it is, in a way. You could have killed his art then to punish him. Instead, his art is dying because I'm around, and now all the other art is completely freaking out." I grip the counter as I recall with pinpoint clarity the moment I noticed the first bit of damage on the piano girls—a few days after art came alive for me. A few days after I came into my own as a human muse.

"I was punishing him for not believing," Thalia says, but there's a defensiveness in her voice.

"If he believed in human muses, he'd be after me, Thalia. And he's not. All along, he's been trying to stop Clio. He's been trying to prevent her painting from being hung. He's always been after her," I say, and a cold dread stretches through me. Maybe he is still hunting her, not just pigment. Could he have been casing the museum the other day to figure out how to cut her canvas from the frame, roll her up, and walk off with her in his sweatshirt sleeve, then closet her away forever? It's not implausible. I can count off dozens of museums that have been victims of unsolved theft, from the Rembrandt heist at the Gardner in Boston to the robbery of several works by Matisse and Picasso at the modern art museum here in Paris. The art has never been recovered because that's the thing about art theft—masterpieces are nearly impossible to sell, but they're incredibly easy to hide. Forever. "Look, all I care about is Clio, and the art. We need—"

She cuts me off. "How is Clio? I need to know."

"She's great," I say quickly, wanting to get to the pressing matter.

"When is she coming back? Are you going to bring her back? Are you going to let her out of the museum?"

"Um, yeah. Soon," I say, but the truth is it's up to Clio, not me.

"What has she been doing?"

"We've been hanging out."

"Hanging out? What is that?"

I laugh, because Thalia doesn't seem like a woman who blows off work. She wouldn't really know what hanging out is. "We talk and we row boats and I draw things for her, and we eat dessert, and it's the best time I've ever had in my life."

"You love her," Thalia says, but it's hardly a statement. It's more like an expression of wonder.

"Yes."

"And she is in love with you?"

"Yes," I say and I can't help myself from grinning as I think of her, and last night, and the words we both said.

"What is it like? That kind of love?" Thalia asks, as if it's the first time the subject of this kind of love has ever come up.

I start to speak, to tell her what it's like—it's like you can do anything, it's like the stars exist for you, it's like you can stop time and fill it with the way your whole heart and mind clicks perfectly with another person.

That it's like the impossible has become possible.

Instead, I put it in terms that she'll understand. "It's like finding a lost symphony."

Thalia smiles, and she looks peaceful with my answer. "That sounds wonderful."

"It is. So how do we reverse the curse? It's obviously infecting the other paintings, like the ones at the Louvre. For whatever reason, it's spread beyond the Renoirs you cursed. Clio tried to fix it. She placed her hands on Renoir's painting of Gabrielle last night. She even tried flicking it with Muse dust. It didn't do anything."

"I'm not surprised. I tried myself this morning."

"What?"

"Well, of course I would try! I was at the Louvre the second it opened. I laid my hands on all the damaged paintings," Thalia says, and like I'm lining up the edges of a drawing I've traced, I can place her red hair. The mane of it that I saw on the steps of the Louvre this morning.

"I saw you. I saw you at the Louvre."

"I tried to stop it. I had to wait until the museum opened, but as soon as it did I was the first one in," she says, and it's almost funny how pedestrian being a Muse can be—she can't just appear and disappear in museums at will. She has to go through the doors, like everyone else. No free pass is given even if you inspire what's on the walls.

"I even sent Calliope over to the National Gallery in London too," Thalia says. "They're having the same problem with their Turners. The curse is spreading quickly now."

My heart sinks. "They're flooding?" The National Gallery is home to so many beautiful J. M. W. Turners, gorgeous seascapes with dappled sunlight on the water.

"All over the floors, Calliope said." Thalia's already been on various assignments today. I get why Clio would want to skip out for a few days. I don't want to think about what happens when Clio returns to being a Muse. Maybe we can meet up in La Belle Vie, or Bonheur's basement. There will be time to figure it out. There will be time to plan a stolen kiss here, a brief moment there. It will be worth it.

But first things first. "Clio tried to fix the paintings, Calliope tried, and you tried. And it didn't work. What are we supposed to do next?"

Thalia looks at me. "Well, have *you* tried?"

CHAPTER 25

Healed Rose, Sliced Skin

I bolt from the rue de Rivoli, nearly knocking over a young family pushing a baby carriage on the pedestrian bridge over the river.

"Sorry," I mutter, but I'm gone, sprinting toward the museum.

My legs have never been this long. My body has never moved so fast. I've never been powered by such ragged desire.

The lines for the Musée d'Orsay snake around the block. It's summer and high tourist season. The museum will be packed inside. I run to one of the side entrances, slide my card key through, then grab hard on the door. Down the stairs, into the administrative wing, and back up to the main floor. There are crowds everywhere, visitors packed into the galleries and halls, just like any other June afternoon. I force myself to walk to *The Swing*, even though I want to shove everyone aside and see if it could possibly be true.

There it is. The painting I touched this morning.

A group of young children sit cross-legged on the floor in front of the image. A teacher explains to them how Renoir tried to capture the effects of sunlight through the trees and on the fabric of the woman's dress. I inch closer to the canvas, and I nearly collapse to my knees, so strung out am I now on a raw and naked kind of hope.

It's perfect. It's absolutely perfect. I want to fold my hands together and say thank you to the only gods I've ever believed in because this is my holy ground, and this feels like the closest I've ever come to witnessing a miracle. I can't even contemplate that it happened because of my hands touching that painting, but there it is. The evidence in front of me. The woman's white dress is luminescent again, the blue bows on it are radiant. I nearly stagger back, so humbled, so awed that I've somehow done something no restorer could ever do. It's only fitting—the curse was over human muses; the antidote is one.

I want to shoo the visitors out the door and lay my hands on the Renoirs. I want to fix them this second, but I can't touch the paintings with these people here. Tonight, I'll take care of the others. I scan the room, mentally ticking off the half dozen or so Renoirs that have just begun to wither—the kind only I can see, and only I can stop.

I notice Gabrielle is missing. Her picture had hung next to *The Swing* just a few hours ago.

I head to my mother's office downstairs to see how bad off *Gabrielle* must be to have been shuttered away. Her door is open and she's on the phone. Her expression is deadly serious. She motions quickly for me to come in. I take a seat as she finishes her call.

"Oh, that's terrible. I'm so sorry to hear. I've been talking to forensic scientists and even the canvas makers themselves to see if they know."

She pauses and listens.

"They don't have any ideas. No one's seen anything like this before."

She waits again. "I've got a new team of restorers coming to look at our Renoirs. I'll let you know what I find out. And please do the same for yours."

She hangs up then, and sighs deeply. She slumps back in her chair.

"Who was that?" I ask.

"My colleague at the Met. They've got one of the sun-damaged Renoirs, and now a Vermeer—the one with the sleeping maid— well, apparently she's snoring and drooling. She drools in her sleep, evidently. So far, it's the Louvre, the National Gallery in London, and the Met in New York with this new spate of problems," she says, and it's so weird how the curse manifests once it infects other paintings. Only the Renoirs seem to go simply, with a leaking of their colors. The others unravel in a mad exhuming of their insides. Perhaps the curse morphs into a new strain of sickness when it stretches beyond the Renoir hosts. "I'm sure we're going to have even more problems any minute, like the other museums. None of this makes any sense."

But it makes perfect sense, I want to say. It makes all the sense in the world and it will all be fine. "Did you move Gabrielle? She's no longer upstairs."

"Storage," my mother says heavily. "The Met's taking the Vermeer down to its storage too. God knows that's where most of our paintings will wind up eventually."

"They'll figure it out. They have to, right? Art doesn't just decompose," I say, doing my best to comfort her.

"Well, that's certainly what I thought for the longest time. But everything I've ever learned is useless right now, Julien. Completely useless."

I want to tell her about *The Swing*. I want to shout happily that it's healed, that all the others soon will be too. I don't know how I'm going to get myself to Boston or New York. But I can start here, and I can start by fixing *Gabrielle*.

"How happy would you be if all Renoirs were suddenly fixed?" I ask.

She manages the tiniest grin. "Ecstatic. And can you pull the moon down from the sky for me too?"

"I'm on it, Mom," I say, then glance at my watch. "I don't have a tour for another hour. Would you mind if I visited the storage room? I'd love to see Gabrielle."

She slides open a drawer to her desk and hands me a key. I head for the stairwell, and I go down one more flight of stairs to the lowest level of the museum tucked far belowground. The storage room is at the end of one hall and hardly anyone is ever in there. I stop in the men's room, wash my hands thoroughly, and then head back down the hall. I unlock the main storage room, then relock the door once I'm inside. The storage room is a way station for art—it houses works that are coming or going, as well as a handful that are on sabbatical as they make room for the traveling paintings that come through. The art here is shelved in specialized units, not hung on the walls. The lights are always dim, and the temperature is cool. There are drawings, paintings, prints, and more. I find *Gabrielle*'s frame easily; it's resting quietly next to other small paintings, since the art is arranged by size.

I slide the frame out carefully, resting it against the nearby wall. I glance back at the door. It may be locked, but plenty of people here have keys. I have to be fast. I'm not even sure what I did this morning, if it was where I touched *The Swing* or how, but I don't have time to parse out the details. I look at the shawl. It's barely visible, so I start there, pressing my hands gently against the canvas. Should I leave my palms on the painting and wait for the colors to fill in like it's some kind of paint-by-numbers magical ink? But I only touched *The Swing* briefly, so I take my hands off and wait. Nothing happens. I stand up, walk around, and wander through the other works. I look at my watch. Ten minutes pass. I check *Gabrielle* again. Still the same. What if my eyes were playing tricks on me with *The Swing*? What if desperate hope fooled me into believing?

I head to another darkened corner of the storage room. I force myself to lie down and close my eyes, and I'd love to take a nap, but I can't because my insides are twisted and torqued, and I am so full of wishing that I am like a coiled wire. But I must be more tired than I think, because the next thing I hear is my mother's voice. "Julien, are you still here? It's time for your tour."

I rub my eyes and sit up. I'm groggy and my head is fuzzy. "Sorry, I fell asleep."

"Well, obviously."

"Any more news?"

My mom nods sadly. "More bad news from the Met. They had just tried moving the Vermeer to storage, but the painting got worse there. I'm told the same thing happened with the other museums. So just to keep the art stable, they've all left them hanging in their galleries. Roped off but hanging. Just in case," she says, then gasps. "Oh my God, oh my God. It's better. *Gabrielle* is better."

I jump up and rush over to the wall where I left her frame. My heart soars when I see that my handiwork has done the trick again. Gabrielle is restored, and her shawl is glorious. It must take more than a few minutes for the healing to spread, but spread it does.

My mother turns to me, and tears are streaking down her face. She clasps me in a hug, though she has no idea what I did. "The paintings love you. Look, you come to visit them and they feel better."

Indeed, it seems something like that has happened.

❧

As the day winds down, my mother receives a happy call. It's the curator in Boston. It seems *Dance at Bougival* is starting to get its color back too. She tells me this as she leaves. "Maybe it was all in our heads," she says, laughing, as she taps her temple. Or perhaps the art is healing in the same way it turned ill. The curse spread from painting to painting; maybe healing spreads too. Tonight, I'll fix ours and hope for the best at the museums across the river and the ocean.

But for now, I'm hungry, so I walk out with my mom, say good-bye to her, and meet Simon down the street at a café. I order french fries, a croque monsieur with chicken instead of ham, since I can't stand ham, and then one more to go, just the same.

Simon raises an eyebrow. "Eating for two?"

"Maybe," I say, then drink my coffee. I shift gears. "Want to see something really cool tonight?"

"A boxer? Or have you found a female sumo wrestler to tackle me next?"

"Better. All you have to do is watch this time. Because I can do something totally awesome with these here hands." I hold my palms up to him and explain how I can heal art with them.

He looks skeptical but amused. "The thing about you, Garnier, is I know what you're saying is crazy, yet I almost believe you."

I hold up a french fry victoriously. "See. It's my sweet innocent face, isn't it?" I give him my best angelic smile, then dip another fry in a ketchup bath.

When we're done, Simon says, "Let's go see the show."

It's later now, and the sun is dropping below the horizon. Gustave opens the front door for us and we head to the faraway galleries to the paintings I need to repair. They're a few rooms down from Clio, and I'll go see her soon to tell her the good news.

Then I hear footsteps, and they're not Gustave's. They're awkward and clunky. I know that sound, and it turns my marrow cold. I take off and run to the sound, my backpack smacking against me as I race.

There's another sound now. A muffled cry, but close by, and I turn the corner into Clio's gallery to see Max scraping off the paint of the signature.

Clio's no longer in the picture.

Next comes a low moan, laced with pain. My heart thuds, heavy in my chest, as I swivel around to find Clio on the ground, bleeding.

CHAPTER 26

The Reckoning

I wish there were two of me, but in some ways there are, thanks to Simon. I grab Max first, tearing him away from the painting, and slam him to the ground.

"Hold him down," I say. Simon pins him. Max, possessed by Renoir, is far easier to hold than Cass Middleton.

I rush to Clio and reach for her. "Clio, are you okay?"

She shakes her head. "It hurts. Oh God. It hurts so much."

She moans like a wounded cat, and I'm sure Simon must be wondering who I'm talking to, since he can't see her. But he can hear her.

"I was starting to come out, to see you. It happened so fast . . ." She trails off, wincing, contorting her gorgeous features.

I look over at Max. "How did you get in here?"

Max jerks his head away, like a petulant child refusing to answer. Simon twists the collar on Max's shirt. "He asked you a question. How. Did. You. Get. In. Here?"

"Stairwell," Max chokes out.

"You were in the stairwell all day?" Simon asks. "Hiding out till the museum closed?"

Max manages a quick nod.

"And to think, I was just about to save all your paintings, Mr. Renoir," I say and watch as his eyes widen with a grotesque kind of happiness.

I turn to Clio. She's cut across the stomach. "We have to stop the bleeding." It's all I can think of. I know nothing of medicine, but I know common sense.

I take off my shirt and press it to her wounds, keeping my hands on them to stem the flow of blood.

She cries out at the pressure. "It's going to be okay, I promise," I say, but I don't know what to do. This isn't the type of cut a Band-Aid will work on. "Should I try some Muse dust?"

"It won't work," she says.

I keep my hands on her, wishing she were a normal girl and I could whisk her off to the emergency room to see a doctor.

A doctor.

There is a doctor in the house.

"Clio, I have to lay you down for a second. I have to get Dr. Gachet, okay?"

But her eyes are closed and her breathing is slowing and she barely acknowledges me. She is fading in and out as I lay her head gently on the floor, not far from Simon's bewildered eyes watching Max and watching me, as I race to Dr. Gachet's frame on the second floor. My hands are bloody, and I don't want to touch his canvas. But I need to wake him up. I wipe my hands off on my jeans, leaving a trail of crimson on me. I touch the frame with my elbow and call his name. "Dr. Gachet! Dr. Gachet! Please help!"

He yawns and his mouth stretches out first. "Yes?"

"Come out. We need you!"

Then the rest of his face, chin, cheeks, forehead, hair, and now his body squeezes out in his shimmery, shiny royal-blue coat. I bring him down to the first floor.

"She's cut." Clio is curled on the floor, twisted in on herself. She's holding on to her middle, a trail of wet blood between her fingers. A small moan escapes, like air slowly freed from a balloon.

Dr. Gachet bends down and begins to tend to her. Soon, Olympia takes notice. She jumps out, and the sight of her naked form strutting in heels and nothing else still surprises me. She hovers nearby, watching.

Dr. Gachet turns to me. "She needs to be stitched up."

I hold up my hands. "How the hell are we supposed to do that? We don't have a single painting of a hospital to go into. Or of medical equipment for me to reach and grab."

Doesn't he get it?

But Dr. Gachet knows more than I do. "She's not like us, Julien. This is real blood, not paint. We can't treat her inside a painting. She needs real stitches for the real blood." He tips his forehead to the red that leaks out of Clio and lists off the tools he'll need. Scissors, thread, a needle, and a little painkiller would be ideal.

"There's no way I can get that all in time." I run my hands

through my hair, and my heart is beating so fast, so crazy, pumping from fear alone.

"Julien."

It's the tiniest little whisper, like a bell. I fall to the ground, kneeling at Clio's side. "What is it?" I ask softly.

"Draw them," she says. "Draw them for me."

Yes!

She grabs hold of my left hand, flicks a bit of silver dust into my palm.

I fumble for my backpack with my right hand. I grab my notebook, slam it open, and listen as Dr. Gachet describes in detail the instruments he'll need. I draw like a surgeon, fast and precise, then trace the lines over in dust. In seconds the flat whiteness becomes shape, turns tactile under my touch.

I give the painkiller to Clio, and the tools to the doctor in the house. Dr. Gachet begins his work.

"Holy crap," Simon says, and I glance over at him. Simon's sitting on Max now, like the street artist ghost host is just a lumpy air mattress, and Simon's watching a fascinating show. His jaw hangs open. He's pointing at the scissors Dr. Gachet holds. Simon may not be able to see Dr. Gachet or Clio, but he can see a needle being threaded by invisible hands. A needle stitching up an unseen wound.

"Yeah, so this is the girl I was telling you about. You can't see her, but she's amazing," I say to Simon, then turn back to Clio. She reaches feebly for my hand, wraps her fingers around mine, and winces. "It'll kick in soon. Just hold tighter till it does," I tell her, urging her to channel all her pain into my hand.

"It's coming along. Hang in there," Dr. Gachet says in his calm, doctorly voice as he makes neat stitches through Clio's flesh.

Clio's tight grip on my hand starts to loosen, and her knitted eyebrows relax. The medicine is working now. She's no longer flinching as Dr. Gachet sews. His hands are steady. He finishes, making a knot. "There." He wipes one hand across the other, then turns to me, handing me back my shirt. I pull it on, bloodstained and filthy. "She's going to be okay. She'll need some rest, but she's going to be okay."

"Can you watch over her, Dr. Gachet? You and Olympia, please?"

"Of course, love." The words come from Olympia, and she kneels down to stroke Clio's hair. I give Clio a kiss on the forehead. "I'll be back soon, I promise."

"I know," she says, and her eyes flutter closed.

I turn my attention to Max. "C'mon," I say to Simon. "Let's take him to another room."

Simon yanks Max and drags him to the next gallery. I move closer to Max, face-to-face with him now. "Don't you get it? Don't you finally get it? This is happening no matter how many of your paintings you remake, no matter how many times you try to chip paint off a canvas for your signature."

"I didn't mean to hurt her," he manages to say. "I just wanted the pigment to make my paintings."

"But you did. You did hurt her. You hurt her then and you hurt her now. You have to stop. It's not just your art that's being ruined. Have you been to the Louvre? Have you seen the Rembrandt? He's one of your idols. And your own work. Just look around. They're all dying because of you."

I point to *The Swing*. "If you were hiding out here all day, then you know it was fading this morning, and now it's not. I fixed *Gabrielle* too. Fixed it with my hands and I'm not even a great artist or an Eternal Muse. I'm not even a very good artist. I'm just a guy who likes art, and I'm the only one who can fix your paintings. I can fix all of these." I pull him over to each and every one of his paintings that have started to wither. "But you have to let it go. You have to move on. Your legacy isn't the only thing that matters. There are bigger things at stake. For God's sake, the guy whose body you've taken over is teaching caricature to kids. The security guard out there is showing wire art in a subway. My friend makes ceramic calves and they're awesome. Art is everywhere, and it's not just for great artists. Anyone can do it, and anyone will. You have got to let this go."

Renoir swallows hard. His pupils flare with desperation. "You'll fix my paintings? You'll save them?"

"Yes," I say, exasperated. "I hate what you did to her, but I'd save your work anyway. Your legacy is safe in my hands, I promise. But you need to leave us alone, and you need to go kill your fakes."

He mutters a strangled apology. "I'm sorry."

"Don't apologize to me. Say you're sorry to Clio."

I drag him back to Clio's gallery, where she's resting on the bench, Dr. Gachet on one side, Olympia on the other.

Simon has Max's hands gripped behind his back. When Max gets closer, he bends down and speaks in a low, remorseful voice. But he doesn't say he's sorry. Instead, he tells her, "Thank you. For inspiring me."

Then he rises, and Simon and I escort him out the front doors, where Gustave looks on with surprised eyes. "I'll explain later," I tell our security guard.

We hail a cab, and I give the driver the address of the church in the Marais. The three of us are in the backseat, Max in the middle.

"Kind of surprised the driver stopped, given your, um, your shirt."

"Yeah, it's kind of a mess, isn't it?"

"So you're in love with a painting?" Simon says.

"Yeah, I'm in love with a girl who's stuck inside a painting. Oh, and get this. She's also a Muse."

"Yeah?" Simon raises an eyebrow. "As in one of the nine Muses?"

"Yeah."

"Sounds like she's perfect for you then," he says, and there's no teasing in his voice.

"She is."

We reach the church, and Max leads the way to the basement, past the altar, down the steps. He turns on the light and takes out the knife with his claw hands, the same blade he tried to use to retrieve the missing piece for his forgeries. He closes his eyes as if this pains him, then opens them and slashes the fakes—the piano girls, the boy with the cat, and the *Gabrielle* that Cass had started next. Each one is gashed down the middle, the canvas split open.

I grab Max by the shoulders. "Now you can go." His hands knot up and cramp. But then he flexes them and stretches his fingers. There's a gust of wind, and it carries the trailing, telltale scent of rose perfume on it. I hope I never smell roses again.

Max shakes his head, as if he just woke up from a strange dream. "What the . . . ?"

He looks around, completely at a loss as to where he is. His hands are his hands again. The hands of a young artist who makes art the way he wants.

"Hey bud," Simon says. "You've been sleepwalking. Let me take you back to your pad."

"Thank you," I mouth to Simon.

"I'll watch over you for a bit," Simon says to Max as they leave. "Make sure you don't sleepwalk again."

I leave too, and I stop at a souvenir shop that's still open. A customer sees my shirt and steps away from me. I grab the nearest I LOVE PARIS T-shirt and buy it. Out on the street I yank off the one coated in dried blood, toss it into a trash can, and pull on the fresh shirt.

I return to the museum, where I scrub the blood off my hands and begin to heal the Renoirs. First a party scene, then a portrait, now a damaged landscape. I watch as they rewind to glory, becoming as perfect as the day they were made. By the time I've laid my hands on the fourth painting, the next two heal on their own. Just as the curse spread, the cure spreads, as if the paintings are linked. Like dominoes falling, all I have to do is touch a few and the rest follow.

I take the nearest stairwell to the administrative wing, wanting to leap and clear all the steps in one big jump but restraining myself as I sneak into my mother's quiet office to check her e-mail. She always leaves her programs running, so I click on her screen, tap on the in-box, and scroll through her latest e-mails to find a message from the director of the museum in New York. It's only six in the evening there, and the museum is still open, so I'm not surprised, but I am thrilled, to find a note from minutes ago. The subject line is all exclamation points, and proclaims the sun-damaged Renoir has been restored. I read the rest of the note. "My fingers are crossed that the Vermeer makes a similar miracle recovery soon."

I'm so tempted to write back and tell my mom's colleague to check the Vermeer in a few minutes, maybe in an hour, because I have a hunch that once all the Renoirs have recovered so will the other sick paintings.

The cure has started.

I mark the note unread, leave her office, and walk upstairs, feeling a sense of calm for the first time since art came alive for me.

Everything is going to be fine. Everything is going to be better. I inhale deeply, relieve Dr. Gachet and Olympia from their bench-side post, and take Clio to the South of France.

CHAPTER 27

The Calm Before

I'm telling you, it was Thalia's idea. She was all like, 'Well, have *you* tried it?'" I say, imitating Thalia's pointed statement.

"I don't care if it was her idea. *You* did it, Julien," Clio says.

Soft waves lap our feet. Warm sand forms a pillow for our heads. We are lying on the beach, inside a Cézanne. The perfect place for rest and relaxation, which is just what the doctor ordered for Clio. I am all too happy to be her companion on a quick trip to the painted seashore in Marseille.

"Just think right now of all the sick paintings that are starting to feel better. Because of your touch," Clio says, as she squeezes my hand happily. Her other hand rests on her wounded stomach. Her face is still pale, but she drank some water and ate some of the sandwich I'd picked up for her before we escaped to a quiet patch of beach deep within a Cézanne on our walls.

"I'm going to hang up a shingle that says ART DOCTOR FOR HIRE,

AT YOUR SERVICE." I tuck my hands behind my head and let the warm sun of the Mediterranean beat down on my face. Outside of the painting it is deep in the middle of the night. "By the time we leave, the reports will be pouring in from all the other museums."

"I can't wait to hear the good news," she says. Then she shifts gears. "What else did Thalia say when you saw her this morning? Did she ask about me?"

"Yes."

"Did she want to know when I was coming back?"

"It's like you can read her mind," I joke.

"What did you tell her?"

I prop myself up on my elbow and run a finger along her bare arm. "Clio, that's entirely up to you."

"Do you think I should go back?"

"If you want to, you should."

"But will I still see you?"

I laugh. "I'll see you as much as I possibly can. But I'm not the one being called upon all the time. As far as I can tell, being a human muse is infinitely easier than being an Eternal one. I'm allowed to do things like lie on a beach all night, and something tells me you won't be able to just hang out like this."

"Maybe I can convince Thalia to let me work less. So I can see you," she suggests, her voice rising a notch.

"Part-time Muse."

"Well, it's not implausible. Besides, I did kind of predict human muses would come to be. So maybe the human muses are here so we Eternal Muses don't have to work all the time."

"Ha. You think you can just push off your workload onto me."

"I could meet you in between assignments. See you here and there. Would that make you crazy?"

"Totally. Totally one hundred percent insane and then some, and I'd happily do it. Clio, if I could see you for five minutes a day I would. If I could see you for five minutes a week I'd sign up for that too. All I want is for this not to end."

"Good. Because I think I can convince her. You know, play up the whole pity case of having been trapped for more than a century," Clio says and bats her eyes in mock plaintiveness, then pushes out her bottom lip, pretending to make it quiver. "How's that?"

"Just add a sniffle to the mix and she won't be able to resist," I say.

"Maybe a crocodile tear or two?"

"Oh totally. Besides, you know she feels guilty for what she did anyway, so this is your chance," I tease, even though it's true. Then I shift gears. "When do you think you'll leave?" My heart hurts to think I might not be able to see her every night here at my home away from home. But I also think it'd be the cruelest torture for her to be trapped in a painting for the rest of her days. She'll be free, and we'll have the chance at least of something. A little something has to be better than nothing.

"I want to rest up for another day or so. It still hurts," she says, gently pressing her hand to her belly. "But then, I guess I'll go."

She sounds so sad, and her voice breaks again. "But we'll see each other," she adds, and she bends to me, her lips brushing so gently, so sweetly, I'm sure I'm dreaming again, or flying. The ends of her hair brush across my shirt, and an intoxicated sigh that becomes her name escapes my lips as she lies against me.

"We *have* to see each other, Julien. I want more of this world. I want more of you," she says, and I wrap my arms around her and hold her, inside our faraway painted land.

We fall asleep on the beach, and I dream of nothing but all the possibilities of her.

I blink. There's sand in my eye. I blink again, and scrunch up my nose, because now my eye is starting to water. I sit up. So does Clio. The sand is blowing, like a breeze is sweeping up the seashore. The wind picks up quickly, and soon it's hardly a warm breeze, or a welcoming one. Within seconds, it's a thrashing wind, and Clio's hair is whipping across her face. She grasps at strands that lash her, and I fumble for her hand to pull her up. The water from the sea pounds the shore, sloshing harder with each break, as if someone were rocking the landscape. We run toward the green fields near the edge of the canvas, but the sand swirls and buries the path. The painted grass turns brown and crackly.

The waves pursue us, snapping at our feet, and I hold a hand over my eyes to keep the sand out. We trudge uphill, and with each step the ground is looser, crumbling under our feet. "We're almost out," I say, but I'm panicked to the core, even as I stick a hand through the end of the paint and slide onto to the museum floor, slipping in a slick pile of sand. We're on the other side at last, but the view isn't that much better. I stare in disbelief at the wet sand on the museum floor.

Clio coughs and sputters. She wipes a hand across her lips,

trying to get the sand out of her mouth. The avalanche has stopped, and the beautiful Cézanne has sloughed off its insides, its heart and guts in a sad pile on the floor. I peer down the hall. The rest of the rooms are quiet. But it's as if a bolt of lightning clapped and we are waiting for the thunder that's sure to follow.

This wasn't supposed to happen. I gave the art its medicine. The medicine was supposed to spread.

"We have to check on the others," I say. Even with her wounded midsection, Clio takes off with me on a mad hunt through the galleries, surveying all the paintings on our walls, from the far ends of the first floor to the hidden nooks on the second floor.

Everything else is fine, except for a Degas of an orchestra. There's music coming from the frame now, only it's out of tune. The notes of the orchestra have become warped and scratchy.

Clio covers her ears for a second. "Oh, that's not how it sounded when he made that painting."

I swivel around and look hard at her. "Right. You were there when he made it. What year was this?" I look back at the plaque, and it reads 1870.

Then I do the math.

This painting and the Cézanne that pulverized itself were made before 1885. But the Van Goghs, the Matisses, the Toulouse-Lautrecs came after and they're unharmed.

Eighteen eighty-five is the dividing line. Before Clio. After Clio.

I can feel the puzzle pieces sliding into place. I turn to Clio and place my hands on her shoulders. "I think I know what's going on. It's all the art that you inspired that's having trouble. Everything modern is fine, the other Cézannes, the ones that came after you were trapped, are fine. But the Cézanne we were in is an earlier one. It was yours. The Degas was yours. It's like the art you inspired is starting to crumble. That has to be what's going on. It wasn't the Renoir curse that made the other art sick. They were never even sick in the same way. It's that the art misses you. You have to go back to being a Muse. We need to free you."

"When did it start? When did these weird problems with the art really start? Not the fading of the Renoirs, but the art truly acting up?"

I think of the dancers twirling in the halls, of Olympia's cat coming out to play. But that's art coming to life. I flash to the first time I saw trouble brewing—the flame, and the feathers, and the transforming of Bathsheba. "A couple days after Bonheur's party. Why?"

Clio darts into the main hallway and looks to the glass doors. "The sun is rising. I have to go."

"Right, right. I know. Let's go. We have to set you free from the painting."

She shakes her head. "No. I can't go yet."

"Clio, c'mon. You'll be better soon. You can rest. Thalia will let you."

"I don't think that's the problem with the art."

"Then what is it?"

"It's daylight. I have to go back or—" She runs to her canvas and slides back inside, cut in her stomach and all.

I call out to her, but she's gone still.

CHAPTER 28

When Paintings Weep

I clean up the Cezanne, bagging up the sand and leaving it at the foot of the frame, as the other museums around the world have done.

I glance at my watch, wishing more than a few minutes had passed, wishing it were miraculously evening and Clio was breaking free, rather than running away. I can't even fathom how to make the time pass until then, but soon enough I find a way by tracking the body count that grows during the day. Several more paintings fall. A Goya in St. Petersburg, a handful of Vermeers in the Met, as well as a Morisot at the Art Institute of Chicago. As the list of unspooling art lengthens, I can't help but feel like a bigger failure. Fine, the damaged Renoirs have all been restored, and that's making museums happy. That debt has been settled, but something far more dangerous has infected other art.

As I grab a late-afternoon coffee to go, Emilie calls.

"Hey," she begins. "I wanted to see how you're doing. I've been following all these crazy museum reports."

"To say it's bad would be an understatement."

She sighs sympathetically. "I'm so sorry. Does anyone know what to do?"

"Possibly," I say, thinking of Clio. She's the only one who might have a clue. "But enough about the art. I could use some good news right now. Anything exciting going on with the Paris Ballet?"

"As a matter of fact, I won a solo in *Sleeping Beauty*," she says, and I can hear her grinning through the phone.

"That's fantastic. And can I just say I told you so?"

"By all means, please do," she says in happy voice.

"Told you so," I say as I quicken my pace up the museum steps. "Hey, I have to run inside now. But you'll get me tickets, right?"

"Of course."

Maybe I can take Clio to see the performance. The thought that she'll be free by then brings me a speck of a smile.

⚜

When night comes, I nearly pounce on Clio as she escapes from her paint.

Her face is ashen, her eyes weary. "I know what's going on with the art. I figured it out," she says in a dead voice. She slumps against the wall, and I sink down too, sitting across from her. She drops her head into her hands. "It is all my fault."

"Clio, it's not your fault. It's just one of those things we never could have known. The art was fine when you were sort of frozen in time. Trapped in there. But now the art you inspired needs you back. We'll get you back. It'll be fine." But if that were true, she would have walked out the doors this morning.

"That's not it, Julien. That's not it at all." Her voice is heavy, as if the words have a weight attached made to sink them deep into black waters.

"What is it then?"

Clio lifts her face and looks at me. "I caused it. They're dying because of me." She gazes at me with a sharp clarity in her eyes, a criminal come of her own volition to confess before the court. "They're dying because I love you more than them."

I start to protest, but I can't form words. My mouth is sawdust.

"It has to be the reason. No Muse has ever been in love before. We only love art, or literature, or music. We love each other, and the art form we're inspiring. Our magic is for inspiration and our love is for preservation. That's it, nothing more. When I started caring about you, all the art I inspired, all the art I loved, got sick. It can't be any other way, Julien."

"That's just . . . ," I say, but I don't know how to finish the thought. I feel as if I've been called on in math and I don't have the answer. I'm just stumbling and bumbling along.

"I thought about it all day. The Géricault—that was the first to die," she says and puts a hand on her heart. "That painting was so hard for him. Remember how I told you that? How I had to give it so much of my love to bring it to being, and to keep it alive. The Ingres at the Louvre too. And Rembrandt. I've loved them all," she says, recounting the works as if she's weaving a sonnet on the spot, crafting an ode to the art she loves. "All I've ever done is put my love into paintings. Until I stopped working and stopped inspiring. Then you came along and I started wanting you. And I can't have both."

"That's not true. Don't say that. You still love the art," I say, as if the power of my conviction can rewind Bathsheba's broken body into the frame, can call back the waves in *The Raft of the Medusa*. "Besides, the art started changing before you even came here," I point out, hunting for any other answer, any other reason. I latch on to the idea, spilling out a theory. "I saw the art changing before anyone else did or could. Back when you were still at Bonheur's house. The day after his party, I was at the Louvre and *Bathsheba* was getting sick. And this La Tour, the flame in it died out. That happened before you ever stepped out of your frame. So how can it be your fault?"

She shakes her head with such heavy sadness. "I wish. Oh, how I wish. But I fell for you before I even came here to the Musée d'Orsay, Julien. I started falling for you the night you talked to me for the first time. Remember? When I was trying to break out at Bonheur's house? I wanted to see you. As soon as I felt the first inklings of something for you, that's when the paintings began to change. All the feelings I had invested in them were starting to shift to you. And the deeper I fell for you, the sicker the art got."

I can't help myself. I have a grin on my face. "You liked me then?"

She smiles. "Yes. You're so easy to like. Falling for you is the most wonderful thing I have done. It's more like floating," she says, and she looks radiant, like she's glowing because of me, and the incongruity of the moment—of this admission in the midst of this destruction—is not lost on me, but even so I am unable to resist touching her. I grab her and kiss her hard on the mouth, holding her face.

These lips, this face, this heat, this life. More, more, more.

But then I flash onto the paintings, to how the sickness started at the Louvre, slowly at first, with a few coughs and sniffles. Until the fuse was lit in *Starry Night*, and the morning after the Géricault drowned in its own waves.

We stop kissing.

"So how do we do it?"

"I have to do it," she says. "I have to heal the art. There are sick paintings in London and New York and at the Louvre, right?"

"And St. Petersburg and Chicago now too. And you need to touch the paintings, right? You need to be able to go to all those museums and touch the art, right?"

"Yes," she says in a careful, measured voice. "But it's not just that."

"What is it then?" I ask, but I doubt I want to hear the answer.

"I need to try it first. Where is the Cézanne from last night?"

"Where it was last night, so it doesn't get any worse. But roped off."

We walk a few rooms over to the Cézanne. The bag of sand is nestled at the foot of the frame. The canvas is a messy stew of mottled oils.

"So, first I'll just touch it," she says, and places her palms on the remains. Nothing happens. "Now, I'll concentrate on putting love back into it." She lays her hands on the canvas once more, closes her eyes. Her lips part, and she looks so beautiful, the way she looked when she first told me she was in love with me. It makes my chest hurt, and it makes me want her at the same awful time.

As she stands like that, the sand from the bag swirls around her, a gentle wind, then dances back to the frame, where it returns to paint and the colors become grass and sea and trees again, reforming a ravaged landscape into the luscious one Cézanne created.

I have seen so many amazing things. I've had my mind blown many times, but watching art repaired, like time-lapse photography run backward, has got to be the top.

When Clio opens her eyes, she looks the slightest bit different. It's hard to pinpoint the change, but she looks a bit less like Clio and more like Thalia. Not in her features, but in her demeanor. As if she's been sharpened.

"The thing is, it's not enough for me to love the art. I have to put the love I feel for you into paintings. To save the art, I have to stop loving you."

CHAPTER 29

Travel Plans

She is the poison and she is the cure.

"It's like a debt. And I have to repay," she says.

I always knew we were stolen. I always knew that we existed in a strange and wonderful *otherness*, but I thought we'd simply have to part. And that would have been hard enough. But this is worse. Because I won't stop feeling for her.

I sink to the floor. My body feels like stone. Clio is crying. Tears streak down her cheeks. "I'm sorry. I'm so sorry. That only took a tiny bit away." She touches my cheek, so soft and tender that I have to close my eyes just to contain all the feelings that threaten to burst out of my heart. "I'm still crazy about you now, Julien."

Now. But soon, not at all.

"So I guess I should let you out the door." My voice is empty.

"No. As long as I'm part of the painting no one can see me except you. But once I leave the museum, I'm no longer bound to the painting. Anyone can see me then, and I'd have to go into the front doors of all the museums, and I might not be able to touch the art long enough to fix it. When Thalia touched the paintings yesterday, she said it was only for a few seconds, right? That's why no one stopped her, plus there was so much commotion, I'm sure."

I nod.

She keeps talking. "But for this to work, I really have to focus. You saw what it takes. I'll need a few minutes with each piece. I have to hold my hands on the art and send them my love. I can't do it when there are crowds, or guards would stop me." The selfish part of me wants to scream *how is that my problem?* But I can't. I love the same things she loves. "To repair the art, I need your help."

"Like how? Am I supposed to smuggle you in? Be your Sherpa?" I say in a cutting voice that makes me feel like a jerk.

"We don't have to go in through the front doors, Julien. We go at night through the bridges. Remember? The Japanese bridges, how they all connect but only when we touch them together? Most of the museums with the sick art have Monets in them with bridges. Because he made all the bridge paintings after me, they'll be intact. We can travel through them almost instantly."

I want to kiss her and tell her she's brilliant. I want to pump a fist high in the air because breaking into a museum through a painting is the smartest, coolest thing I've ever heard. But it hardly feels like we're on the same team. "Okay, so we'll go together," I say, and it hits me—I have to witness my own execution. I'll have to watch her fall out of love with me.

"Let's go now," I say and walk over to the nearest bridge painting. I want to get this over with. I want to drop in and out of the world's museums in the dark of night, and then I want to open the door and say good-bye to her because I will barely be able to stand this at all.

"There's only one problem with going now."

"What's that?"

"The Louvre doesn't have any Monets, or any other Impressionist paintings of the bridge. We can't get into the Louvre that way. And I think we should start at the Louvre," she says, and I can see the logic—the outbreak, for whatever random reason, started at the Louvre.

"Let's go there now. Walk over. It's just across the river. There's got to be a door that's open somewhere," I say even though it's a horrible idea—you can't just walk into the Louvre at night—but I feel horrible.

"It'll never work that way. You know we can't get in there now," she says, and wipes a hand across her cheeks. She dries her tears and steels herself. "Look, this is my problem. I'll have to do it myself during the day after you free me and try to be fast. I'll take the risk."

"That's crazy."

"I should never have asked you. It's not fair."

"Of course it's not fair. It sucks in every way imaginable. But I'm in this with you, and we have to fix it together. I want to protect you, and I will. The trouble is anyone can see me anytime. So how do you suppose I not get caught in the Hermitage or the National Gallery in the middle of the night?"

"I actually have a few ideas," she says with a grin. "But what about the Louvre? Is there any way we can get one of the Japanese bridges from the Musée d'Orsay into the Louvre?"

I shake my head several times. "I can ask, but I seriously don't think I can convince my mom to let me take one of our bridges on a sleepover."

"Do you know anybody, any private collectors maybe, who have a bridge painting? Anyone at all?"

In a flash, I picture dusky-blue light on the slatted bridge. I smile wickedly. "As a matter of fact, I do know a collector."

We spend the rest of the night mapping out a plan. We study the layouts of the Art Institute of Chicago, the Met in New York, the National Gallery in London, and the Hermitage in St. Petersburg. I look up the floor plan for the Louvre too, double-checking where the sick paintings reside and plotting the fastest course to the art. The Louvre is a beast and has several sick paintings. But my primary focus with the Louvre maps is in locating the best restroom.

Next, we search through interactive maps, along with pictures of the galleries in each museum that houses one of the Monet bridges, writing down the names of the nearby works and whether they were painted before or after 1885 so we'll know which are safe. We hunt for photos online of the benches inside those rooms. I study the map of the Monet exhibit that's at the Hermitage right now. I try to ignore the fact that we were once planning a date at the Hermitage and now we're preparing for our demise.

The last order of business for Clio is with Gustave. She slips a hand into his pocket, carefully takes out his cell phone, and scrolls through his calls for the one that came from his friend who runs the night shift at the Louvre. She memorizes the number, drops the phone into his pocket, and gives me the digits.

Somehow, I don't think Gustave will mind the small part he's going to inadvertently play. He's always liked art.

Then Clio heals the warped Degas, and the orchestra stops playing out of tune. I'm afraid to look at her, afraid she won't care for me anymore, but she gives me one more kiss good night, and I do my best to savor it.

As I leave I send a group text to Bonheur, Sophie, Simon, and Lucy, letting them know I desperately need their help and could they please meet me in the late morning. I tell Bonheur and Sophie that the girl they've been protecting all these years is a Muse and that she needs our help to fix the art. They don't write back. They're all asleep. I manage to go home and snag a few troubled hours myself. I've had better nights of sleep, that's for sure.

❧

The thing about museum security is this—it's a myth. Those movies where master thieves break into museums inside horse statues and then rewire cameras to show video from the day before, or the ones where infrared lights shine at unpredictable angles and the hero executes a series of acrobatic moves while suspended via ropes? That's all Las Vegas–casino–level stuff. That's the sort of security you need when you have millions of dollars in cash on hand. Because cash is nameless. Cash goes anywhere. Paintings don't.

The reality is most museums have little more than simple alarms on doors and a couple guards yawning as they stroll a few galleries after dark. It's just not that hard for thieves to slice canvases from frames under the cloak of night, or even in the bright light of day, and slip out among the afternoon crowds with invaluable art tucked inside a shirt. The real security system museums rely on is the astronomical difficulty in selling a priceless work of art. It's virtually impossible to fence a museum piece anywhere, even in countries where it once was popular, like Japan or Switzerland.

Sure, there are some camera systems in the museums I'll need to visit. The Louvre has the most secure setup, but I won't be seen there. If cameras catch me in any of the other four locations, I'm going to have to rely on the sheer logical impossibility of having been anywhere else but Paris in the same night.

Even so, I'd rather not be spotted by camera lenses or human eyes, so once my friends join me at a cafe I run down the basics of the who, why, and where of the mission. I leave out the part about Clio falling out of love with me. I don't want pity.

"So, here in this room in the National Gallery. That's where I need the pencil and paper," I say as I tap the layout of the museum in London where the Turners have been weeping waves. "Who knows someone in London who can get over there today?"

"I've got a friend there," Simon says. "My buddy Patrick. He'll do it."

I down my third coffee of the morning and take a bite of a chicken sandwich. There is a huge plate of french fries on the table that we've been sharing. A grandmotherly old woman with white hair and an even whiter Maltese sits at the table next to us, feeding her dog pieces of ham.

"Next, Chicago. Lucy, you used to live there, right?"

Lucy nods excitedly. She and Simon are done eating, so he's braiding her hair. She leans back into him, as he loops one brown-and-emerald strand over another. I try to quell my jealousy over him being out with his girlfriend during the day, over him likely being out with her tomorrow, and the next day, and the next. "For a year. And I know just who to call."

"Better not be a guy," Simon says.

"Oh, Simon. I never ever dated anyone before you, don't you know that?"

"Impressive," I say, tipping my forehead to Simon's hair-dresser handiwork.

"I have many talents."

I show Lucy where the pencil and paper should go in the Art Institute. "I'm on it," she says and dives into her purse for her phone.

Simon loses hold of the braid. "Look at that. I'll have to start all over."

"Oh, boo-hoo. I know how you hate having your hands in my hair," Lucy says.

"All right, where else do we need people?" Simon asks.

"Well, I'm guessing the chances of knowing someone in St. Petersburg are pretty slim?"

Everyone shakes their heads.

"That's okay. I've got another plan for the Hermitage. What about New York?"

Bonheur waves a hand. "I have plenty of friends in New York. Where do we need to plant this clandestine sheet of paper and pencil to help you and the Muse?" he asks in a Sherlock Holmesian voice.

I show him the location in the Met.

"Consider it done. Americans are so friendly. They do love to help, you know," he says as he whisks off a quick text message.

When he's done, he looks up at me.

"Something else?"

"That's going to be the easiest thing you do today, Bonheur," I tell him. "The next part is going to require you and Sophie."

"Good, because I was feeling left out," Sophie says.

"Oh, you won't feel left out now, trust me."

Sophie's eyes widen, and Bonheur's face turns white when I tell them what they have to do with their priceless Monet. "Just look at it this way—it's much easier to get a painting into the Louvre than out of the Louvre."

"Oh, well then. Piece of cake. But how are we going to get it back? My mother will kill me if anything happens to that painting."

"Nothing is going to happen to it. It's going to be in the safest place in the world for a piece of art."

"So I just walk back in tomorrow morning and say, 'Excuse me, did I happen to leave my Monet here?'"

Sophie rolls her eyes and swats her brother's arm. He's in a sleeveless red top today. "Seriously. Mom bought that painting at Christie's, you dodo. Everyone knows it belongs to us, so we'll get it back."

"Actually, you'll get it back tonight. Or at least, it'll be safe tonight. I promise. Besides, the worst-case scenario is you look like an idiot in front of your mom. It's not like you might get caught in the Louvre after midnight. And if you have to explain to your mom, something tells me she'll be cool with you having helped out on an Avant-Garde mission to save the world's art." I look at my watch. "But you should probably get going soon. You have a lot to do, and I'm guessing you'll want to get over there a few minutes before closing time. I'll wait outside for you guys for moral support."

"I'm going to need some absinthe for real after this," Bonheur says as he slinks down into the wicker chair.

꿎

For once, Bonheur does not stand out in a crowd. He's outside the pyramid at the Louvre and he's wearing jeans and a brown T-shirt. Sophie has ditched her trademark tap shoes in favor of sneakers. They're about to do something totally legal, but completely unusual, so there's no need to draw attention.

Bonheur pats the side of his messenger bag. "It's like carrying around a freaking diamond."

"More like thousands of diamonds," I correct.

He rolls his eyes. "Don't remind me. My heart is already beating ten thousand times a minute. That's fast, right?"

"Very," I say with a small laugh. "Okay, let's go through this. The Monet canvas is inside the bag, right?"

"We took it out of the frame and off the stretcher bars," he says, referring to the wooden bars that keep canvases taut inside frames. "Then we put it into a padded envelope and caught a taxi because there was no way I was taking a Monet on the Metro."

"Correction. I took it off the stretchers. Your hands were shaking too much to do that," Sophie points out.

Bonheur holds up a palm to his sister. "Whatever."

I continue to review the plan. "So you're going to go through security. They'll scan your bag, just like they scan every bag. There's nothing in it to alert them, and even if for whatever reason they looked through the bag, there's no law that says you can't take a work of art you own out for a stroll."

"Right. Right," Bonheur says and nods several times, as if the repetitive motion will calm his nerves. "Then we go to the ladies' room on the second floor."

"The one by the far stairwell," I add. We picked that bathroom because it's unlikely anyone from museum security will patrol a small, two-stall restroom at night.

"And that's where I come in," Sophie says and bounces on her toes. She's game for anything. "I have the double-sided tape in my purse." She shows me a small purple purse. "I take the canvas from the envelope and hang it under the sink, so no one will see it. Then we leave the padded envelope behind in the bathroom."

"There you go," I say and clap them both on the back. "You can do it. I'll see you in a few minutes. You better get in there now because it's going to close soon."

Bonheur salutes me, and Sophie grabs his elbow. I watch as they head into the pyramid entrance. I'd go with them, but I know far too many people who work there and I can't take any chances today. So I wait and I wander, and twenty minutes later, they rush out, breathless and full of adrenaline.

"We did it!" Sophie declares, then tells me how she hung their prized Monet. It's now out of sight, suspended on the wooden underside of the sink counter with sturdy, double-sided tape Sophie pressed against the unpainted outer edge of the canvas, the white border that's normally wrapped around the stretcher bars. That way the tape won't mar a brushstroke of Monet's nor affect the value of the art.

Now all I have to do is hope no one goes into that bathroom for the next several hours.

CHAPTER 30

Last Dance

I don't have any carry-on luggage. This trip doesn't allow it, since you can't take anything into a painting. All we need are hands and wits. I hope they're mightier than the sword, or the nightstick, I should say.

"Ready?"

"I just need to do one more thing. Come with me," Clio says and walks across the main floor. I follow her and we stop at a Toulouse-Lautrec. She tilts her head and offers a faint smile, tinged with regret. "A proper good-bye?"

That is something I can't resist. I take her hand and the museum is gone, wiped clean by the sounds of the cancan, the dance that originated at a cabaret with windmills at the top of Montmartre. How I wish I were truly dancing with her in Montmartre. But this is as close as we'll come. We've fallen into the festivities as only Toulouse-Lautrec could imagine them, surrounded by turn-of-the-century-dressed men and women with high-laced boots and ruffled skirts who don't notice that we've crashed their painted party. Music plays from a band on the stage, drinks are shared freely, and everywhere are revelers. It's always a fete at the Moulin Rouge, but it is bittersweet tonight.

She holds her hands out, ready to dance. "May I have this dance?"

"But of course," I say with a smile, trying my best to keep the sadness at bay.

"This is what I want you to remember of me, not what happens next. This is what I'll remember. The before," she says, and her eyes are so tough and so earnest at the same time. I know she wants to believe what she's saying. I know right now she suspects she'll never forget this. But she won't *feel* it again. I will be just another memory, the same as all her other memories. Nothing special, just the week she ditched work. *What made it so compelling?* she'll wonder days and weeks from now, barely able to recall what it was like.

I wrap my arms tight around her as she leans into me, and I take my here and my now. I layer kisses on her neck, I plunge my hands into her soft curls that have come home underneath my fingers. The dancers kicking their legs high in the air onstage might as well be in Peru. *This* is all there is. *This* is all I want. "I will never forget you."

"You saved me, you know. You saved me from being trapped. You're the reason I can be free of that painting," she says, and with her words my heart is both caving and pounding. "I want you to know how much I wish there were another way. I love you, Julien. More than art."

That, in a nutshell, is the problem.

I fold her into my arms, and we dance for a few minutes inside a Toulouse-Lautrec, aware the whole time of a ticking bomb on the other side. But I let this moment stretch into itself, here in our sliver of time.

I wish I could say I don't care if I ever return to the real world.

But I can't say that.

The enemy was never really Renoir. The real enemy has always been the impossibility of us.

I kiss her once more, a last kiss that has to last for all time.

CHAPTER 31

Night at the Museums

It is midnight. We're starting now so we can reach all the museums while it's nighttime in their time zones. I leave my backpack and phone under a bench, a home base here in Musée d'Orsay. A few feet away is the Japanese bridge Monet painted. I step inside it with Clio, and we place our clasped hands together on the railing.

"To the Louvre," she says, and we step forward, our feet landing on another bridge, this one in Bonheur's painting.

I jam my palms out but still smack the tiled floor of the ladies' room hard with my hands. Clio falls out next, banging her forehead on a metal pipe.

"Ouch," she mouths.

"You okay?"

She nods and rolls from under the sink. She stumbles as she stands up, getting tangled in her long dress. I reach out for her hand, so she won't trip and attract attention. She steadies herself, and I crawl out next. I smile at my partner-in-crime, or rather, my partner-in-uncrime. "It worked," I whisper, relieved that the painting's been safe from people and water since closing time.

"It's showtime," I say and hold open the door for Clio. This part of the job is easy for me, since the Louvre is the one museum where we could control the arrival spot, giving me a place to hide. Clio takes off for the Géricault, and the halls are eerily silent.

I focus on my small tasks. I kneel down at the sink and carefully remove the tape from the painting. I move onto the padded envelope, which the canvas will need for a safe return. Sophie left the envelope between the trash can liner and the trash can itself, stowed out of sight. I take it out and tuck it under my arm.

A few minutes pass, and Clio must have healed *The Raft of the Medusa* and has to be onto the Rembrandt now. I hear someone's voice. I tense and shrink into a stall. I close the door quietly and hop up onto the toilet seat, holding the Monet and the envelope. Someone opens the door. I don't move a muscle. The light goes on. Through the crack in the stall door, I see a security guard. She looks into the mirror, bares her teeth, and seems to inspect them. She pinches her thumb and index finger together and grabs at her two front teeth. "There!"

She flicks the stray piece of food into the sink and turns on the water to flush it down.

She turns off the water and opens the door to leave when her radio crackles.

"Problem at the *Mona Lisa*," the garbled voice says.

I hold my breath. *Please be safe, Clio.*

The guard brings the radio to her mouth. "What's the problem?"

"It's talking dirty."

The guard scoffs. "Really?"

"Something about a priest and a rabbi in a bar."

"I'm on my way," she barks into the radio and slams it onto her belt. The door swings shut, and she's gone.

I exhale, and then it hits me—the Mona Lisa is unspooling her insides, telling her dirty joke. I'm tempted to pop out of the bathroom and listen in the halls, but her gallery is too far away.

"... And the bartender says, 'you can sit on my lap.'" The voice is a boom, like it's coming from a speaker system, so I guess I don't have to leave the bathroom because the whole museum can hear it now, as Mona Lisa unwinds, telling her bawdy joke over and over.

Several minutes later the joke stops, and in sixty seconds Clio opens the door. She's breathing hard. I unlock the stall. "I had to fix the *Mona Lisa* too," she says with wide eyes. "The guards had already taken off her glass when I got there, so all I had to do was touch her. Must have been the Moulin Rouge that did her in."

That shouldn't make me happy, but in a sick way it does, the collateral damage from one last dance.

I position the padded envelope right next to the door and then lay the Monet on the tiles. We return to the Musée d'Orsay.

We step inside the familiar blue-walled gallery, still grinning because we pulled it off, still holding hands. The touch of her is almost enough to make me believe there's room in her heart for both art and me. But already she's not quite holding my hand the way she used to, she's not touching the inside of my palm with a finger, or tracing lines on my wrist. I'm more like a guy she likes, not the guy she loves.

I call Bonheur. He answers his phone as if it's been implanted in his head. "Please have good news."

"The paintings at the Louvre are healed. Now, go call the number I gave you and let the security guard know you left your Monet in the ladies' room this evening. It's on the floor, and the envelope he can carry it in is by the door."

He sighs happily. "Thank you."

I have no doubt Gustave's friend will take good care of the Louvre's temporary overnight visitor.

I turn to Clio. "How was the art? What did it look like?"

"Titian's mirror repaired itself. Bathsheba regrew. The flame in the LaTour relit and it's flickering in paint now," Clio says, and she's so animated and excited to tell me the stories of the reformed art.

"And the Géricault?"

"It was as if the water had crashed backward and the waves rolled right into the frame. Then the canvas just sort of slurped it all up. It looks just like the day it was made."

"It's amazing," I say. "Russia now?"

"To St. Petersburg we go."

❧

Clio might not be visible to anyone but me, but she's audible to everyone. Including a guard who happens to be one room over from the Monet exhibit at the Hermitage. To complicate matters, the museum hasn't updated its website lately because the layout we saw of this gallery is just a tad wrong.

The guard jerks his head when he hears the sound of Clio's footsteps race past him on the way to the Goya. But when he swivels around and sees me, I must appear—though it would be impossible—to be the source of the footsteps. At the very least, I'm an intruder. I'm about to jump into the closest Monet, the one I picked in advance for protection, but all the Monets near me are his earlier works that Clio inspired—*thanks for nothing, Hermitage website*—and I'm not about to take shelter in a painting that could collapse in on itself.

I scan the room quickly as the guard calls out to me in Russian. I don't know what he's saying, but he's not happy. He moves toward me. I spot a later Monet, one of the haystacks. It's a few feet from me. I step toward it as the guard comes closer. I reach my hands inside the painting and take out the haystack. It's big, but it's not heavy. I hold it in front of me as a shield. I don't think he can see the haystack, since he's not a muse. But like Olympia's cat and Cézanne's peach, the haystack is real and it occupies space.

More Russian words fall from his lips. I shrug my shoulders but stay silent. Accents won't disguise me. The guard is now mere feet from me and he tries to get closer, but he can't. There's a buffer between us, and it's a thick mound of straw only I can see. He tries to grab me, but he bumps up against the crackly mass and flinches. He reaches for me again, but I move away, and we're now engaged in the most awkward of dances. He keeps lunging and keeps getting bounced back by the invisible haystack. It's as if I have a bubble surrounding me. He fumbles for the radio on his belt and calls for backup. He goes for his phone next and snaps a picture of me, of the Teflon guy he can't touch.

C'mon, Clio. It's only one painting.

I hear another set of footsteps, but the soles of the shoes are heavy, and they carry another guard. More Russian words are fired off at me, but no one pulls a gun. Seconds later, Clio's racing through the halls, and they both turn their heads at the noise. She slides into the gallery and sees the guards, the haystack, and me. She rushes past the second guard, knocking off his cap. He swivels around. She comes up behind the first guard and speaks rapid-fire Russian. His eyes widen, and he looks down at his pants and his face turns red. It's enough of a window for her to grab the haystack from me, drop it on the ground, and take my hand. We run like hell to the bridge.

"What are we going to do about the haystack?" I ask as soon as our feet touch safe ground.

"I'll go there tomorrow morning. I'll put it back. It'll take two seconds, but we didn't have time right then," she says.

"Right. How was the Goya?"

"Oh, it was beautiful." She lays a hand on her heart. "I was so happy to see it again."

Happy. I wince.

"But I still like you," she says, and she sounds like herself, or as much of herself as there still is. She's got that shy and sweet look about her, and part of me thinks she may even dive in for one more kiss. But she doesn't.

"What did you say to that guard in Russian?"

"I told him his fly was down."

I laugh, and she smiles, and we're still in this together.

"Hey, Clio. I have a favor to ask you. Can you try to be just a little quieter when you run down the halls? I'd kind of like to not run into a security guard if I can."

"Maybe you should draw me some padded socks," she says with a wink, and I have a feeling it's the last time we'll have an inside joke.

⌘

The Impressionist room at the National Gallery is blissfully quiet. So is Clio as she taps Muse dust into my hand and I close my fist around it, then let the dust loose in my front pocket. She takes careful, quiet steps away from the Monets and heads for the Turners, a few rooms away.

I spy the bench. Simon's friend Patrick came through. There's a sheet of paper and a pencil taped to the underside of the seat. I untape them, lie flat on my stomach and sketch quickly. I tuck the paper under the bench, then go camp out inside a painting of water lilies. I'm soaked to my knees the second I enter the painting, but it's peaceful here at Monet's pond, and I won't be wet when I leave, so I sink down and float on my back. I count the seconds until I reach fifteen minutes. I don't want to lose track of time, and I know she'll need time here. There are more than half a dozen damaged Turners.

I stand up in the tranquil pond, surrounded by water lilies.

I'm in the most beautiful place, and I'm about to enter a terrible one—I can't imagine she'll feel much of anything for me after the Turners take her love.

Inside the room, I'm dry again. All the water is left behind on the other side of the frame. The room is still quiet, but just in case a guard comes, I return to the bench, pluck the paper from its hiding place, and pinch some Muse dust from my pocket. I stand by the Japanese bridge and wait.

Two sets of footsteps. Heavy boots and soft slippers.

I curse silently, and my chest tightens. Still, I'm glad we planned for this, so I trace my drawing with silvery fingertips, and a blond mutt comes to life, along with a tennis ball. Clio rounds the corner into the Impressionist room, and I toss the ball as far as I can in the direction of the boots. The dog barks happily and scampers after it, his nails scratching the hardwood floors. He careens around the corner after the ball, and I can hear the guard say, "What the bloody—" as Clio and I step back onto the bridge. Inside the painting she tells me about the magnificent sight of the waters and the sunsets being remade, of how the light streaked across the paint in just the way Turner had always envisioned. As I listen to her, it occurs to me that in some ways she's not that different. She isn't cold or callous. She's still warm and glowing, but she only has eyes for art now. She is slipping away from the girl she was with me and reverting back to the Muse she was made to be. I want to share this moment with her, to rejoice in the saving of the art, but each reborn painting crushes me a little more.

She almost forgets to reach for my hand when we walk onto

the bridge on the way to the Met. I feel as if the ground is starting to sway as she changes.

"Oops, sorry," she says, like it's no big deal, and it isn't to her, because she no longer has the desire to hold my hand.

❧

I take shelter in a church. I'm in front of a gothic cathedral now that bends and waves, its skyscraping spires cutting skies with a tower that was once the tallest in the world. The real Rouen Cathedral in Normandy is damaged after bombs rained down on it in World War II and one of the towers burned. But the painted one is still perfect. I grab hold of the metal knocker on the heavy wooden door, pulling as it groans and creaks open. It is beautiful inside, with stained-glass windows that fly from floor to ceiling and pews in a rich shade of chestnut that seem to billow and swell, paint marks that sway like a breeze blows through them.

I wander through the pews, past the altar, and back again, wrapped in silence in the crystal quiet of this other world.

But it's too quiet, and too lonely in here. I leave the painting, find the paper Bonheur's American friend left for me, and draw a blue jumpsuit, like a janitor would wear. Then, a broom. I could draw a cloak, or a mustache and glasses, but blending into the surroundings as if I belong here will be better than hiding my features. I flick dust on the paper, then step into my drawn set of clothes, pulling them over my jeans and shirt.

There's a cry from another room. Clio. All my instincts tell me to run to her, and I don't ignore them. I leave the broom and bolt down the hall in her direction. I see a shadow by the exit to the next gallery.

My heart stops. I survey the room in seconds. I'm surrounded by modern art, so I dive into the nearest painting. My jaw drops when I reach the other side of the drip marks, and I think I may laugh harder than I've ever laughed in my life. Jackson Pollock always said his abstract art was about the art, and the paint itself, nothing more.

Pollock lied.

I'm inside a gigantic refrigerator. There's a jar of pickles, a container of mustard, and some yogurt that is probably way past its expiration date.

This is what art historians and modernists have been ruminating on for years?

Ladies and gentleman, I'm here to say Jackson Pollock painted appliances.

I leave and double back to our exit. Clio is waiting for me by the bench. She looks nervous and worried. She motions for me to run. I do as instructed, moving quickly even in my double outfit. But she surprises me by grabbing my hand and pulling me under the bench, shifting so I'm on top of her. The bench has a front that hangs down, and I'm shielded, so there's no need for my new garb to hide me. But this is the cruelest torture. I'm pressed against her, and I can feel her heart beating against mine. I want to smother her in kisses, but she's simply my accomplice now, nothing more. She presses a finger against her lips. Footsteps pass dangerously close. I don't breathe until they leave the room, my temporary jumpsuit dissolving to dust in seconds. Then she rolls out from under me, and we head for our final destination.

"Why were you crying back there?" I ask once we're safely on the bridge.

"It was the Vermeers."

"Well, are they okay? Did you fix them?"

"Yes, they look so beautiful now." Her voice breaks. "I was overcome."

∽✄

We go to Chicago.

The sick Morisot is only a few rooms away, and I'm so pummeled now by witnessing Clio lose her love that I barely care if I get caught. Besides, she's arrived at the final destination, and what's the worst that can happen? She doesn't need me anymore so she could just slink out of the museum in the morning and find the Chicago entrance back to her Musely home. As for me, I suppose the worst is happening so I don't bother to draw a jumpsuit or a dog. I've never been to Chicago, and I've always wanted to see Edward Hopper's *Nighthawks*, his image of three lonely people in a diner. Why not? I've made it this far. It's a few rooms over, and I go inside and order a chocolate milk shake.

The guy at the counter nods and hands me the drink.

It's fantastic, and I feel as if I could stay here all night. No one talks to each other. The other three people just stare off with empty eyes at their lonely worlds.

But I have friends back home, and I could really use them now.

More than ever. So I leave, and I walk to the Japanese bridge where Clio's already waiting. A guard sees me, calls after me. I understand him perfectly.

"What the hell are you doing here?"

"Getting a milk shake," I tell him, and keep going.

The guard grabs for the belt buckles on my jeans, and I roll my eyes.

"Seriously? That's the best you've got?" I speak to him in English but don't bother with an accent. Let him report back to the Chicago police about the boy with the French accent who drank milk shakes in his museum.

"You want to be arrested, smart aleck?"

I pull away. He's no Cass Middleton. He's sluggish and I'm nimble, and I suppose all things being equal, I'd really rather be in Paris right now, so I run to the bridge painting and dive into it with Clio.

I don't make it all the way in. He's grabbed a boot. Clio's got me by the forearm and is pulling me farther into the Monet, and the guard is yanking harder on my boot. With the sole of my other shoe, I push the boot off and slide into the painting, picturing a guard in Chicago bewildered by the worn black boot in his hand.

CHAPTER 32

Freedom

Good night, Gustave."

"What happened to your other boot?"

"Lost it somewhere. Go figure," I say.

"Maybe your prince will find it, Cinderella," he teases. "Hey, did you hear about the Monet that was left in the bathroom at the Louvre a few hours ago? Some crazy collector left it there, along with an envelope too."

"Your friend found it?"

"Yup. Packed it all up and has it ready to be returned."

"Ah, but that's the real Cinderella story," I say, and head for the doors, Clio by my side.

I pause when I lift the handle to leave the museum, remembering when she told me how easy it would be to free her. *You don't need a crazy car chase or knife fight to free me. Nothing violent, nothing dangerous. It's simple because art is grace. Art is class. You can free me by holding open the door and letting me out.*

I do the thing Clio didn't want me to do a few days ago. Because there is nothing for her on this side of the door. There is nothing to tie her to the museum. Not her frame and not me.

She crosses the threshold and her feet touch outside ground for the first time in a hundred and thirty years. If I were to look back at Gustave right now, he'd probably be as shocked as the Chicago guard with the boot in his hand, because now there is a girl beside me who wasn't there before.

Anyone can see her. She's no longer bound to the painting Renoir trapped her in. She's bound to being a Muse, and she can't wait to start up again.

We walk down the steps, like two acquaintances, like two coworkers who did a job together. A job well done, but now they move on. To the next city, the next assignment. I walk her across the river, and to the block with La Belle Vie. Bonheur has alerted Thalia to meet Clio there. I called him a few minutes ago and asked him to let her know the missing Muse would be coming home.

I stop on the rue de Rivoli. "Good-bye, Clio."

"Good-bye," she says, her voice clipped and cheery. She doesn't even use my name.

"Do you even remember what happened with us?" I ask tentatively because she seems like a robot, like she had her chip erased of all past memories.

"Of course I remember. We had a nice time together," she says and smiles brightly, but her eyes are empty. There's nothing there for me. "And now I get to go back to work."

Get to.

"It's been so long," she continues. "I can't wait to find out what's next, what new assignments are waiting for me. I've missed it so."

No, you didn't, I want to tell her. *You didn't miss it. You were tired of it. You wanted more.*

I know it's not personal. I know it's not me. But that doesn't stop me from feeling, from wanting, from aching.

Thalia steps out of La Belle Vie and beams, like a mother welcoming back a long-lost child. Clio rushes to her. She doesn't look back at me. Not once. But I can't take my eyes off her. I can't stop watching her.

I will never stop seeing her everywhere I go.

My heart is a padlock on the lovers' bridge as it's sliced. I am all the *cadenas* ever placed there, chopped off at once.

CHAPTER 33

Drawn to Dust

Paris is quiet, and the sun is peeking over the horizon, like a small child checking the covers before pitter-pattering out of bed. Pink streaks leak across the blue of night as I find my way home and crash in my bed.

I think my mother tries to wake me and urge me to come to work. She is unsuccessful and she gives up.

When I finally make it out of bed in the late afternoon, she's sent me several texts. They are full of exclamation points and many smiley faces. The reports have come in from the museums, and all the curators are rejoicing. I send her back a smiley face. Bonheur has texted me too, letting me know his mother was thrilled with the part their painting played. *Awesome,* I write back. Then he tells me he's having another party soon, and that I better be there. I can even see my Muse again, he adds. He doesn't know what happened to us last night, and I'm not ready to tell that story. I don't answer either of his messages.

I turn on my computer so I can read the news.

First, there was the Cézanne and the Degas miraculously restored at the Musée d'Orsay a day ago, the stories note.

Then, more tales of strange goings-on at museums came from around the world last night. Perhaps the oddest of all is the story of the security guard in St. Petersburg who had a picture of a young guy standing in front of the Monet exhibit at the Hermitage. My mother calls when the photo surfaces.

"Look at that picture," she says and she's laughing wildly. "He almost looks like you."

I laugh too. I do look pretty silly with my arms stretched out wide as if I'm holding on to something awkward and large. Like a haystack. "Yeah, that guy does kind of look like me," I say.

Then there's the story of the boot. One lone boot that a guard claims he tugged off a teenage boy who hopped inside a painting at the Art Institute of Chicago.

"The Cinderella Boot," the news is calling it. It's a fairy tale, they say, since all the sick paintings have been healed. And so the stories go, like a song, a chorus passed from one group to the next, singing of the healed Vermeers, the cured Turners, the Morisot restored. It couldn't be anything but magic, right?

They'll all forget about it soon enough. We always do.

❧

The next week, I guide a group of tourists through our galleries, including a brief stop at *The Girl in the Garden*. Hope rises in my chest when I see the painting of Clio, as it does every time, every day, with every look. But the canvas has been quiet at night. No girl has come alive, not even a painted version, like Emmanuelle or Dr. Gachet. I keep waiting for the night when she might break free, even if she's only a shadow of the Clio I once knew. I'd take that. I'd take anything.

A girl with a Brown University T-shirt raises a hand and begins speaking. "Isn't that the Renoir that was missing for years?"

"Yes. Since 1885," I answer as clinically as I can.

"What happened to it? How does a painting just vanish for so long, then reappear?"

Another girl on the tour chimes in, probably an art student at another college. "There's a story that Renoir and Monet were both in love with her," the second girl starts to say, and it's a knife digging around in my chest, on a blind hunt for any organ. "And the family hid the painting to protect her reputation or something."

"Is that true?" the girl in the Brown shirt asks me.

I flinch, as if she's just raised her fists, then I let it all out, the truth of the missing Renoir, once lost, now found. "It's possible. Or she could have been a Muse trapped in a painting and was just set free to save the world's art," I say without a smile, without a knowing wink. No one says anything. "Or maybe she's just a girl and she comes out at night when the museum is closed," I offer.

Both girls look at me quizzically, then laughter kicks in. I've just made a joke, or possibly two, they think.

"Or maybe it's just a painting," someone else says. "Sometimes a painting is just a painting."

"And sometimes lost paintings are lost again," I say, and conclude my tour so that we can all escape from my melancholy.

I walk past Emmanuelle, then Dr. Gachet. Imprints of who

they once were long ago. An idea comes to me then, a crazy one, but I have to try. Maybe there is a version of Clio out there who still cares about me.

I'm done for the day and it's only early afternoon, so I go to Gare Saint-Lazare station and buy a ticket. An hour later, the train rattles to a stop and I disembark. I walk from the station to Monet's garden, a little less than an hour by foot. The gardens are closing when I arrive, and the ticket taker tells me I will only have a few minutes.

"That's fine."

I have seen the gardens. For real and in paint. I'm not here today to catch the tail end of a tour or to snap photos of the kaleidoscope of colors. But the place Monet once called home is, empirically, gorgeous. Summer has stolen into Giverny, bringing with it the glory of reds, yellows, and oranges that blaze under the sun.

Some might say it's better than a painting.

They have never gone into *her* painting.

I walk through lush fields and past blankets of petals and stems. I make my way to the pond where a raft of water lilies floats lazily in the blue-green waters. The other visitors begin to file out as the bell signals closing time. I let them leave, and the sun dips farther. Long shadows fall across the pond, and the weeping willow brushes its branches against the earth.

I close my eyes and I'm back in time.

"I used to pretend there was a door at the end of this bridge. A plain, simple wooden door with an old-fashioned ring handle. Dark metal. You pull it open and there. The other side. I'm finally on the other side."

I open my eyes and remove my notebook, sketching the door she described in painstaking detail. I take the last pinch of silver dust that I stashed away in London, and voilà. The door materializes. Clio always longed for escape when she was trapped. Maybe *that* Clio is here. Maybe *that* Clio misses me. I reach for the handle and pull it open.

There's nothing but a weeping willow on the other side.

I press a palm over my eyes. Stupid me. Stupid mind playing stupid tricks. She is gone, and all that's left is this emptiness, this loneliness, so terribly alive, in her place. No drawing will ever change that.

I flop down in the grass and lie there until the door disappears and an old man who tends the gardens tells me it's time to go.

CHAPTER 34

Dancing in the Streets

Simon has a plan. Forget clubbing in Oberkampf. Don't even think about bolt cutters. This one is guaranteed to eradicate any longing for any girl who's stomped on your heart, he declares as he escorts me along the street vendors across from Notre Dame. He gestures grandly to the secondhand booksellers who peddle old books along with postcards of landmarks and matted prints of famous destinations in the green boxes by the river.

"Here's the plan. We apply for a *bouquiniste* license and we set up shop."

"What will we be selling exactly? If memory serves, neither one of us has a collection of antique books or access to a stash of cheap postcards."

"Ah, but see, postcards will just be our loss leader. What we're really going to be selling is our ghost-removal skills. The book vendor thing is just going to be a front for a ghost-removal shop."

I manage a small "huh."

"Picture it," he continues. "We're practically pros. Can you name anyone else who has successfully exorcised a spirit, let alone the spirit of a great artist?"

"Can't say that I have."

"All we have to do is convince the tourists that Marilyn Monroe or Jim Morrison is inhabiting them, and we'll work our hocus-pocus again."

"We'll be rolling in the euros," I say without much enthusiasm.

He pats me on the back. "Someday you'll be happy again, Garnier."

ॐ

I honor a commitment to another girl. The one at the Paris Ballet.

The lights are low. The music swells. I feel more human than I have in days here in the opera house where the Ballet performs. Maybe because the dancers aren't shadow girls. Dancers keep moving, keep swimming. Emilie looks as if she is gliding through waves, a dolphin, sleek and mammalian, as she performs her solo in *Sleeping Beauty*.

The only music I hear is coming from the orchestra pit. Emilie feels confident onstage, and it shows. I lean back against the cranberry upholstered chair in the second row and watch, glad to not be at the museum with its phantom people. In here art is alive for real, and it is flying.

When the ballet ends, I join the rest of the audience in a standing ovation. As the dancers take their bows and curtsies, I lock eyes with Emilie. She can't stop smiling, and I feel the first touch of happiness in days, even though it's fleeting.

The balletgoers in their tuxes and suits, their gowns and evening dresses, make their way out through the arched doorways. I follow the directions Emilie gave me to the stage door. When she emerges, she's in jeans and a tank top, but her hair is still in a bun and she has full makeup on.

"You were magnificent," I say as I give her kisses on each cheek. "Do I know what I'm talking about or do I know what I'm talking about?"

"Was I really good?"

"The best. So good that I don't even hear music right now."

She snaps her fingers, a faux regretful gesture. "Darn. I thought it was kind of cool that you heard things."

"Cool? Really?"

"Sure. All artists are a little bit insane. I was hoping that was your crazy."

"An artist I am not, and that's okay. But I've got all kinds of crazy, so don't worry there. Coffee?"

"Always coffee."

We walk to the front of the opera house, and Emilie gasps when she sees a girl dancing on the steps.

"Look at that," Emilie whispers to me.

"Yeah, she's dancing. Just like you were."

The girl wears jean shorts and high black heels. She has a boom box and is moving to some kind of balletic hip-hop.

"I wish I could dance like that."

I give her a curious look, but then it hits me. Emilie doesn't have the abandon to dance when no one's expecting it.

"You are afraid to dance on the street," I say, calling her out.

"Nooooo," she says in a long, drawn-out, and obvious denial.

"C'mon. You just danced for thousands of people who paid plenty of money, and you won't dance on the street outside the opera house?"

"Another time." She grabs my elbow and pulls me away.

At the café we order espressos and talk about the ballet. She tells me how nervous she was before her solo, but how she left her fear backstage when she stepped under the lights.

"I could tell," I say, and Emilie smiles.

"I love talking to you like this. You really understand what it's like."

"I try."

"But it's more than trying. You just *get* it in a way that so few do, and so—" She stops when the waiter brings our drinks. After he leaves, she lowers her voice. "Listen, I'm really glad you came, and I was just wondering, because, you know, we get along so well, if you'd want to go out on a date-date sometime?"

I'll admit the offer is tempting, but I could never do that to her. "I would love to, really, I would. But I can't."

Emilie covers her face with her hand. "I'm such an idiot. You have a girlfriend, don't you?"

"No. But I had one."

"She broke your heart?"

"You could say that. I'm pretty much wrecked for relationships for a while."

"We'll be friends then. Like we already are."

"Of course. That won't change. But I'm going to have to insist you dance in the streets."

She laughs and shakes her head.

"Okay, how about this? My friend Bonheur is throwing an apron party. I hate the thought of going, but he won't take no for an answer, and if I have to go, you should have to dance at the party."

"An apron party? What is that?"

"I've obviously never been to an apron party. But if I were you, I'd get one."

"You're not going to wear an apron, Julien?" she asks with a bit of mischief in her voice.

"He's making me go to the party. He can't make me wear an apron."

"Something tells me no one could make you go to a party. Maybe you actually want to go."

Maybe I do.

✣

Bonheur wears a light-blue apron with red cherries. Sophie has gone meta and her apron has prints of mini aprons on it in orange, yellow, purple, and blue. Lucy is dressed to the nines in a black-and-white-striped skirt topped with a pink apron with black piping, like a sexy ice-cream-parlor girl. Simon can't keep his hands off her.

Emilie has on leggings and a pink tulle apron.

"I told you I could bring back aprons as an accessory," Bonheur declares as he invites us into his home. The Japanese bridge is on the wall. I force myself not to look at it. I force myself to look anywhere but the door that leads to the basement. The door that leads to her.

Sophie brings around a tray of *macarons*—combos of saffron and peach, of caramel and pistachio, and a grapefruit-wasabi one.

I pass.

"You never take the food I try to give you," Sophie says, narrowing her eyes. "It's like with the falafel. I swear I don't have cooties."

"Just not in the mood for *macarons*."

"Suit yourself. Someday you'll regret it." Sophie heads to another group of partygoers as Bonheur drapes an arm over my shoulder.

"I've got the music file you sent me. Just say the word when you want me to cue it up."

"I will."

Then he lowers his voice. "Don't you want to see her again, Julien? You haven't come by at all. Have you just been going through La Belle Vie?"

"She doesn't want to see me," I say.

His jaw drops. "What? After all that? After all you did?"

"It's just one of those things about Muses," I say, and explain briefly what happened to us when Clio saved the art. "So, if you ever see me go near that trapdoor, handcuff me and keep me away."

His eyes are sad. He was looking forward to being my Muse wingman. But he perks himself up quickly. "Well, let's just find you an aproned girl here who likes boys then."

Everywhere I turn, one of my friends is trying to set me up.

He introduces me to more girls than I can count, girls from his school, girls from the neighborhood, even a girl from New York with sharp brown eyes and a droll wit who says she's going to be studying art history at Columbia in the fall. She'll be here for the rest of the summer, she says, and leaves the veiled offer hanging there. But I am hopeless, so I say it was nice meeting her, and I return to Lucy, Emilie, and Simon. Maybe we'll be something of a foursome after all. One couple, one set of friends.

"Hey, Emilie, you owe me that dance," I remind her.

She covers her eyes, embarrassed.

"Oh, c'mon. Didn't you once say you wanted to do *Swan Lake* to some sort of techno pop? Like Protracted Envy," I say, reminding her of the band-ballet-mash-ups we brainstormed the last time we were supposed to go to a Bonheur party.

She takes her hand off her eyes and looks stunned. "You didn't."

I tip my forehead to Bonheur. "Cue it up."

He switches music on his portable stereo system, starts blasting the mix I made for Emilie, and ushers all of us through the courtyard and onto the cobbled sidewalk outside his house.

"You're terrible," she says to me.

I just shrug and wait for her to dance. Everyone else is looking on too, and soon they start urging her to show her moves. "Dance, dance, dance."

"You can do it, Emilie," I say gently, just to her. "This is how you wanted to dance."

"Okay," she says in a shy, quiet voice. She looks around, then twirls once across the cobblestones. As the music shifts to a poppier sound, she shifts too, moving to a faster beat, a clubby rhythm, but with the grace of a ballerina. She looks classical and totally trendy. Lucy joins in, bringing Simon to the impromptu dance floor, and Sophie jumps around too. The girl from New York moves her hips, and Bonheur takes Emilie's hand.

I watch them all. Dancing the way they want, listening to the music they like, and I think of Gustave and his subway art, of Max and his caricature classes, of my friends and their random toasts to things like aprons and five-legged calves and flash mobs on the curving corner of a hilly street in Montmartre.

I don't know that Renoir would have liked this party. But I do.

I'm pretty sure Clio—or at least the Clio I knew—would have liked it too.

❧

Later, Bonheur disappears for a while. When he returns to the party he pulls me aside. "Thalia wants to see you tomorrow morning. Can you meet her?"

"Why?"

"She just asked if you could be at the bridge between the two museums at nine. What should I tell her?"

I don't know if I like Thalia. I don't know if I want to see her. But I still say yes.

CHAPTER 35

Write Me Anew

Thalia is prompt. She waits on the Louvre side of the bridge, one hand resting on the links with the padlocks, the other on her waist. She wears slacks and a blouse. Her red hair hangs loose.

"Thank you for meeting me," she says.

"Well, it's not often I'm requested to meet with the head of the Muses."

She manages a small smile, the kind that doesn't show any teeth. "I wanted to thank you. For all you did for the paintings. We couldn't have done it without you, and I've been remiss in not extending my gratitude."

"What else was there to be done? It was the only way."

"No. There was another way. You could have let the art die. But you didn't. You saved it. You lost yourself to save it."

"Yeah," I say and look at the water, gray and murky, floating by under the bridge. The Seine reminds me of me. "Yeah."

Neither one of us says anything for another minute. Thalia breaks the silence. "You really loved her, didn't you?"

"Yes," I say with a huff. "Isn't it obvious?"

"How? How do you love her?"

"You asked me that before," I point out, because I'd rather not flay myself anymore. I've already been splintered a thousand times. I've somehow got to find a way to put myself back together, and I'm finally starting to, thanks to my friends. I don't want to just keep rewinding to Clio.

"Would you mind, though, telling me one more time what it was like?"

"What it was like," I repeat.

It was my everything. It was all my days and nights, and I am ruined for anyone else. Because there is only her. She was a revolution and she staged a coup d'état in my heart. "It all seemed possible with her, even though I knew it was impossible. She made me feel that way, like the stars were ours."

Thalia nods and she seems peaceful, the corners of her lips turning up.

"Thank you for your sacrifice. I cannot thank you enough, Julien."

I nod. I have nothing to say.

"You have good friends," she says, and I raise an eyebrow to ask what she means, but she keeps talking. "I have a gift for you. Just something to say thank you."

"I could use some more silver dust. I'm all out. I used the last bit drawing a stupid door that didn't work."

"I'll be right back."

I stare at the water, this snake of a river that washes away all the promises, all the keys to all the hearts. Thalia's gone for a few minutes, and a part of me figures she's not coming back. She's said her piece. She's probably moving on to her next assignment—a violin somewhere is weeping away notes, a poem is drowning in the tears of its words.

She returns and she's not alone. She's walking with Clio, who's wearing jeans and green flats. Her dress is gone. She's so beautiful it makes my chest hurt. It feels like a cruel game to bring her to me when I know she doesn't feel the same. But I can't look away. Maybe that's my curse now. I will always see her. I will always want to see her. They stop when they reach me.

"Hi," Clio says.

"Hi."

"How are you?"

"Um, fine. You?"

"Good."

Thalia speaks. "Clio and I had a long talk last night. I asked her about her time at the Musée d'Orsay."

"Oh?" I ask carefully, because I feel as if I'm in trouble, though for what I don't know.

"I asked her to tell me what she did during those days. Or nights, rather. The things that the two of you did. The reasons why she didn't come home right away."

"Okay."

"And they are not things Muses usually do," Thalia continues in that commanding, teacherly tone she has. "Actually, they are not things Muses ever do. Hanging out. Going to the beach. Rowing boats. Dancing. Picnics. That made me think that I had an opportunity to right a wrong from years ago."

Thalia looks to Clio and nods.

Clio holds up her hands, letting the sleeves of her shirt fall to her elbows. Her wrists are naked. "No more bracelets," she says to me.

"You're not a . . ."

Clio shakes her head.

"It was my decision," Thalia says. "I can't keep making the wrong choices, so I took off her bracelets. I made her a Muse, and now I have unmade her. She's a girl." Thalia turns to Clio. "I will miss you so, so much."

"I'll miss you too. But you'll take good care of the art, right?"

"You know me. It's on my to-do list forevermore," Thalia says, and taps her heart, then her own bracelets. She has a set of two on each wrist, double the number she had before.

"You're not going to see each other again?" I ask.

Thalia shakes her head, and her voice breaks. "Not often. I'm quite busy, and I'm even busier now that I have nearly all the painting preservation work on my plate. But I don't mind. I love the work, and I've had more than a century to get used to not seeing my Clio. We had to get along without her then, and now we have help, thanks to a human muse."

"Right, of course. I'm on it."

"Will you take care of her now?" Thalia asks me.

"Yes," I say, but I don't know if Clio wants me to. Whatever Clio told Thalia last night was surely just a clinical account. Thalia clasps Clio in an embrace and then lets her go. The redheaded Muse walks away.

I turn back to Clio. She looks nervous, and so am I.

"How did it work? She just took them off?"

"It was incredible. She didn't need pliers or a crowbar or anything. She just took them off, and she put them on her own wrists."

"So all the paintings you inspired? They're fine? She's going to hold them up now?"

Clio nods. "It's like she let me go on permanent vacation and took all over all my chores and now here I am. Look," she says and flicks her fingers. No silver dust comes out.

"Wow. But how do you . . . ," I start to say, but then I stop. I don't know how to ask, or even if I should. Just because she's human doesn't mean she's fallen back in love with me. She fell out.

She swallows. "But how do I feel? Is that what you were going to ask?"

I nod.

She looks at me, those sapphire eyes as fiery as the first night I met her, but soft too. Like she always was with me. She takes my hand and traces a jagged line across my palm. Her touch sends shivers through me, then she whispers, "Sing in me, Muse, and through me tell the story. Of a new way back to you."

My heart bursts from my chest. "Really? You really . . . ?"

"I feel like I'm dancing at the Moulin Rouge, like I'm on the beach in the South of France, like I'm spending a thousand starry nights with you. I want to spend all my days with you."

I can't speak. I am overwhelmed with all I want becoming real.

"But mostly I feel like a girl who's in love with a boy," she says.

I run my thumbs along her naked wrists. "You look so good without bracelets," I say. "You look so good in the sun. In the daylight."

She is no longer for my eyes only, and I am so glad that anyone can see us as we kiss on the bridge over the river. But hardly anyone is looking because this is what we do in Paris. I place my hand on her cheek, then down to her neck. We are just another pair of young lovers becoming another set of ornaments in this city.

We kiss all through the morning.

Sometime later, I ask a practical question. "So what do we do now? Where are you going to live? Maybe that sounds silly."

"I don't know," she says and laughs.

"You should stay with Bonheur. His family would love to have you. He has tons of room. He's going to be so excited to meet you. And Simon, he's great. You met him at the museum that night. But you can meet his girlfriend, Lucy, and we can all do stuff together. You have to meet my friend Emilie too," I say, and I'm rushing because all these ideas are coming to me now of how amazing it will be to just hang out with her.

"I can't wait to meet all your friends. And you know, I also thought I might try my hand at painting. I have quite a good eye, and lots of ideas about what to make," she says, and that sly smile of hers is back. "The only thing missing is . . . a muse."

"Oh, that's right. You'll need a muse. Wherever would you find one?"

"I wonder, wonder, wonder. Maybe you would be mine?"

I pretend to think about it. "Let's see. Do I have the time? Yes, I think I could fit you in. It's binding though. You can't have any other muse."

"I could never want any other one."

"Are you hungry? Because I could really go for a chocolate croissant. Funny thing, I know this great bakery and I'd love to take you there."

"Take me there, Julien."

We walk along the river to the best bakery in Paris.

AUTHOR'S NOTE

While some aspects of the history of art were altered for the purposes of this novel, many are rooted in fact. The following information is based on research into art and history.

• All the paintings cited in the story as hanging in the Musée d'Orsay do hang in the Musée d'Orsay, such as Van Gogh's *The Portrait of Dr. Gachet*, Manet's *Olympia*, Van Gogh's *Starry Night*, Toulouse-Lautrec's *Dancing at the Moulin-Rouge*, Cézanne's *View of the Gulf at Marseille*, Renoir's *The Swing*, as well as all the other Monets and Renoirs mentioned.

• All the paintings in the Musée d'Orsay, Louvre, Hermitage, Art Institute of Chicago, Metropolitan Museum of Art, Boston's Museum of Fine Arts, and the National Gallery of London are actual paintings and are described accurately, and the dates and stories surrounding these paintings and their history are described accurately. There are two exceptions to this. The first is the missing Renoir, known as *The Girl in the Garden*. This painting was made up for the story. The second is the character of Emmanuelle. While she is based on a Degas painting that hangs in the Musée d'Orsay, her heritage and relationship to the dancer Emilie are made up.

• All the details Julien imparts on his tours as to the history surrounding certain paintings, the prices they have commanded at auctions, and the style and technique of certain paintings is accurate. This includes Julien's description of Renoir's hands near the end of the artist's life.

• Suzanne Valadon was the first female painter admitted into the Ecole des Beaux-Arts. She and Renoir were contemporaries, and she appeared as a model in three of his paintings.

• Rosa Bonheur dressed in men's clothes when she painted *The Horse Fair*. She also kept a pet goat on her balcony.

• Many French families hid paintings in cellars during the Siege of Paris in the Franco-Prussian War and during the Nazi occupation.

• During the Nazi era, Nazis looted countless pieces of art across Europe. Today, reputable museums and dealers are expected to research and know the provenance of European paintings that changed hands during this time to ensure that restitution of any once-looted ones has been made.

• Renoir reportedly likened female painters to five-legged calves in a quote attributed to him as: "I consider women writers, lawyers, and politicians as monsters and nothing but five-legged calves. The woman artist is merely ridiculous, but I am in favor of the female singer and dancer."

• As for paintings that come alive, well, that is for you to decide.

ACKNOWLEDGMENTS

In many ways this book began more than twenty years ago, not so much as a story but as a moment of inspiration. From the second I set foot in Professor Kermit Champa's Survey of Art History class my sophomore year of college I was enthralled. I have never loved a class more nor been so enchanted by a subject. Professor Champa's knowledge of art was limitless; his passion for the beauty in a painting immense. Thank you, Professor Champa, for inspiring me to study art.

As for the book itself, I am indebted and awed by the brilliance of my two editors, Caroline Abbey and Michelle Nagler, who had so much vision for what this story could become. My agent Michelle Wolfson found the absolutely perfect home for this book. Thank you, Michelle, for being a dedicated, driven, and most entertaining advocate.

Theresa Shaw is my best friend in the universe, and having

her on my side makes me feel invincible at times, and simply happy at others.

Courtney Summers helped me replot the novel in one weekend, and offered so many incisive suggestions on twists and turns, big and small. Courtney, you have mad plotting skills. Cynthia Jaynes is the best type of critique partner—she gives great feedback, and she cheers you on. Cheryl Herbsman helped guide me through an early draft. Love you madly, girls! Big hugs as always to Stephanie Perkins, Kiersten White, and Malinda Lo.

I also must extend my gratitude to Cammi Bell, Kelli Anderson, Jill Ciambriello, Marylee George, Ilene Braff, and Ingrid and Eric Kettunen. Cammi, in particular, shared useful medical input on sewing up a wound. Thanks, Nurse Cammi!

Stéphanie Ngo served as my on-the-ground eyes and ears of Paris, sharing stories of high school life, of teens, and of young love on display every day in the city. She also assisted me with French phrases and has been a wonderful friend. Translation help also came from my French teacher, Anne-andrée.

None of this would have happened without the generous support of my mother-in-law, Barbara, who has taken me to Paris the last three years. We do have fun in our favorite city, don't we? Thanks to Paul, as well. I love our times at the markets and restaurants and shops.

My parents have always supported and encouraged me in all my endeavors, from studying art to writing books, and the biggest thanks I owe them is this—THANKS FOR SENDING ME TO COLLEGE, MOM AND DAD!

I relied on many books to inform this story including *Planting Schemes from Monet's Garden* by Vivian Russell, *The Judgment of Paris* by Ross King, *Alias Olympia* by Eunice Lipton, *Daily Life of French Artists in the Nineteenth Century* by Jacques Letheve, catalogues from the Musée d'Orsay and the Louvre, as well as the websites of the museums featured in the story. I must also give credit to two movies that inspired me—*Night at the Museum* for its playfulness and *Shakespeare in Love* for its beautiful heart.

My son and daughter are the lights of my life and my greatest joys, and they are always encouraging and loving. My daughter accompanied me on a trip to the Musée d'Orsay, where I shared secrets of what the paintings are up to at night. Her response: "When you describe it like that, I really do think the paintings come alive at night."

I believe in the magic of art too.

Then there is my wonderful husband, who manages to put up with me. Oh, and he also found me another dog! So big love and kisses to Violet Delia and Flipper McDoodle, my four-legged coworkers!

Enter Aria's fiery world, where the stakes are higher than life and death—and nothing can stop forbidden romance from igniting.

THE FIRE ARTIST

DAISY WHITNEY

BLOOMSBURY

Read on for a selection from *The Fire Artist*, a wholly original fantasy from **Daisy Whitney**.

Lightning Strikes the Heart

A plume of flames erupts from my fingertips and rises high above me. As I widen my arms, the fire curves in a brilliant arc. More flames burst into the inky night at my command.

I call them down, luring them back into my scarred and hardened palms, like scarves of silk being pulled back into a magician's top hat.

Then, with a graceful bend, I grasp a pair of arm's-length chains I've left on the ground for this moment. I raise my arms above my head, wirelike whips in my hands now. A quick flick of my wrists and sparks race to the metal on the wires. A crack, then molten drops rain over me, a willowy canopy of sizzling hisses that light up the faces of the crowd. They are packed tightly into every inch of the bleachers, their bare arms glistening with sweat in the muggy night.

My fireworks hail down from the cloudless sky, falling gently at first, then quickly, like bullets and gunfire. Another snap and sparks leap higher. And another, until I can no longer distinguish the crackling sound of the fire from the gasps and cheers of the crowd.

On summer evenings like this, the metal bleachers are jammed with the young, old, and everyone in between, clasping tight their crinkled, hastily printed flyers advertising our lineup of fire, ice, earth, and wind. I'm the final act, and I'm nearly done, so I drop the chains to the ground and show my palms to the audience. I'm not the only one who can do this. But no one in or around Wonder, Florida, is tired of coming here to watch flames fly from human hands, with fire that flies higher, burns brighter, and curls tighter than any other fire artist's in a long time.

This is the big one, when I extinguish all the fire, the park goes dark for one long, silent moment, then a spectacular torch flares from me high into the sky. I glance at the onlookers. They are tense, jaws tight, bodies hunching forward in the stands. I look away, and it's then that a pair of phantom fingers pinch a corner of my heart. My shoulders pull in as my chest constricts. My throat tightens for a moment.

Like a glass being knocked off the corner of a counter, I've spilled fire all over the ground. I can't blame it on stage fright. I'm not nervous.

I'm losing my fire again. It's not the first time. It won't be the last.

The fire skitters away from me, racing over the hard grass and packed dirt, hell-bent on the front row. I fall to my knees to coax the sparks back to my hands, before they burn off the feet of the girl with the ratty pink sneakers who has been kicking the ground absently as she watches. Now, fear fills her eyes, and she leaps up onto the bench. Her mother grabs her and holds her tight.

My heart sputters, like it's gasping for a last breath. There's a hole in the show, a patch I must fill in. Like an actor forgetting a line and covering it up with an ad lib that doesn't quite fit, I grasp the long ribbon of blazing orange and tug it back into my hands.

As if I meant to nearly roast the audience.

To maintain the illusion I jump back onto my feet, thrust my arms high in the air. I'm a gymnast who's expertly dismounted, covering up the broken bone inside her. The little girl has tucked her head against her mother's chest, but the mother is softening. It's a show, after all, and I have shown them that my little stumble must have been scripted.

Now there is clapping, and hollering, and so much whistling too. Fingers inside mouths making the sounds that draw taxis to the curbs in cities I've never been to. The audience is swallowed in cheers. They got their money's worth and then some. Our shows don't cost much, not at this level or this venue, a part-time ballpark a few miles from swampland and a few blocks from the abandoned amusement park that used to be Wonder's greatest draw. Had this night been two years ago, we might have also heard the cranking of the roller-coaster cars chugging up tracks, or the groans of the circling Ferris wheel nearby. But the Eighth Wonder of the Modern World amusement park has since closed down, and all that's left are the skeletons of the rides that peer over the wooden fences.

Together, the ten of us in this latest cast of performance artists—including my best friend, Elise, who can harness the wind—lower our heads in unison, all while my heart thumps against my chest as if it has a repetitive injury, an insistent hiss in the pipes. My heart is not like the others'; it's not whole.

It's missing parts.

I walk inside to the locker rooms that house ballplayers on other nights, guys with big, broad chests and beefy arms and mouths that chew gum or spit tobacco. I slow down, waiting for Elise, and I pull her aside into a quiet corner.

"It's time for another renewal."

Her eyes are sad. "I know. I could tell when the fire jumped away."

"Will you do it for me again?"

"You know I will. You don't even have to ask. I always will," Elise says, and I can hear the heaviness in her voice. "I'll start tracking the morning storms for tomorrow."

———

The weather forecasters were right, but we're behind the first flash storm. We catch a glimpse of a streak of lightning far off, and Elise jams the gas. But the thunder comes nearly forty-five seconds later.

"It's at least nine miles away!" I shout, even though I'm next to her in the front seat of her brown hatchback that used to be painted pink. "But there's more coming. There has to be."

We fly down the Wilderness Waterway, sprinting past mangrove islets.

Elise points. "There."

Lightning pierces the sky, ripping it apart with a bright

scratch. We count out loud, reaching thirty seconds before the thunder rumbles toward us.

"Closer," I say, and Elise nods. She is pure determination now, focused and instinctual as we race toward the brewing storm. We cross into the curtain of rain, and she barely slows her car at all, cruising over the soon-to-be-slick highway as raindrops turn heavy and hammer the car. Elise's parents gave her this car when she turned sixteen, a pink hatchback, since pink has always been her favorite color. She drove it in all its girly glory for a few months until she realized it would be far too conspicuous on days like this. She and I painted it brown one afternoon, and I bought her cherry ice cream when we finished. Her parents simply shrugged and figured her change of heart was the capriciousness of a teenager, when the truth is she changed it to protect me.

To protect us. If she's caught helping me, the consequences for her and her family could be dire.

The rain pounds harder into the windshield, and Elise grips the wheel, her arms like steel cables as she steers through the wet onslaught.

Another flash of lightning. Seconds later, a clap of thunder. She slows down and squeals to a stop on the side of the road, empty beach alongside us. She looks around, scanning the deserted beach to make sure we're alone. Then she throws open her door, and I do the same, following her as she rushes across the sand, still glancing behind and around in case there's someone who'd see us. But we're all alone here. The air is electric. I keep pace with her, ankles digging into the sand as we run closer to the storm. There's an outcrop of rocks near the edge of the water, and Elise races to it, giving us a shield in case anyone driving by can make out what we're doing from a distance.

I'm battered with rain when Elise stops short, breathing hard. She plants her feet firm and holds out her hands. Her palms are open wide, and, like a switch turned on, gusts of air burst forth from her, powerful blasts that stir the sand into swirling gales at our feet. She lifts up her hands, bringing them over her head, the squalls rising with her. I squint, trying to keep the sand out of my eyes.

The wind she weaves intensifies. Her arms move as she fortifies her elemental creation, layer by layer. Some air artists can execute beautiful flips and twists in the air, can contort their bodies in strange and gorgeous ways through wispy blasts of air, but Elise's gifts have always been more blunt. Her true ability is in the sheer strength of the air she can make, the way she can guide it with the precision of an atomic clock. Soon she's crafting a miniature tornado around us, the wind a creature that bends at her command.

She peers up at the gray and crying sky, then turns to me and gives a quick nod.

All I have to do is stand and wait.

When the next jagged needle rends the sky a few hundred feet away, she yanks her man-made air with the strength of an Olympic weight lifter. Her cocoon of wind tugs the lightning bolt into her orbit. With the control that I wish I had, she sends the razor edge of the bolt into my heart.

In an instant, my nostrils fill with the smell of burning flesh. All the nearby air heats up, roaring up hundreds of degrees for a split second or more, and Elise runs out of the line of fire. There's a choking in my chest as my heart digests the electric current. And just like that, it's done. My heart is a ravenous beast, blind and hungry and needy as it gobbles a force of nature.

Then comes the thunder. It howls in my ears, the sound wave vibrating through my molten insides.

The crack deafens me, and everything goes dark as I collapse to the ground.

Monsters and Makers

My chest caves in and back out. Hands shake my shoulders hard, the back of my head hitting the sand. I cough and gasp and flip to the side.

Elise falls off me, panting, her own chest heaving too.

She pushes her soaking wet hair away from her forehead. "You were unconscious for a couple minutes this time. I was shaking you. Trying to get you to come to. That's the longest, Aria."

I cough a few more times, then rub a hand against my chest. It's burning, like a fever. My toenails are toasty. My kneecap is broiling. Even my eyelashes are hot.

The rain has slowed; it's merely drizzling now, and the clouds are breaking, making way for the sun.

"Sorry," I manage to say as I pull myself up, sitting now. I'm always knocked unconscious after a lightning strike. No big surprise there.

Elise drapes an arm around me. "Don't say sorry. Are you okay?"

I nod.

"God. I'm a wreck. My heart is beating fifty thousand miles an hour. Do you have any idea how awful it is to strike your best friend with lightning?"

I laugh weakly, making a wheezy sound. "Can't say that I do."

"It's totally traumatizing. I'm going to be in therapy for life, you know. I'm going to have some shrink when I'm old, and I'll still be talking about you and how it was like killing you each time I replenished your fire."

"I'm sorry I made you do this. But you're not killing me. It's just a blackout for a few minutes."

"You didn't make me, dummy. I wanted to. I'd do anything for you. You're my Frankenstein."

"You're my Frankenstein's maker then."

Elise wraps me in a hug, holds me tight. "Actually, wasn't Frankenstein the scientist? Didn't we study that book in English class?"

"Yeah, we did study it, but that doesn't mean I paid attention."

"I'm sure you read the SparkNotes online."

"As always," I say with a slight smile. Elise knows I'm hardly a model student. I haven't had the time, and my family hasn't pressured me when it comes to classes, grades, or school reports. All my pressure comes from my father and has to do with fire and art, not classic literature or trigonometry. My mom used to care. She used to sit down with me every night to work on spelling and vocabulary, on multiplication tables and long division, praising, always praising, when the grades came home.

Now she's sick, and she's stopped caring. I've stopped trying so hard. Now I try for one thing, and one thing only—to get out of town.

"Well, as I recall, Frankenstein was the doctor. Dr. Frankenstein," Elise says.

"I guess you're Dr. Frankenstein then. I'm the monster."

"You're my monster and I love you."

"I love you."

"Now, show me what you can do."

The beach is empty. I stand, clench my fists, then open them, unleashing a gorgeous torrent of flames. Elise laughs wildly as I extinguish the fresh, beautiful, and wholly new fire.

"Daddy will love it," I say sarcastically.

Elise narrows her eyes, shakes her head. "You should give him a taste of his own medicine someday, Ar."

"Yeah, I should but I won't."

I'm stronger than my father. My fire is far more powerful and potent than his ever was, and now his fire has faded, time suctioning it away as time does.

Elise grasps my hand in hers and we return to her car. She shakes her head at me as she backs out of the spot and turns onto the road. "Someday, we won't have to do this, right?"

"Yeah. When they stop expecting me to make fire. When I'm in my midtwenties." I touch Elise's arm so she's looking at me. "It's never run out of me this fast, Elise. Never."

She squeezes my hand gently and doesn't let go. "Don't worry. I'll always help you get it back."

"But what if you're not here?"

"We'll find a way," she says, then we return to the mainland, where I take her out for cherry ice cream. I order a lemon sherbet for myself. In a cup, rather than a cone. Even so, it melts quickly.

Soon, we're joined by Elise's boyfriend, Kyle. He shows up in his tricked-out truck, tires jacked up high, the rims glistening and shiny.

"Babe, I missed you today," he says to Elise, and wraps her in his arms. Big and broad with close-cropped hair, he leans in to kiss her, and she kisses him back. I briefly wonder what it would be like to kiss like that, with abandon. Then I look away and tap on my phone, calling up a photo I found the other night, when I was looking at some snapshots of performers in the New York Leagues. One of the girls on the team has been posting pictures of herself with a new boy. A beautiful boy with dark hair and dark, brooding eyes. There's a distance in those eyes, like he has secrets too.

Secrets he keeps from her.

Maybe I could join the Leagues and find a boy like this. A boy like me.

I trace his face with my fingers, imagining what it would be like to be with someone who knew my secrets, who knew my half-baked heart and didn't mind.

Elise and Kyle stop kissing. "But I'm right here now," she says with a smile that's just for him.

They're so into each other it makes my chest hurt. It makes me feel hollow all over again because I don't know how she does it. I don't know how she gives so much, how she can be so into him, and do so much for me at the same time. It's as if Elise has this endless reserve inside her and she can keep tap-tap-tapping into it.

"C'mon, lovebirds. We need to get to practice," I say as I jam my phone into my pocket.

The Aria Opportunity

Every inch of me is wet with my own sweat. You could wring me out and there would still be more. There will always be more, because my body temperature is higher than average all the time.

But my fire is back, and that makes me happy, because it will make Daddy happy, and when Daddy's happy I am safe.

My fire is too intense though, as it always is after a renewal, until I can escape to the canals and let some loose. I spray a fireball at the flame-resistant concrete wall, specially built next to the park's bull pen. Our little arena is also home to hopeful ballplayers trying to eke out runs and hits and strikeouts for their Triple-A team, even though baseball, like most other professional sports, is dying.

The flames escape from my fingertips, then race toward the wall like a kamikaze fighter pilot. I swear I see the wall shake from the impact.

"Damn, you have some serious power today," Nava says.

She's perched on the metal bench. She wears a white T-shirt and pink basketball shorts. Her legs are all muscle, corded and sturdy. Her wild curls flare out from under the brim of her ball cap, a baby-blue mesh thing.

"Too much," I say under my breath as I throw another explosive fireball.

This is how it goes. When my fire fades, I lose control. When I replenish my fire, I have far too much. I am an unnatural balance, swaying one way or the other. Tonight I'll go to the canals to restore the precarious balance of me.

"Why don't we try just a tiny little flicker? You can work on your starlight," Nava says gently.

I bet Nava never saw these problems in her native Israel years ago. Her mother was a top-tier fire artist for years, performing into her early twenties. Nava is nineteen and she's fire too, but she suffers from too much stage fright to perform herself, and she's told me that's one of the reasons she likes working with me—I don't have any stage fright. Her family moved here, and she's the fire coach for all the farm-league teams in southern Florida, traveling from ballpark to ballpark to guide the fire girls and boys she trains. Her mother coaches the rookies at a facility in Miami, where all the teams in the M.E. Leagues start training, even though the M.E. Leagues are headquartered in the former Middle East. There are other elemental arts leagues in the United States and around the world, but the one run by the M.E. is the largest and most prestigious. Those who are good enough to be recruited to the M.E. Leagues are then sent to the biggest cities in the United States, to Chicago, Los Angeles, New York, and some even perform abroad. I have posters on my walls of some of the M.E. Leagues performers. They have stage names like Flame Rider and Night Wind.

I bring my fingertips together as if I'm snapping. When I release my clenched hand, I unleash a huge spray of angry orange flames.

I turn to Nava, embarrassed. I hate that it's not night. I hate that I have to be here at practice hours after a renewal. "I'm sorry."

"No, you're tired. You're exhausted. This is your body's way of saying you need to rest. We'll try again tomorrow."

I nod, then my stomach twists as I ask the next thing. "If my dad asks, can you tell him I did fine?"

"You always do fine in my book. So, yes. I will tell Mr. Kilandros so."

All the tension fades away for a moment. "Thanks."

She tips her forehead to the stands. "But he's been watching you."

JEFF BROOKS

DAISY WHITNEY is also the author of *The Fire Artist*, *The Mockingbirds*, *The Rivals*, and *When You Were Here*. She lives in San Francisco, California, with her fabulous husband, fantastic kids, and the two best dogs. She spends her days reporting on television, media, and advertising for a range of news outlets, and her nights dreaming of Paris, the most wonderful city in the world. Daisy earned a degree in art history at Brown University and has always believed paintings have great stories to tell.

www.daisywhitney.com

@DaisyWhitney